LEAVING THE MIDDLE LANE

LEAVING THE MIDDLE LANE

CLAUDIA WILLIAMS

ISBN: 979-8-9887703-0-5

Dedicated to my husband, children and grandchildren.

Table Of Contents

Table of Contents

Table Of Contents

Chapter 1
The To Do List

Maeve Carey sat at her gleaming, new oak kitchen table and studied the to do list that she had written for the day on the five by seven yellow legal sized lined paper tablet in front of her. First on her list: Call Clare. She picked up her cell phone and dialed Clare's phone number. After five rings, the call went into phone mail. Sighing impatiently, Maeve left a message, "Clare, this is your mother, please call me at once. It is 8:55 in the morning."

Next, Maeve texted a message to Clare. *Please call me. Important. Love, Mom.* Maeve estimated that Clare would call or text her within the hour, as usual. She picked up her ball point pen and checked number one off her list.

Second on her list: Call Mom and Dad. She checked her watch. It was nine o'clock sharp. She always called her parents at the same time. "Hello Dad," Maeve said. "How are you and Mom this morning?"

Sitting by the phone in his kitchen, Paul O'Connor picked up Maeve's call with his left hand on the first ring. "Hello Maeve," he said cheerily as he edged his cane closer to his side with his left foot. His right arm hung at his side.

Paul shifted in his seat and looked at the dishes in the sink that had not been done for two days. "Doing just fine, Maeve. Thank you for asking.

Mother is still sleeping, but she will be up soon. I have things under control here."

"Good. Please say hello to Mother for me. I will stop by tomorrow to take you and Mom out to eat."

"That's my girl," Paul said with a smile. "Talk to you tonight at 8:00 P.M. sharp."

"Yes, have a great day Dad." Maeve hung up her phone and checked number two off her list.

Maeve peered at number three on her list: Return her newly altered pants to the dry cleaners for the second alteration. The cleaners hadn't taken in the waist of her new pants properly, because the pants still hung too loosely. She had made the mistake of not trying on the pants at the cleaners when she went to pick them up after their first alteration. Upon arriving home, she tried them on and they still didn't fit well at the waist. Why not return them for another alteration? She had already paid for the service and expected satisfaction from the seamstress. I may be a bit of a pest, she thought, but people should be held accountable for their work. I know that   Jeremy agrees with me. Look at his company. His success comes because he delivers superior service to his clients. She then called the dry cleaners.

She placed her cell phone in her jogging pants pocket and glanced at her watch. Oh, no, she thought. The new landscapers are late. This is not good. They said they would arrive at 9:00 A.M. sharp. I'll just call the main office and ask where they are. A moment before she started dialing, she had a change of mind. No, you are being too rigid, she chastised herself.   Give the landscapers ten more minutes to arrive and if they don't appear, call their office.

Maeve frowned. No, don't frown she reminded herself.   She hurried to the hall mirror and stared at the small furrows between her eyebrows.   She recalled an article she had read recently   about how to prevent aging.   Make an effort to smile at all times, it suggested.   This will improve the appearance of wrinkles and keep a pleasant look upon your face.   A frowning face is an old face.   She turned the corner of her mouth up determinedly and forced a smile.

She strolled into the living room of the stately home that she and Jeremy had bought in East Lake Forest twenty-five years ago and gazed out the massive floor to ceiling glass window that overlooked the winding, tree lined brick driveway in front of the house.   No landscapers yet.   For the next ten minutes she held the smile position carefully while observing the birds, squirrels and chipmunks scamper about the two acre lot she and Jeremy enjoyed next to a ravine that led to the Lake Forest beach on Lake Michigan.

It's not bad enough I have to hold this excruciating smile, but here I stand wasting my time waiting for these landscapers to arrive, she groused. Finally, at 9:15 A.M., she heard the landscapers' truck rumbling onto the grounds.   Four Mexican men hopped out of the truck and quickly tackled their separate jobs: mowing, edging, trimming and blowing.

It's about time, Maeve thought.   Against her better judgment, she again glanced more closely into the mirror.   To her surprise, the lines that creased around her eyes and lips seemed less prominent. The new face cream she recently bought seemed to be working, she thought. It had cost a small fortune, but the ad on television promised that women's aging skin would look younger in just one week of using the product. Maeve knew that the cream wouldn't do any good if she looked sour, so weary or not, she clenched her teeth and pulled her lips up to form another plastered smile on her face as she walked into the kitchen.

She stepped to the kitchen sink, washed her chapped and bloody hands, squirted a dollop of hand cream onto them and massaged the cream deeply into her hands until the cream smothered the cracked skin. If only I could stop washing my hands so often, she grumbled to herself.

Chapter 2
The Landscapers

The growl of the lawn mower entering the back yard interrupted her annoying thoughts. She glanced up to see the landscaper who was pushing the lawn mower stop. He appeared to be around thirty years old and was sweating profusely. He pulled a soiled towel from his back pocket and wiped his glistening brow. Then he raised his head and looked directly at Maeve. She stared at him and was struck by his sky blue eyes. When he saw her looking at him, he averted his eyes and stuffed his towel back into his pocket. Then he continued pushing his mower over the backyard lawn until he was done.

His much younger co-worker, perhaps in his teens, aimed his blower at the fallen leaves, twigs and cut grass and blasted them into large piles that lay in neat stacks about the back yard. He then stuffed the stacks into the pre-approved Lake Forest lawn bags and he and the men who had been trimming and edging carried them to the front of the house, where they loaded the lawn bags into their green and white landscaping truck along with their landscaping supples.

Maeve stepped outside and followed the men to the front of the house. These landscapers certainly are efficient, she thought. The blue eyed man glanced at her again. Then, for some reason, Maeve felt guilty. "Wait," she called out. "I will be back in just a moment." She hurried into the house and took a plastic pitcher from her pantry and filled it with water and ice and carried the pitcher and some paper cups to the men who were patiently waiting. She gave the cups to the blue eyed man. His eyes are so kind, she thought.

"Gracias," he said. He passed a cup to each of his co-workers who held them out while Maeve poured the ice water into them.

"Gracias," each of the men said. They drank their cups quickly, handed them back to her and climbed into the truck.

"You are welcome," replied Maeve.

Maeve watched as the truck moved slowly down the driveway to the street. She waved goodbye to them. She also wanted to make sure the truck didn't veer off the driveway and leave wheel marks on the lawn. When the truck reach the end of the driveway and pulled away, she admired the manicured, green lawn, so satisfying in its perfection.

Unfortunately, a small breeze blew and shook some leaves from the trees. The leaves dotted the lawn like a sprinkling of orange and yellow confetti. Maeve frowned, then caught herself and immediately smiled, but she wasn't happy. She knew that in a few days, the leaves would completely pepper her perfect green lawn. She shook her head, walked back to the kitchen and threw the paper cups into her new trash compactor and placed the pitcher into her dishwasher. She picked up her to do list and wrote number four on it. Call landscaping company. Maeve picked up the phone.

"Hello, this is Mrs. Carey on Thistle Road in Lake Forest. Your men have just completed mowing our lawn, but the wind is blowing and leaves are already falling on our grounds. I am having guests tomorrow and I need our lawn to look pristine for our party." She listened attentively to the lawn service representative at the other end of the phone. "Yes, tomorrow morning will be fine as long as the men arrive at 9:00 A.M.," she spoke into the phone. "Thank you for fitting me into your schedule." Maeve hung up the phone and checked number four off of her list.

She pulled an eight ounce bottle of spring water from the refrigerator and swigged it down. Thank God I hired this new landscaping company, she thought with satisfaction. They charge more than our previous landscaper, but they are an old and established company in Lake Forest and their contract specifies that they will mow the lawn, keep it free from falling leaves, trim the hedges properly, edge and aerate the grass and plant and weed the flower beds.

I am so happy that I fired the old landscaping company. I had to practically beg them to keep the lawn manicured and free from leaves. Of course we're not having any company tomorrow, but so what. I need a well groomed lawn. After all, we do live in Lake Forest and have appearances to keep, she reasoned as she took an apple walnut muffin from the refrigerator and nibbled on it.

A crumb from the muffin fell to her chin and landed on the table. Without hesitation, she rose and pulled a paper towel from the roller on the kitchen counter, wet the towel and wiped the crumb residue from her face and the kitchen table. She threw the used towel into the built in trash compactor next to the kitchen sink and sighed. What to have for dinner tonight?

Suddenly, she remembered the blue eyed landscaper and the kindness in his eyes. She didn't want him or his co-workers to get into trouble about her lawn. After all, they did their job well and couldn't control the leaves falling. She called the landscaping service again. "Hello, this is Mrs. Carey again. Please disregard my previous request to have the the men return tomorrow. The lawn is fine as it is," she said. "Thank you," she concluded as she finished the call.

Chapter 3
The Help Wanted Ad

The Lake Forest Weekly Press Newspaper lay on the kitchen table. As usual, Jeremy had brought it in from the driveway this morning. Maeve glanced at the front page headline, *Local Sixteen Year Old High School Student Found Dead in Home*. The ensuing article reported that drug use was suspected in the teenager's death because his parents found drug paraphernalia in his bedroom. Maeve shook her head. This is unbelievable, she thought. He must have moved to the area recently from Chicago or another suburb on the south side.

She found another article on the second page. *Drug Use Growing Among High School Students and Young Adults on the North Shore*. She read that drug use among young people who live on the North Shore was growing. New heroin users were now more likely to be white, suburban and in their teens or twenties. "Ridiculous," she murmured. She and Jeremy had raised Clare in Lake Forest for the past twenty-two years and the idea of North Shore teenagers and young adults taking illegal drugs seemed remote.

Maeve licked her finger and swiped to the next pages until she came to the Help Wanted section of the paper. One ad caught her eye. A law firm in downtown Lake Forest was looking for an assistant. Hmm, she thought. I am so tired of my life. All I do is worry about Clare, take care of my parents and Jeremy and obsess about this house and my appearance. Maybe it's time to get a job and see how that feels.   She drew a circle around the ad and dropped the newspaper onto the kitchen table.

Right now, I'd rather think about my newly renovated kitchen. Thank God the contractor finished the job just a few days ago. What a mess! It was all we could do to not move out of the house. Jeremy and I had to practically live in restaurants this past month.   But now it is all over and worth the inconvenience we endured.

Maeve peered with satisfaction at the new cream wood cupboards that hung on the walls of her kitchen. She tilted her head to get a better glance and decided that the cupboards were lovely. Their wood and glass panels blended so well with her new cream dishes flecked with tiny green leaves. But the beauty of the dishes didn't show as well without the LED lighting on. She flicked the electric switch near the bay window. The tiny LED lights that rimmed the inner borders of the glass cupboard doors sparkled brightly, perhaps a bit too brightly, she thought; there is a bit of a glare.   So she softened the lights by gently pressing down on the dimmer of the wall switch.   Now her new cream dishes shone through the glass cupboard doors   like art in a museum display.

A bag containing her old lavender and white dishes waited in the garage, ready for the Cancer Society pickup tomorrow. She had debated for six weeks about keeping the old dishes or donating them for new ones, but after twenty-five years of use, she came to the realization that someone else might as well make use of the remaining set. This past year, she had thrown two chipped cups and three broken dishes into the garbage and decided that enough was enough. So, she bit the bullet and bought a new set of kitchen dishes which she hoped would last another twenty-five years. When the Cancer Society picks up the dishes, I'll file their receipt along with our other donations as a charitable deduction for this year's tax return, she thought.   Every little bit helps.   Even though Jeremy's business is very successful, I still like to watch our finances.

She gently removed one of the new cream cups out of the cabinet and held it under the water dispenser of the new stainless steel refrigerator. Once full, she placed the cup in the new microwave and set the time to one minute. When the buzzer rang, she transferred the cup from the microwave to the kitchen table and dipped a black tea bag into the cup exactly twenty times. That was just the amount of dipping that produced a perfect cup of tea, in her opinion.   She relaxed at the kitchen table while sipping her tea and mulled about what to cook for dinner.

Chapter 4
The Business Meeting On Saturday

Maeve peered into the refrigerator and looked at the leftover meatloaf and mashed potatoes she had bought at the ready made food section of the local grocery store the previous night. I don't want to reheat those and I really don't feel like cooking tonight. Maybe we'll have Chinese carryout this evening, she mused as she closed the refrigerator door. In the background, she heard Jeremy's footsteps as he descended the foyer stairs and entered the kitchen. He placed his briefcase on the kitchen table and looked around. "Have you seen my iPhone?" he asked as he ran his hands over the pockets of his finely tailored suit and searched through his briefcase. "I can't find it."

"Why no, darling," she replied as she took another sip of the tea. "Have you looked in the bedroom?"

"Of course, I have," he growled. Then he spotted his iPhone in the corner of the kitchen counter, grabbed it and placed it in his inner suit coat pocket.

Maeve paused as she looked at Jeremy. "Why are you dressed in a suit and tie on a Saturday morning? Where are you going?"

"I'm late for a meeting," he said. He snatched his briefcase and took a few steps towards the garage.

Maeve frowned. "Why do you have a meeting on a Saturday morning?" She moved next to him and flicked a grey hair off his shoulder. Jeremy is still so attractive after twenty-five years of marriage, she thought. His curly salt and pepper hair hangs in waves over his brown eyes, just like when we were dating. It's a pity he doesn't smile more, though.

"It is the only time the client could make it. He's in from Europe. I'll be home around 6:00 tonight." He gave her a peck on the cheek and continued towards the garage.

She followed behind him and called out, "Would you like Chinese carryout tonight? I don't feel like cooking a meal this evening."

"Whatever you want. I have to get going." He walked into the garage, placed his briefcase into the passenger side of his BMW 7 Series car, got into the driver's seat, started the engine and put the car into reverse.

"My, you're not in a good mood this morning," she called out as she followed him to the car. She sniffed and picked up the spicy smell of after shave. "Jeremy, are you wearing that new cologne I gave you?" she asked.

"Yes," he replied.

"It smells so good. On your way down the driveway, look at the work our new landscapers did on the lawn this morning and tell me what you think. Well, Have a wonderful day and remember I love you."

"Love you too," Jeremy murmured. In a matter of seconds he backed out of the garage.

"Bye, darling," she called out. Jeremy has never been a morning person, but lately he seems extremely grouchy, she pondered. Oh, well, we all have those days. She wrote number five on her to do list: Call Chinese carryout. Then she closed the garage door, strolled into the kitchen and looked up the menu of the Chinese restaurant on her cell phone. She browsed through it and dialed Jeremy's cell phone.

"Hello, Maeve. What now?" he groused.

"What do you want to eat for takeout tonight? Your usual egg rolls, kung pao chicken, fried rice or something else?"

Jeremy rolled his eyes and tightened his grip on the steering wheel and answered in a measured voice, "The usual sounds okay. See you tonight."

"And what did you think about the lawn?"

"It looks fine. I have to go Maeve."

"Bye, darling," Maeve said. She clicked off her cell phone and immediately dialed the Chinese restaurant. When they answered the phone, she gave her name and phone number and placed her order. "Two egg rolls, two kung pao chickens and one fried rice. Please repeat the order back to me."

She listened intently as the employee went over the order. "That is correct," she said. "I will pick it up at 5:30 tonight. Goodbye." She clicked off the phone and marked number five off her list.

What now, she thought? Her eyes moved to the kitchen cabinets again. She opened each cabinet one by one, admiring the way she had arranged the contents in straight rows, like soldiers at attention. Ah, they look splendid.   I certainly do have organizational skills.

The canned goods and spices stood in alphabetical order, the pots and pans perched atop each other, the plastic containers (most acquired from carry out she had ordered from the local restaurants) filled a whole shelf according to size. She let out a sigh of relief. Although she had hired a cleaning lady to come to the house one day a week many years ago, she found it therapeutic to create this island of order and calm around her.

Just then, her cell phone rang. "Hi, Mom," came Clare's voice at the other end. "I just opened your text. Is there anything wrong? Your message sounded urgent."

"Hi, honey," Maeve said sweetly. "Nothing is wrong. I just wanted to talk to you and find out how life is at the advertising company."

Clare let out a perceptible sigh of relief and put her speaker phone on. She shook her head at her boyfriend, Sean, who was sitting on the couch with her. "Please don't scare me like that. I thought something was wrong with you or Dad or Grandma and Grandpa. To answer your question, things are pretty good at work. I have one new account. I must say I'm pretty proud of myself."

"And I am proud of you, too. You know that. How is the new apartment? Are you still enjoying living downtown in River West with Sean after two months?"

"Oh, Mom, I love it here. I'm in the middle of all the action. Sean and I go out to the neighborhood bars, theaters and restaurants. You know I miss you, but I don't miss living in that stogy old Lake Forest neighborhood where nothing interesting happens."

Maeve paused. "Can I come and visit you next Saturday? If you want, we can go shopping."

Clare punched the pillow in her lap and looked at Sean. "Sorry Mom. Sean and I are going out with friends. Maybe we can get together the week after. Is Dad around? I would like to say hello to him too."

"He is working today. He has a meeting with a client. Give him a call on his cell phone."

"Why is he working on Saturday?'

"Oh, a business meeting with someone from Europe."

"Thanks Mom. I'll call him. Love you. Bye."

"Love you too, honey." Maeve hung up the phone and grinned with satisfaction. *Well, I got Clare to get back to me. When a call doesn't work, just text. I think the only way the younger generation communicates is through texting,* Maeve decided. *Clare is a good girl and I'm so proud of her. I just wish we had more time together.*

Maeve spied the cereal bowl, spoon and coffee cup that Jeremy had left in the kitchen sink when he had gotten up this morning. *You'd think he could just rinse them and put them in the dishwasher. I've asked him so many times to do this, but he just forgets.* Annoyed, she put on her rubber kitchen gloves, picked up the dishes and silverware, hand washed them and arranged them in her special order (all dishes facing right) in the dishwasher.

The rubber gloves provided some relief from the pain of the dry, red cracks that covered the top of her hands. For the third time this morning, she took off the rubber gloves, reached for the moisturizing lotion that she kept on the kitchen counter near the sink and lathered the lotion onto her hands. She tried her best to keep her hands soft, but it was a losing battle with all the hand washing that she did.

She dreaded going to social functions and shaking hands with people. When she and Jeremy went to a party, she always had a glass of wine (she didn't drink alcohol or beer) in her hands so she wouldn't have to shake hands with anyone. Usually, this worked and people didn't seem to mind. Oh, well, she thought. At least my hands are clean and free from germs. You just never know what you may pick up from others.

Chapter 5
Drug Use On The North Shore

After she loaded the dishwasher, Maeve spotted the Lake Forest Weekly Press newspaper on the kitchen table. She again looked at the ad she had circled for an assistant at the O'Mara Law Firm in downtown Lake Forest. Why not? she thought. Her typing and computer skills were still good and she was probably the most organized person she knew. She strolled to the guest bedroom closet on the first floor and pulled out a banker's box of her old school teaching files and resumes.

She headed to the den, turned on her computer and started typing. After an hour or so, she read her resume over, spell checked it and decided it was as good as it was going to get. She felt sure that she would never hear from the law firm, but thought, what the heck, what can I lose by sending it in. Anyway, I have an updated resume now in case I want to apply for any other jobs. Then she mailed it to the O'Mara law firm.

She leafed through the Lake Forest Weekly Press Newspaper again to the article about teenagers taking drugs on the North Shore. The article stated that heroin use among teens on the North Shore was becoming more prevalent. Teens who usually started with prescription drugs such as painkillers, easily made the transition to heroin. The emerging profile of heroin users from the suburbs was white and under 25 years old. Alarmed and disgusted, she flipped the paper onto the kitchen table and moved to the backyard lounge chair that faced Lake Michigan.

She thought of her friends. Not one of their children had trouble with drugs and she knew with certainty that Clare never used them. The article reported that younger teens were introduced to drugs through older students in the late teens and early twenties who sold the drugs to make enough money to support their drug habit. It quoted recent studies that suggested there was a shift from injecting heroin to snorting or smoking because of its increased purity and the misconception that those forms of use would not lead to addiction.

What has this world become of? Maeve thought. I am sure I don't know anyone who takes drugs, much less sells them. All of that goes on in the south and west sides of Chicago. I know for a fact that if I ever met someone who took drugs, I would know it right away.

She read the warning signs of heroin use in a side bar to the article: Lack of personal hygiene; tendency toward recklessness; withdrawal from family and friends; items of value being lost or stolen; burnt foil present in one's car, room or in personal effects; mood swings; intense rage; lying and manipulation; sudden drop in grades and excessive ditching at school; finding evidence or prescription drugs; scratching hands and arms; strong craving for sweets, morning, noon and night; possession of drug paraphernalia.

Another side bar described the physical signs of heroin use: Runny nose and constant sniffling; needle marks on arms and/or legs; sores on nostrils and on top of lips; constant hacking cough from smoking heroin off of tin foil; loss of appetite and dramatic weight loss; nodding off during the day and inability to sleep at night; dark circles under eyes and a constant sleepy or groggy expression.

Maeve gazed at the placid blue waters of Lake Michigan in the distance and thought, Yes, I'd be able to spot a druggie in a minute.

Chapter 6
Clare's Complaints

Clare Carey ended the call on her cell phone, shrugged and shifted in her seat on the couch in the small one bedroom apartment she rented in River West, a mecca for young professionals in Chicago.

"My mother absolutely drives me crazy," she complained to her boyfriend, Sean Baker, who sat next to her intently reading the sports section of the Chicago Examiner.

Clare tapped him on the shoulder. "Hey, football jock. I'm talking to you. My mother is driving me crazy!" Sean picked up the bottle of water next to him and took five long gulps of it. He then resumed reading.

Clare stared at him and threw her phone onto the pine coffee table in front of the couch where she rested her bare feet. The phone hit her foot hard. "Ouch," she cried as she felt a sharp pain sensation on the top of her foot. She kicked the phone off the table and burrowed her head into one of the two fake fur throw pillows that lay on the arms of the couch.

Sean stirred and looked at her. "Are you hurt?" he asked as he reached for the bottle of water again.

"No," she answered. "But you are ignoring what I am saying. Put down that water and the paper."

Sean took another gulp and burped afterwards. "No, I'm drinking this water to keep from throwing up again after eating that expensive meal last night at the

French restaurant with your friends. We usually don't eat foods rich enough to clog our arteries and induce a heart attack in one dinner sitting, even though the portions were the size of a thumbnail and the prices large enough to buy a new car."

"Funny," she declared.   "Now put down that paper."

"Look, I enjoy reading the sports section in the morning.   At least give me that.   I listen to you complain all the time."

She threw the pillow at him hitting the paper our of his hands.   "The problem is that you think you're still the football jock you were in college. You're not the quarterback any more.   You don't call all the plays.   All you think about is sports.   Can't you see that I am upset?"

"Uh, huh," Sean replied.   He picked up the throw pillow that landed on his paper and placed it next to him.

"I am going to the bathroom," Maeve shouted. She grabbed her clothes and shoes that lay scattered on the floor from the previous night.

"When you're in there, don't forget to brush your teeth.   Your breath is awful this morning," Sean retorted.

"You have some nerve telling me that," she grumbled.   "Look at you who spent the whole night throwing up on the bedroom floor.   I had to tiptoe over the mess this morning.   You had better clean it up," she hissed.   She stomped into the bathroom and banged the door behind her.

"I'll clean it up later," Sean snapped. He turned to the next page of the sports section where he scoured the news about the status of the Chicago Bears.

Clare sat on the edge of the tub. What am I going to do about Sean? she thought. For all of his faults, he certainly is handsome with his dark brown hair and pale blue eyes. When I started dating him I knew he was a sports addict. I knew he played football in college. I spend more time than I care to think about going to football games, basketball games and ice hockey games with him. But I love Sean and want to be with him. And he is a good sport about going to the movies with me to see the chick flicks I enjoy. I'm even able to get him to attend an occasional broadway musical in downtown Chicago.

Clare marched back into the living room, grabbed her phone and promptly returned to the bathroom where she checked her text messages and email. No new messages. Just the last text message from her mother which she had dutifully answered promptly. She knew if she didn't reply, her mother would continue to hound her until Clare gave up.

Chapter 7
The Night Before

Clare curled up in her bed with two pillows propped behind her and a soft, white blanket around her as she thought about the previous night. What a mess. She had invited her best friends, Lyndsey and Drake to a ritzy French restaurant to celebrate their first wedding anniversary. She had chosen the restaurant because some of her co-workers had recommended it. Also, the newspaper reviews claimed it was the hottest place in town. The chef was a finalist on the Cooking Channel's 'Up and Coming Chefs' contest on television for goodness sake. The place was so popular, she had to book their reservations two months in advance.

When they arrived, the restaurant was jammed with customers drinking at the bar while they waited for their tables. Normally, she didn't drink that much, but by the time they were seated an hour later, she, Sean, Lyndsey and Drake had consumed three glasses of wine apiece. Even worse, at the table, Drake ordered a very expensive bottle of French wine. Throughout the meal, Lyndsey and Drake seemed very happy, giving each other small kisses. They even talked about starting a family. But Clare noticed that the more they drank, the more they started criticizing each other, giving each other little personal jabs.

Lyndsey bent toward Clare and whispered in her ear. "We love each other; we just can't stand living with each other," Lyndsey said with a slur.

Clare shook her head and bit her lip. "I'm so sorry," she whispered back. "Do you need any help?"

"No," Lyndsey replied quietly. "Just don't tell anyone." Then she picked at her food and continued drinking while listening to Sean and Drake talk about the upcoming Bulls basketball game and the price of the tickets.

"Speaking of the expensive ticket prices that you bought," Lyndsey interjected angrily, "what's about that new car I want?" At that, both Lindsey and Drake started arguing about their finances.

Clare kicked Sean's leg under the table and put her hand over her mouth. "Wow, things really change after the honeymoon, don't they?" she murmured to Sean. "Finding out that the person you married is not the person you thought he was must be pretty disappointing, don't you think?"

Lyndsey overheard the comment and looked as if she had been punched in the stomach. "Drake, did you hear what Clare said?" she asked with tears in her eyes. Drake looked at her, then at Sean and Clare. "No comment," he replied.

Lyndsey grabbed her purse and stated, "It's time to go home."

Clare tried to make amends. "I was only joking," she began, but it was too late.

Lyndsey grabbed Drake's arm and they got up and walked away.

"What a rotten night," Sean exclaimed with a scowl on his face as he looked at the bill the waiter gave to him. He reached for his wallet, took out his credit card, paid the bill and left a small tip for the waiter.

Once Clare and Sean returned to her apartment, Clare lay on the couch and fell asleep for a few hours. When she woke up, her head started spinning, so she undressed quickly and dropped her clothes onto the floor next to the couch.

She shuffled to her bedroom and plopped into her bed where she held tightly to the sides of the mattress to keep from falling off. Her dizziness lasted for an hour or so and finally she fell asleep. She vaguely remembered Sean coming to bed at 3:00 A.M. or so. He kept her awake the rest of the night with his relentless vomiting over the side of the bed. At 10 o'clock in the morning, Sean opened the blinds in the bedroom and the morning sun shone in upon Clare. She woke up to face the dread day after the night before.

Now, fighting a splitting headache and nausea, she walked to the bedroom mirror and stared at the dark circles under her bloodshot green eyes. She hated the sprinkle of freckles that covered her refined straight nose. People had always complimented her on her looks, telling her she was beautiful, but she didn't see it, especially now.

Sean interrupted her thoughts. "Want to go to the Bears game tomorrow?" he asked. "A friend offered me the tickets but I have to let him know by noon today. I think it's a safe bet that Drake won't be interested after last night," he commented sarcastically.

"Sure, Sean," she replied. She ran her hands through his hair. "You know, my mother is the neediest mother in the world," she murmured staring out toward the wall. "I wish she weren't so helpless, Sean. I feel like she is incapable of doing anything and I feel guilty about not seeing her that often."

Sean sat in silence for a minute. He was convinced that any reply he gave about Clare's mother would be incorrect, so he decided to keep quiet.

Clare waited and then cleared her throat. She put her head on his shoulder and asked, "What are we going to do tonight?"

Sean picked up the arts section of the newspaper and looked through the movie reviews. "Want to go to the show? There are some good new movies out."

She shook her head. "I'd rather we get a pizza and watch a movie here," she said.

Sean pulled away from her. "You know, you do this all the time. You ask me what I want to do and when I suggest something, you turn it down and want to do something else. Why didn't you just tell me you wanted to get some food and stay in to watch a movie for the evening?" He stood and folded his arms across his chest and looked down at her.

"Well, you've got a chip on your shoulder this morning," she retorted angrily. She rose from the sofa. "Are you saying I can't make any suggestions about what we could do?"

He stared at her and shrugged his shoulders. "I'm saying it's difficult to communicate with you. It's like we're on two different wave lengths."

Clare wondered if Sean was right and decided to take a more conciliatory tone. "Let's not argue, Sean. If you want to go to a show, we'll go. What movie do you want to see?"

Sean was surprised at Clare's response and answered, "You choose."

"No, you choose. You're the one who wants to go to the show. I'd be just as happy staying at home and watching a movie."

Sean looked at his watch. "It's ten thirty. We have to get going. The Northwestern football game starts at one o'clock."

"Oh, I forgot. Who is Northwestern playing?" she asked.

"Michigan. We'd better leave now. I don't want to be late because we still have to buy the brats, buns, chips and beer and load it all into the car to tailgate with Brad, Mike and Taylor. Maybe some of their girlfriends will show up to keep you company. Right now let's load the charcoal grill, tent and chairs into the car. The traffic will be heavy with all the Michigan fans and I want to make sure we get a good tailgating spot in the parking lot."

Maeve yawned and sat up. "I'm not going, Sean. I want to do some shopping this afternoon."

His face turned red and his shoulders slumped. "You could have let me know last night," he shouted.

"Next time just give me some advance notice, okay?" He grabbed his keys and left.

Sean's reaction shocked Clare. This was the first time she had told him she didn't want to attend a football game with him and he actually seemed disappointed. Maybe he likes me more than he lets on, she thought.

Chapter 8
The Chinese Take Out Order

At five forty-five promptly, Maeve drove to the Chinese restaurant in Lake Forest. She stood in line behind two other people at the takeout counter and waited for the harried employee to get to her. Five other people lined up behind her waiting to pick up their orders. Finally, after ten minutes, the woman at the take out counter said, "What is your last name?"

"Carey," Maeve answered.

The employee searched through the many bags that filled the counter behind her. She found Maeve's order and placed it on the front counter. "That will be $35.00 please," said the woman.

Maeve placed her purse on the counter, remembered to smile and said, "I want you to pull out all the cartons from the bag and double check each one against the order I called in." The man standing behind her heard what she said and let out a large moan.

She heard the man's sigh, turned and smiled at him and said, "It will be just a moment." He rolled his eyes and made a clicking sound with his tongue.

Maeve ignored him and turned back to the counter. The take out woman patiently pulled out each little white carton from the bag. "These are your egg rolls, these are your king pao chickens, and this is your fried rice," the woman explained. "Is everything satisfactory?"

"Perfect," answered Maeve.

"Good," said the carry out woman.   She beamed a large smile at Maeve and returned each carton back into the bag.

Maeve unzipped her purse and pulled out exactly $35.00 in cash from her little pink cotton change purse and handed it to the take out woman. Maeve tried to pay for most purchases in cash and not use her credit cards.   Cash made spending money so much more painful.   Cash forced her to decide whether or not she really needed the goods or just wanted the goods. She didn't keep money in her wallet because she didn't want to fish for paper money or change with all the credit cards and identification she kept in it.   This way, her wallet seemed so much more secure.

"Thank you Mrs. Carey," the woman said.

"You are welcome," replied Maeve keeping a smile on her face.   She waited a moment and then held out her hand.   "I need my receipt, please," Maeve said.   The take out woman complied and handed her the receipt. Maeve promptly placed it in the small pocket of her purse. She zipped her purse shut, picked up the bag of food and turned to leave the restaurant.

The man behind her scowled at her, but she paid no heed to him because she always made sure that her order was complete.   Sometimes it was so frustrating to have to keep checking up on people, but otherwise how could you guarantee that you are getting what you pay for, she thought.

Chapter 9
The Memories

Maeve returned home, turned on the oven to warm and placed the Chinese take out food into it.   Then she wrapped a red cotton sweater around her slender shoulders and eased onto a lawn chair on the bluestone patio in the backyard and waited for Jeremy.   She hear the sound of the waves breaking onto the shore beyond the ravine and marveled at the passage of time.   Can it really be twenty-five years that Jeremy and I have lived in Lake Forest, she thought.

The grind of the garage door opening interrupted her reverie.   She heard Jeremy's car door slam shut and his footsteps as he walked into the mud room adjacent to the kitchen.   She jumped from her chair and hurried into the kitchen just as Jeremy entered the room. "Hi, Jeremy," she said excitedly.

"Hi, Maeve.   I'm going to get changed." Jeremy put his briefcase on the kitchen table, looked at his watch and walked to the master bedroom.

Maeve pulled a beer bottle from the refrigerator for Jeremy and poured herself a glass of wine. By the time she was finished, Jeremy had returned dressed in shorts, a cotton top and sandals.   "What are we having for dinner?" he asked.

"Chinese carryout.   Don't you remember my calling you to ask you what you wanted to eat?" She looked at him in surprise.

"Oh, that's right.   I'm sorry.   I forgot," Jeremy responded.

She offered him the beer and said, "Let's go on the patio and relax for a while before we eat."

"How was your meeting today with the man from Europe?" Maeve asked as they settled on the lawn chairs on the patio.

"Nothing special," he replied taking a gulp from the beer bottle. "He said he would let me know if he wants to place an order."

Maeve exchanged glances with Jeremy, but he averted his eyes and took another long swig from the beer bottle.

She wondered why Jeremy seemed so distant, but she pushed the thought to the back of her head and continued in an upbeat voice, "That's good. You know, Jeremy, while I was waiting for you, I was remembering when we were young and newly married. Remember the small one bedroom apartment in Niles that we rented as newlyweds? At the time, it seemed like heaven, a living room, a tiny kitchen, one bedroom, a bathroom and a balcony overlooking the parking lot. The year that we spent in the apartment flew by. We were so happy then. And then we moved to Lake Forest.

Jeremy narrowed his eyes and stared straight ahead. "Yes, we were happy because life was simple then; all we wanted was a family and a small home." He placed the beer on the side table and looked towards the lake. "Looking back, I always believed that we made a good choice in choosing to live in Lake Forest. Clare thrived in the schools here and you can't beat the place for its beauty."

Without waiting for him to continue, Maeve shook her head and asked heatedly, "What do you mean by believed? Don't you still think it was the right choice?"

He gulped the rest of the beer down, shaking the bottle to coax the last few drops out of it. "It doesn't matter whether or not I believe we made a wise decision now. Clare is grown and we've been here over twenty-five years. What was right then might not be right now." He picked up his empty bottle and stood up. "Do you want anything from the kitchen? I'm going to get another beer."

"No thanks," Maeve answered testily. "I've barely touched my wine." She rose and followed Jeremy into the kitchen. "You know, you're right. Things have changed quite a bit in the years that we have lived here. I felt so happy when we bought our first home here, that cute three bedroom ranch near Lake Forest High School. Remember how we painted all the rooms when we moved in and you mowed the lawn each weekend?" She finished her wine and held out the empty glass to Jeremy who poured her another drink.

"You sold advertising and I taught first grade. We had dinner together every night when you weren't traveling and we usually went out for a hamburger and to the movies every weekend."

Jeremy placed his empty bottle of beer on the kitchen counter and took another beer from the refrigerator. "Yes, but we weren't satisfied. I wanted to be my own boss." He paused and glared at Maeve. "You encouraged me to open my own company selling television advertising."

Maeve smiled. "You don't have the personality to work for someone else. But I must admit, it wasn't pleasant at first. I was frightened because we had to mortgage our home to fund the new company and I hardly saw you the first year. You spent most of your time making sales calls and traveling the country trying to make a success of the new business. But look at how well you have done!" She clicked her wine glass against his beer bottle and said happily, "To you and your success!"

Jeremy looked away and put his beer bottle down. "Do you want another wine?" he snapped.

"No thanks," she answered and wondered why Jeremy was so crabby. She took some hummus out of the refrigerator and scooped it into a small dish and arranged crackers around the dish. "Want some?" she offered as she held out a small paper plate to him. He reached for the plate, scooped some crackers and hummus onto it, dipped the crackers into the hummus and ate them.

As he continued to eat, Maeve took a sip of her wine and asked, "Remember when I found out that I was pregnant?"

"How could I forget? You told me at our second anniversary dinner. It was the best present you could have given to me." His phone rang and he pulled it out of his pocket. "Hello," he said impatiently. Then he walked towards the den. "I have to take this call, Maeve. I'll be back in a few minutes."

Chapter 10
The Beginning

I wonder why Jeremy is so crabby lately? Maeve thought as she pulled out the Chinese take out from the oven. When Jeremy returned, she asked, "Who was that on the phone?"

"It was the European I mentioned today. He wants to place the order," Jeremy said with a sigh of relief.

"All of your hard work has paid off," Maeve commented with pride. "I still can't believe how fast your company grew. I was so lucky when I married you." She placed the food on the table and they sat down.

Jeremy took a bite of one of the egg rolls and swigged another gulp of beer. "I did my best, Maeve." He hesitated and then swallowed hard. "Sometimes I think my best is just not good enough for you," he said sadly.

Maeve couldn't believe what she was hearing. "Why do you say that? Everyone admires you and looks up to you."

"I don't care about other people. I care about you," he answered soberly. He crossed his hands in front of his face and rested his chin on them.

Maeve frowned and was taken by surprise. "Why Jeremy, I care about you too. I look up to you. I always have and I love you." She waited for his reply, but he picked up his fork and started to eat the kung pao chicken.

Maeve shifted in her chair and started eating. "Jeremy, getting back to our conversation before, remember the room we prepared for Clare before she was born? We decorated it in pale yellow because it was a neutral color that would be suitable for a boy or girl. I bought the white wicker bassinet and the yellow cotton coverlet with white dots that fit over the bassinet. We chose a white wood dresser and a white changing table that we placed on the wall opposite the bassinet. At least ten teddy bears sat on the shelf over the changing tale. It was your idea to keep the teddy bears there to occupy the baby when diaper time came, you know."

Jeremy gave a hearty laugh. "I'm more domestic than you give me credit for," he chuckled.

Maeve was relieved that the mood in the room had lightened. This was the first time she and Jeremy had laughed together in a long time. "Do you recall how I called you at work when the labor pains started? I told you to stay at the office since the contractions were two hours apart, but you charged into the house a half hour later. For the next ten hours you held me in your arms on the living room sofa as I sat clutching a pillow to my stomach. When the contractions were an hour apart, you called the doctor. He told us to come to his office for a check up. I was dilating so quickly, that he decided to admit me into the hospital.

Jeremy smiled. "It seems so funny to look back on that now, but it didn't seem funny then. I was worried that we wouldn't make it to the hospital on time because you wanted me to get your overnight bag from our apartment."

"I still appreciate the fact that after we left for the hospital, you agreed to turn around and drive us back home to get my overnight bag that I left at the apartment. I'll never forget how anxious you looked during that ride. Your hands were clutching the steering wheel, your eyes were bulging and your head was bobbling back and forth from the street to me sitting next to you."

He chuckled. "That's a pretty accurate description of how I felt," he said. "And I'll never forget the sight of you sitting in the car taking in deep breaths from your nose and blowing them out through your mouth while I jumped out of the car and ran inside the house to pick up the overnight case you had packed with the stuff to get you through the birth. It was a miracle we arrived at the hospital in one piece because I was driving so fast."

"Boy, you are right about that. By the time we arrived at the hospital, the contractions were coming ten minutes apart and they were squeezing every part of my body. Once I was in my hospital room, I spent an hour lying on the bed panting. It became so bad that I asked you to hand me the paper bag inside of my overnight case," she laughed.

"I wouldn't call it asking. You started screaming and shouted, 'Give me the paper bag now," Jeremy recalled with a grin.

"I needed that bag badly. Then while I was breathing into it, I looked over at you and couldn't believe that you sat next to me sucking on one of the lollipops I had brought to keep my mouth moist."

They laughed together at the memory. "They were good lollipops," Jeremy recalled happily. "And not two hours later, you gave birth to our beautiful baby girl, Clare, with her curly red hair and big green eyes."

"She was a beauty and still is," said Maeve remembering how she felt when she first held Clare. She picked at the kung pao chicken while Jeremy fixed himself another drink, this time a scotch and soda and poured another glass of wine for Maeve. The ringing of his phone interrupted them again.

He looked at his phone and said, "Sorry, Maeve, but I have to take another call. I'll be back in a few minutes." He rose from the table and left the room.

"No problem," murmured Maeve sadly. She sat at the table and nibbled at the fried rice while waiting for Jeremy to complete his call.

Jeremy returned in five minutes, took another gulp of his scotch and soda and looked lost in thought.

"Hey, what's going on?" Maeve asked with concern. "You look preoccupied with something. Who was on the call?"

"Just another customer," Jeremy replied quickly. He leaned forward as if so say something to her, but then slumped in his chair and kept quiet.

Chapter 11
The Large House

Maeve glanced at Jeremy for a moment, then decided to get up and start clearing the plates off the kitchen table.   "Since we were remembering so many happy times from our past, while you were on the call, I was thinking about when we bought this house. After Clare was born, I drove by this home so many times when I used to take her to the beach. I loved it the moment I saw it. It knew it was a bit big for our small family, but thought it would be perfect when we had more children. Unfortunately, we couldn't have more children," she reminisced dolefully.

Jeremy sat straight up and hit his hand upon the table. "No regrets, Maeve," he spoke forcefully. "We have Clare. Let's be thankful for her."

Before he could comment any more, Maeve said," You were never really enthusiastic about buying this home Was it because of its size? I mean five bedrooms, a living room, dining room, large kitchen, family room, library/den, finished basement and five bathrooms is a bit much. But you seem to be getting a lot of use out of your office in the basement."

"You're right. I thought we didn't need such a large home, but you wanted it so much when it came on the market, that I figured, why not?"

"Well, you knew that I always wanted to live on the water. Even as a teen, I drew a picture of a home near the water and tacked it to my bedroom wall. I made a promise to myself that I would live next to the water some day. Besides, your business was thriving and we could afford it."

"I knew that I never could work for anyone else. I decided a long time ago that I wanted to be my own boss. I saw too many people in my industry being let go because of their age and I vowed that would never happen to me," he declared forcefully.

"But the years have flown by so fast. It all seems a blur," Maeve said softly. "Clare is on her own now. I hope she still doesn't resent me for not allowing any teenage parties at our home. I was afraid that her friends would sneak in beer, get drunk and then drive off and get into an accident."

"I think she was upset at the time, but now she knows it was for the best," Jeremy explained.

"Fortunately, you decided to stop traveling when she was eight years old or so. It meant so much to her that you were able to attend her soccer games and parent-teacher conferences with me. But time has passed so quickly."

"It all seems a blur and what do we have to show for it?" he asked harshly. He set down his drink and stared hard at Maeve.

'Why are you so melancholy, Jeremy? Look at all we have now. We have Clare, this house, each other and your business. What more could we want?"

"Let's finish eating," he said abruptly. "I have work to do downstairs." They ate in silence and afterwards, Jeremy walked down to the basement while Maeve cleared the table and put on her rubber gloves.

Jeremy certainly seems different tonight, she thought. I wish he would confide in me. She rinsed the dishes and placed them in the dishwasher. Then she took off the gloves and lathered her chapped hands with lotion. But what am I going to do about me? Maeve thought. Maybe I'll get that job I applied for. All I do now is rearrange this house, take my parents out to lunch, spend every Friday taking them shopping for food, to doctor's appointments, doing their bills and cooking for them. I don't want to go back to teaching and I've never been into luncheons or charity events or women's groups. I want to be more like Clare and spread my wings.

Chapter 12
The Secret

A few days later, Maeve finished her workout in the upstairs bedroom exercise room and walked down to the kitchen to get a bottle of cold water. As she gulped down the water, the phone rang. Caller ID showed the O'Mara Law Firm. Maeve answered the phone. A voice at the other end asked, "Hello, is Mrs. Carey home?"

"This is she," replied Maeve. Her heart started to race.

"Mrs. Carey, my name is Damien Flynn, from the O'Mara Law Firm. Mr. O'Mara received your resume and would like to set up an interview with you. Are you available this Thursday at ten o'clock?"

"Yes," she responded breathlessly as she wiped the sweat off her face with a paper towel. It was all she could do to maintain her composure. "Thank you, Mr. Flynn. I'll be there on Thursday." She couldn't believe her good luck. She actually had an interview. She called Jeremy at work, but he didn't answer, so she left him a voice mail message about her good news. A few minutes later, she received a call from him.

"Maeve," he shouted, "you didn't tell me you were applying for a job. Congratulations on getting the interview! What kind of job did you apply for?"

"A legal assistant in a small law firm in downtown Lake Forest. I really can't believe that I was called in for an interview."

A minute passed before Jeremy spoke. "What's the name of the law firm?"

"The O'Mara Law Firm. Have you heard of it?"

"Not really. I was just wondering." Jeremy paced the floor and started to perspire.

"Are you still there, Jeremy?" Maeve stared at the phone to make sure she had not lost the connection.

"Of course I'm still here. Why didn't you tell me you had applied for a job? I thought we didn't keep secrets from each other," Jeremy said in an annoyed voice.

"I just wanted to surprise you, Jeremy," Maeve answered. "I wasn't keeping a secret from you. I just need to do something for myself, that's all. I decided to apply for the job as a lark. You have your business, darling, and it's time I started earning my keep around here," she laughed. Already she was planning on what to have for dinner to celebrate. "By the way, what time will you be home?"

"Around seven o'clock," he answered quietly.

"See you then, darling. I'll make your favorite chicken marsala for dinner." Maeve pressed the end call button on her cell phone, walked into the den, booted her computer on and looked up the O'Mara Law Firm on the internet. The only entry she found reported that Stephen O'Mara was a sole practitioner with the firm and specialized in wills, trusts and real estate. Beyond that she found nothing except the firm's name, address, phone number and directions to it. She entered Stephen O'Mara's name into the search engine and up came a short obituary of a Sherri O'Mara. The obituary stated that Sherri

O'Mara had died the previous year as a result of a car accident in Lake Bluff, Illinois.   She left only two survivors, her husband Stephen O'Mara and her son, Damien Flynn.   She was cremated and her ashes were scattered in Lake Michigan.

Maeve printed out the obituary, folded the paper and tucked it into her desk drawer.   Although she didn't find much information on Stephen O'Mara, at least she had some background on him.   And the Damien who called her must be Sherri O'Mara's son, she surmised.

Chapter 13
The Mess

After he ended the call with Maeve, Jeremy dialed Stephen O'Mara's phone number. Stephen answered on the third ring. "O'Mara here," he said quickly.

"Stephen, this is Jeremy Carey. I just got a call from my wife telling me that she applied for a job at your firm and that you called her in for an interview." Jeremy sounded very stressed.

Stephen swallowed and his mouth dropped open. "I thought you knew about it, Jeremy," he said cautiously. When there was no reply from Jeremy, he reconsidered and offered, "I'm sorry if you didn't. I'll have my new assistant call her back and tell her I hired someone else."

"No. Look Stephen, I'm all for her getting a job with your firm if you think she is qualified. I just want to make sure you don't tell her about the financial problems I've been having with my company and that I have been considering suing some of my clients for non-payment. Will you keep all this to yourself when you interview her?"

Stephen belted down the last of the scotch he was drinking, his usual pick me up in the morning. "I'm bound by attorney-client privilege, Jeremy. Don't worry about anything. I have your file and a few other ones locked in my desk. My assistant quit a month ago, so you won't have to worry about her discussing your case with your wife," Stephen said soothingly.

"Thanks, Stephen," Jeremy answered.   He pressed the end button, grabbed a tissue from his desk and wiped the sweat that was dripping down the sides of his face.   If Maeve finds out about the precarious state of my business, she will crumble like a cookie, he worried.   Her first question would be, Why didn't you tell me?   Jeremy didn't want to face the relentless questions that she would throw at him and the look of hurt on her face.   He shut down his computer and decided to buy a bottle of wine to surprise her tonight and to celebrate her upcoming interview.

Then he shook his head as he sat at his desk in his office and stared at the spreadsheets before him.   Sales had fallen by seventy percent.   The economy was in shambles and no one wanted to buy advertising any more.   So far, he had laid off all of his twelve employees, including his secretary.   His line of credit at the bank was maxed out and soon he would have to close the business.   The thought made him almost physically sick.   No use telling Maeve about this mess I'm in, he thought sadly.   She would just start crying and ask a million questions.

And I don't have any answers except that we may have to sell the house.   What I need is some good luck and the economy to turn around.   An influx of cash would help too.   Disgusted, he decided to take a break and go out for the rest of the afternoon.   He had three hours to kill before he needed to be home. He rose from his desk, walked to his car and drove to the grocery store where he bought a bottle of merlot.

Then he took a long drive to Lake Geneva, Wisconsin, to clear his head. He sat at a small restaurant overlooking the lake and tried to think of any other options he had to salvage his finances besides closing down the business and selling his home. Three hours later, Jeremy pulled into the garage of his house. He picked up the bottle of merlot, put on his happy face and walked into the house.

"Maeve, I'm home," he call out loudly. He placed his briefcase on the dining room table and walked into the kitchen.

Maeve looked up from the stove where she was cooking the chicken marsala. "You are so sweet to bring me my favorite wine," she said as he handed the wine to her. She kissed him on the cheek, turned and placed the wine on the counter, pulled a wine opener out of the drawer and popped the cork off of the bottle. Then she poured the wine into two wine glasses and offered one to Jeremy.

Jeremy held up the glass and clicked it against hers. "To you and your success in your interview. I am so proud of you," he spoke nervously. He drained half of his glass of wine.

"And I am so proud of you, Jeremy," Maeve answered as she took her sip of wine. "Hopefully, I will be just a smidgen as successful as you."

Jeremy gulped the rest of his wine and poured himself another. "What did I do to deserve you?" he asked numbly, finishing off his second drink.

Maeve smiled. "That is what I ask myself about you every day! Now the chicken is ready. Go wash your hands and you can tell me all about your day while we eat." She tossed the sliced tomatoes into the green leaf salad with the shaved carrots and red cabbage and poured the oil, balsamic vinegar, salt and pepper dressing onto it. "I just can't believe the firm called me for an interview," she said in amazement. "After all, I haven't worked in twenty years. I'm going to look up all possible interview questions on the internet and practice them before this Thursday."

Chapter 14
Preparations for the Interview

Interview day finally arrived. Maeve bounded out of bed at seven o'clock. What would be appropriate to wear for this interview? she asked herself excitedly. She looked in her walk-in closet, where her clothes hung neatly in categories according to color and season. Built in cubicles held her shoes, and her sweaters and casual tops lay stylishly in the glass drawers. She chose a white cotton blouse, navy blue blazer and skirt and navy pumps and laid them on the chair in her dressing room. These will be perfect, she thought as she held them up to the full length mirror. Not too flashy, not too severe.

She had spent most of the previous night going over her responses to the interview questions she might be asked. Since Jeremy was still sleeping, she quietly stepped out of the bedroom and walked into the kitchen to practice her answers again. She washed her hands before she pulled a tea bag out of the tea box stored in the T section of the kitchen cabinet. She meticulously closed the top of the tea box. As usual, she placed the teacup under the water spigot on the door of the refrigerator, filled it almost to the top and then microwaved the cup for exactly one minute. Then she dunked the bag exactly twenty times until the hot water turned a deep rich brown. She took a long sip and felt the liquid warm her throat and soothe her frazzled nerves. "Please let this go well," she prayed fervently. "I really want this job."

She peeled a banana and dropped it into the blender.   Then she added one-half cup of non-fat plain yogurt, one-half cup of strawberries, one cup of ice and one-half cup of orange juice to the blender. She turned the timer on the blender to three minutes and flicked on the frappe switch until the timer rang and the smoothie glistened a frothy pink. She poured the smoothie into a tall glass and drank it while reviewing the answers to the questions she might be asked.

Why have you been out of the workforce for so long? (I stayed home to raise my child.)   What experience do you have? (I taught first grade with twenty children. They thrived in my classroom with a combination of personal attention, discipline and quality lesson plans.) What are your strengths, your weaknesses? (Strength: I am organized and follow up on things. Weakness: I sometimes go overboard in trying to achieve perfection.) She went through the other job interview questions she had printed out from a job hunting website, practiced her answers and finally felt ready to face her interview.

At eight o'clock, she stepped into the shower for a long, hot wash, then wrapped a towel around herself, blow dried her hair and dressed in the white blouse, navy blazer and skirt and pumps she had laid out. She stroked brown mascara onto her eyelashes, brushed rose blush across her cheeks and applied pink gloss onto her lips. She combed her brown hair into a bob and looked at her wristwatch. Eight fifty-five in the morning. Almost time to call Mom and Dad, she realized. I have just enough time to slather the hand cream on my hands before I call them, she thought in relief. I know I'll have to shake hands with Mr. O'Mara today and they feel so dry and cracked. She squirted an extra dollop of cream onto her hands and rubbed them softly until her hands felt smooth. Then she called her parents.

She waited while the phone rang and rang. Her father, Paul O'Connor, took a sip of his coffee and drummed the fingers of his left hand on the kitchen table as he waited for Maeve's nine o'clock call. The phone hung on the wall right next to the kitchen table. When the phone rang, he reached over and picked it up. The stroke he had suffered eight years before had damaged his body, but it did not dampen his disposition.

"Good morning, Maeve. All is well here. Mother is still sleeping and I am minding the house," he said in a firm voice. "Appreciate that you're calling. And how are things with you this morning?' he inquired cheerfully.

"Just fine, Dad," she replied happily. "Give Mom my love. I'll call you both at eight o'clock tonight as usual and I'll see you both tomorrow to do the shopping and pay the bills."

"Talk you you later," Paul said. He hung up the phone and took another sip of his coffee. Maeve was a good girl, he thought emotionally. A bit stubborn at times, but for the most part we raised her well. He looked out the kitchen window to the street in front of their house. I hope Therese feels well. today. I don't know how much longer I can take care of her. The dementia is getting worse. He sighed and took another drink of his coffee while he waited for Therese to wake up.

By now, it was nine fifteen. Maeve grabbed her purse and flicked the basement lights on and off. It was her way of saying goodbye to Jeremy who was now working in his basement office.

"Bye, Maeve," Jeremy call out. "Good luck with the interview. Kill them with your smarts."

Chapter 15
The Interview

Maeve arrived for her interview thirty minutes early. She smiled brightly when she walked into the office. A young man greeted her. He looked about twenty years old and could have been a Brooks Brothers model. Reed thin, he dressed impeccably with a starched white shirt, well cut tan suit and green silk tie. His short, blonde, curly hair was combed back neatly in waves, not a hair out of place. "You must be Maeve Carey," he stated cooly. His dark brown eyes peered at her from under his wire-rimmed glasses. For a moment she thought he looked angry, but then he smiled at her. "I'm Damien. Please have a seat. Mr. O'Mara is in a meeting. He will be finished in a few minutes." He sniffled and wiped his nose with a tissue.

"Thank you," Maeve replied, her broad smile intact. She sat down in a comfortable tan stuffed chair and glanced around the reception area. Paintings of horses lined the brown walls and the dark wood doors and floors shone as if they had just been polished. Tan and white striped drapes hung from the windows. All in all, she felt a bit claustrophobic.

She picked up Sports Illustrated and leafed through it, all the time glancing up at Damien once in a while. He kept his head down and seemed preoccupied with some papers on his desk. A short time later, the phone rang. He answered it, then rose and walked over to Maeve and said, "Please follow me." He led her down the hall and opened the door to a large office.

Stephen O'Mara was just finishing up a phone call. He put his hand over the phone and snarled, "I told you to give me a few minutes, Damien." Then he looked at Maeve, smiled and motioned to her to come in. "Sit in that chair," he said pointing to the wood chair in front of his desk. Then he pointed at Damien and said brusquely, "Close the door after you and finish that special project I gave you. You know the one I am talking about."

"Yes, Stephen," Damien said politely with a frown on his face as he left the office and closed the door.

When Maeve sat down, Stephen took his hand off the phone and said tersely, "Nice talking to you, Rubin." He rose to his six foot five inches height and continued, "We're ramping up to go to trial in a few months. Don't worry. You're going to collect a lot of money. Talk to you tomorrow." With that, he hung up the phone and extended his hand to Maeve.

Maeve gritted her teeth and prayed that the hand lotion was still working as she held out her hand and shook Stephen's hand. If her touch felt rough, he didn't show it. "Very please to meet you, Mr. O'Mara," she said smiling. Stephen O'Mara looks like a former football player, Maeve thought. He must weigh 250 pounds and his hands are thick and stocky.

"Call me Stephen," he responded warmly. He sat down. "I read your resume and was impressed. My assistant moved out of state, so I need someone who can start right away. Tell me about yourself." He cracked his knuckles and leaned back in his tan leather chair.

Maeve responded with the answer she had practiced at home. "I used to teach school before our daughter was born. I've spent the bulk of the past twenty-one years caring for her. Right now I'm looking for full time work. I'm detail oriented, enthusiastic and a quick learner." She hoped he didn't notice her nervousness.

Stephen's brown eyes stared at Maeve. "You know, you remind me so much of my late wife. She passed away suddenly in a car accident last year. She had been a school teacher too. I always admired her ability to deal with the kids in the classroom every day. She was so organized and so dedicated to them." His phone rang again. He pressed a button and spoke into the intercom. "I told you to hold all calls," he snapped in a tight voice. He slammed the phone down, pushed back his chair and walked to a table on the other side of the room. "Would you like some coffee or tea?" he asked quietly.

"Tea, please. Just black," Maeve responded quickly.

He poured the tea into a large cup and brought it to her. "I told you I need someone right away and I mean right away. Can you start on Monday?"

Maeve almost dropped the teacup in her lap. "You've made your decision already?" she asked incredulously.

"Yes, I have," he replied frowning. "Well, what's your answer?"

"What exactly does the job involve?" she asked quickly. She tried to balance the teacup on the arm of the chair, but it teetered a bit so she held it in her lap.

"Answering the phones, keeping the files and taking care of my calendar. I do a lot of the work myself, but I need someone to keep me organized. I have a student, Damien, who has been working part time this month, but he'll start his senior year in college shortly," he explained as he sat down next to her.

"I have no doubt that I can keep you organized," Maeve said with the confidence she didn't feel. She cleared her throat and took a deep breath. "I do have a few more questions."

"Well, shoot," said Stephen. He stared at her intently.

"How much does the job pay and what are the hours?" Her heart was pounding in her chest.

Stephen smiled. "I'm offering $40,000 per year to start and the hours are eight A.M. to five P.M. Monday through Thursday with an hour for lunch. I don't work on Fridays unless I have to appear in court. You might have to work a few Fridays if I need you. I'd like you to start this coming Monday. Does that seem acceptable to you?"

"That is perfect," she replied happily. "I accept your offer." She placed the teacup on Stephen's desk.

"Fine," said Stephen. "Come with me and I'll walk you to the reception area." He held the door for Maeve and followed her to the lobby. "See you at eight A.M. sharp on Monday." He turned towards Damien, and said, "Please show Maeve out." Stephen then returned to his office.

"Congratulations," Damien snapped.   He rose and escorted her to the front door.

"Thank you," Maeve replied. She walked onto the front steps of the building and waved goodbye to Damien. "See you on Monday."

"I'll be waiting for you," Damien responded quickly. "Have a good weekend and drive safely." He waved to her and closed the door.

I cannot believe my good luck, Maeve thought as she crossed the street to her BMW. When she started the car, she noticed an alarm sign appear on the dashboard.   The red letters stated SERVICE NEEDED. I'll make an appointment for next Saturday, she promised to herself. Right now, I cannot wait to tell Jeremy and Clare the good news!

Chapter 16
The Good News

Jeremy answered his cell phone as he pulled into the driveway of his house. "Hi, Stephen," Jeremy said while he parked the car in the garage.

"Just wanted you to know that I hired Maeve," Stephen said. He turned the key in the lock of the bottom right hand drawer of his desk and hooked the key on his key ring. "As I said before, your file is locked in my desk, so you don't have to worry about her finding out about your financial problems."

"Stephen, thanks for calling and letting me know you hired Maeve," Jeremy replied slowly. "If she's half as organized in your office as she is at home, you'll be very happy you hired her." He ended the call and thought for a moment. Maybe this will keep Maeve so busy she won't ask any questions about the business and won't realize it is in danger of going under. Jeremy walked through the garage door into the mud room and then into the laundry room and kitchen.

"Hi, Maeve," he called out as he pulled a bottle of beer from the refrigerator and placed it on the kitchen table. "I'm going upstairs to change." He returned a few minutes later dressed in jogging pants and a casual cotton top and picked up the beer.

"How was your day?" Maeve asked with a grin on her face. She could hardly wait to tell Jeremy the good news.

"Fine," he answered nonchalantly. "How was your interview?"

Maeve could not contain her excitement. "I have some good news to tell you. I got the job!" she exclaimed happily.

Jeremy put down his beer and put his arms about her. "I am so proud of you! Congratulations! When do you start?"

"Monday. And the hours are perfect. I have most Fridays off, so I can still go to my parents' home to help them."

Jeremy gave Maeve a kiss on the cheek, then he took the beer and went into the family room and sat in his favorite brown leather lounge chair. He placed the beer on the small wood side table, turned on the television and promptly fell asleep.

Maeve peeked into the family room when she heard Jeremy's loud snoring. He must be so tired, Maeve thought as she finished cooking the pork chops and apple recipe from a new food magazine she had bought. At dinner time, she tiptoed into the family room and gently shook Jeremy. He woke up quickly. "Maeve, what time is it?" he asked sleepily.

"Six o'clock," she responded cheerfully. "Dinner is ready."

"I'll be right in," he said quickly. He jumped up, turned off the television, picked up his beer and brought it into the kitchen. As they sat eating the pork chops smothered with baked apples, spinach sauteed with garlic and baked potatoes, Jeremy put down his fork and looked at her as if he had just flunked a test in school. "Oh, Maeve. I'm so sorry I didn't ask you how the interview went. Tell me all about it."

"Jeremy, it was the quickest interview in the history of the world. He asked me a few questions about my background and all of a sudden, he offered me the job. I asked him a few questions, such as hours and salary and I accepted the job." She waited for Jeremy's response, but could not tell by looking at him whether he was happy or upset about her taking the job.

"How much did he offer to pay you?" Jeremy murmured.

"Forty thousand dollars a year and the hours are Monday through Thursday, eight o'clock to five o'clock with an hour for lunch. Doesn't this sound good?" she asked proudly.

"This is wonderful! I am so proud of you! After we eat this delicious meal, I'll treat you to an ice cream cone down at the beach to celebrate your new job!" Jeremy exclaimed excitedly.

When they were finished eating, Jeremy cleared the dishes from the kitchen table. Maeve put on her rubber gloves and rinsed the dishes in the sink before placing them in the dishwasher. She pulled out the garbage bag from the trash compactor and left it next to the refrigerator.

"I'll take out the garbage," Jeremy offered. "Do you have any recycles to take out too?"

"Thank you," Maeve replied gratefully. "No recycles."

Jeremy picked up the garbage bag and placed it in the garbage bin in the garage and returned to the kitchen. "Are you ready to go to the beach?" he asked hopefully.

"Almost ready," responded Maeve as she rubbed on the hand lotion. Then, she changed into a pair of sandals and shorts.

Chapter 17
The Meeting on the Beach

Maeve and Jeremy descended the wooden steps at the back of their yard that led to the Lake Forest beach. As they strolled the sidewalk next to the sandy shore, they observed fresh faced teenagers playing beach volleyball near the boat dock. Passing the breakers, they gazed at the sailboats skimming across the lake and the speed boats slicing through the lake leaving tall wakes of water behind them. Maeve and Jeremy paused at the playground where mothers and fathers pushed their young children on the playground swings and stood guard as they slid down the slides near the sidewalk. Finally, she and Jeremy admired the bronzed fishermen who stood on the pier and cast their rods into the lake.

"We are so lucky to live here, don't you think?" Maeve asked as they approached the ice cream stand.

"There's not a better place to be," Jeremy replied quietly. "What flavor of ice cream do you want?"

She read the menu and said, "Butter pecan. What are you going to have?" she asked. Before Jeremy could answer, she noticed a man walking towards them. As he got closer she realized that he was Damien.

"Damien," she call out to him. He glanced towards her, but just kept on walking with his head down. "Damien," she called again and waved to him.

"Maeve," he answered quickly. He continued towards her. "I forgot to wear my glasses and I couldn't see who you were from where I was. I'm sorry."

"Oh, that's all right," Maeve said calmly. She turned to Jeremy. "Jeremy, this is Damien Flynn. He works at the O'Mara Law Firm and was kind enough to set up a time for my interview."

Jeremy shook Damien's hand. "Nice to meet you, Damien," he told him. He sure has a weak handshake, thought Jeremy and his hands are cold and clammy.

"Pleasure to meet you, Jeremy," Damien commented uncertainly. He pulled back his hand abruptly and placed it in his pocket. "You made a great impression on Stephen today, Maeve. He couldn't stop talking about you after you left." Damien sniffled, then reached into his pocket and pulled out some tissues. "Pardon me," he spoke slowly as he wiped his nose. "I have allergies."

"No problem, Damien. I have allergies too. And thank you for telling me about Stephen. I know he won't regret hiring me. See you at the office on Monday."

"Yes, but I want you to know that I am leaving in a week. I'll show you the ropes next week, but after that you'll be on your own."

"Damien is starting his senior year in college," Maeve mentioned to Jeremy.

"How do you know that?" demanded Damien angrily.

Maeve looked stricken. "Because Stephen mentioned it to me at my interview today," she answered defensively.

Jeremy interjected quickly. "What are you majoring in?"

Damien paused and then responded, "Business and then I'll go into law."

"Well, good luck," Jeremy said heartily.

"Oh, that is wonderful," Maeve smiled. "Will you go to work with Stephen when you graduate?"

Damien spotted a man in the distance and waved to him. "Well, I have to get going. My friend is over there. I'll see you on Monday."

"Very nice to meet you, Damien," said Jeremy. He extended his hand. Damien pulled his hand out of his pocket and shook Jeremy's hand and then stuffed it back into his pocket and walked away.

Jeremy frowned. Maeve noticed his frown and asked,"Why do you have that sour look on your face?"

"There's something about that guy that I don't like. I don't know what it is, but he sure doesn't look a person in the eye. And he said he didn't recognize you because he wasn't wearing his glasses, but he sure spotted his friend in the distance right now."

"Oh, he's just young and shy, that's all. He was very polite at the firm today. But he certainly got upset that Stephen told me he was starting his senior year in college." Maeve shook her head and took Jeremy's hand. "Let's not talk about him and get our ice cream."

They ordered the ice cream and sat contentedly on a bench facing the lake and watched the parade of people passing by. When they finished the ice cream, they climbed the wooden stairs that led to the backyard of their home and entered their house.

"I have some work to do," Jeremy mentioned quickly.   He then took the stairs down to the basement.

Maeve sat at the kitchen table and sent a text to Clare telling her about her new job. Clare sent a reply text stating simply: Happy for you!

Clare then sent a text to Jeremy. Daddy, good news about Mom's job, but bad news for me. Lost my job. One hundred people laid off, poor economy. Can I borrow a couple month's rent from you? Don't want Mom to worry.   You know how she obsesses over things. Love, Clare.

Jeremy texted back: Sorry about the bad news, but don't worry.   You'll have a new job soon. Will send you the rent money. Love, Dad.

Chapter 18
The Accident

The hands of the alarm clock glowed green in the dark of Maeve's bedroom. Three fifteen in the morning. Maeve hated these sleepless nights. She tossed and turned, kicking off the blankets. A hot flash rolled over her, leaving her flushed and sweating. After a few minutes, she shivered and pulled the covers up again. Then another hot flash consumed her. She pulled up her legs and jammed them into the covers and pushed the blankets to the bottom of the bed.

This went on until five thirty in the morning when she jumped out of bed, washed her hands and threw on a pair of shorts, a top and her socks and gym shoes. She took a bottle of water out of the fridge and jogged back up to the upstairs exercise room. She flipped on the lights, pressed the remote to turn on the television and climbed onto the treadmill. She set the control to the manual medium level for three minutes at a 2.3 rate and started the slow walk to warm up. After three minutes, she set the rate to 3.5. The treadmill moved more quickly and she picked up her walking pace in order to keep up with the machine.

Maeve turned to Channel 2 news. Nothing much was happening in the news domestically or internationally, but the weather man reported that a strong thunderstorm was blanketing the Chicago area and would soon arrive in the northern suburbs.

Heavy rains were producing a slow and treacherous commute to work.

Good thing I don't have a long way to go to work today, she thought eagerly.   After all, this is Monday and my first day working for Stephen O'Mara. After thirty minutes, she climbed onto the stationary bike and rode for another fifteen minutes. Then she pressed the off button on the television remote and headed to the master bedroom to take a hot shower. Jeremy was still sleeping, so she quietly tiptoed into the bathroom, washed her hands, stepped into the shower and turned on the water. The spray of hot water from the shower head felt comforting. The soap left a film on her skin that made it feel softer. She washed her hair once, rinsed it and washed it again and rinsed it again. She liked being clean.

She turned off the water, stepped out of the shower, placed a towel around her hair and dried herself off. Then she put on her bra, panties and robe, pulled out the hair dryer, turned her head upside down and blew her hair until it was dry. She placed two large rollers in the front of her hair and padded back into the bedroom.

By this time, Jeremy had woken up and ambled out to the driveway to pick up the morning newspaper.

With a quick flick, Maeve turned on the electric lights in the bedroom. They glowed brightly. As she walked into the closet, she tried to determine what to wear. She chose the tan blazer and tan skirt. Then she pulled a white cotton top over her head and finished dressing. The mound of clothes she had worn the previous day lay neatly folded on her dresser, so she scooped them up and threw them down the laundry shoot to the laundry room on the first floor. Then she walked to the kitchen where she washed her hands again.

"Wow, it's pouring out there," Jeremy exclaimed as he took off his soaked jacket. He pulled the newspaper out of its wet, plastic lining, threw the plastic lining into the garbage and laid the paper onto the kitchen table. "I'm going to work out upstairs," he said quickly, "and then I'll be making some calls in the basement. See you later."

Thinking of the coming day, Maeve alleviated her stress by   automatically washing her hands. Then she poured one-half cup of orange juice into a glass and one-half cup of Cheerios and skim milk into a bowel and sat at the table.   As she skimmed through the paper, she sipped the juice and nibbled at the cereal.

She paused at another article about heroin use in the northern suburbs of Chicago.   The article reported that heroin users from the North Shore were typically white and under twenty-five years of age. They usually started with alcohol or tobacco, then progressed to drugs such as marijuana, then to prescription drugs such as painkillers and on to heroin due to its relatively cheap price. With just a car trip or a train ride to the city or with local peddlers, young people could obtain the heroin easily.

Maeve frowned as she finished the article. Nothing like this would happen in Lake Forest, she thought.   She folded the paper and laid it neatly on the table for Jeremy. She glanced at the clock on the microwave which glowed seven o'clock now. She slipped her hands into her rubber gloves and washed the breakfast dishes and placed them neatly into the dishwasher. Then she removed the rubber gloves, rubbed hand lotion into her hands, strode into the master bathroom, stood in front of the mirror and started to apply her makeup.

The little cracks in her hands began to burn. She had washed her hands four times so far this morning, not that she was counting, but the washing was a necessity to keep her hands clean and avoid getting any illness from the spread of germs. Small drops of blood oozed out of the cracks. She tried applying more hand cream, but now even the hand cream didn't improve the blood caked cracks. It was a source of embarrassment to her, but she couldn't help washing her hands when she was under a lot of stress. All she could do was hide her hands and continue to put cream on them to try to heal them. She dipped her fingers into the cream jar next to the sink and slathered dollops onto the tops of her hands and rubbed them together. A few minutes later, her skin seemed to have absorbed the cream.

She pulled the paper bag lunch she had made the previous night (three slices of turkey on whole wheat bread topped with mustard, lettuce and a tomato slice, an orange cut into slices, and a bottle of water) out of the refrigerator. The kitchen clock now displayed seven forty in the morning. This gave her twenty minutes to drive to Stephen O'Mara's law office. As she left the house, she turned the switch to the lights in the basement off and on. "Bye and good luck!" Jeremy shouted from his basement office. "Drive safely. It is pouring out there!"

She found it difficult to see as she pulled her BMW out of the garage. Leaves littered the driveway and a strong wind blew the rain in torrents across it. The car's headlights automatically turned on when she backed the car a few feet. She clicked the close button on the garage door remote, then waited in the driveway to make sure the garage door was completely shut. While she waited, she listened to the beating of the window wipers flapping back and forth, rapidly trying to wipe the drenching rain off the windshield.

She turned the car forward and as she approached the end of her long driveway, she looked to the right and left, eased out, pressed the gas pedal and headed north. The road was empty except for one car behind her. She pulled onto a winding road that headed west towards downtown Lake Forest. The car behind her had disappeared and now she was alone on the road. She pressed the brakes lightly to stop the car from moving too quickly on the slippery road and was alarmed to hear the brakes making a grinding sound. At that moment, a squirrel darted in front of her BMW. Maeve saw it at the last minute and jammed on the brakes to avoid hitting the animal, but the brakes failed and the car slid violently on the wet road. Maeve felt herself straining at the safety belt. The last thing she remembered was the car flipping over and resting on its top.

Chapter 19
The Hospital

Maeve heard the sound of a siren wailing in the distance and voices around her. "Miss," one voice shouted in a worried tone. "Miss, can you hear me?" the paramedic repeated. Maeve felt herself fading. She closed her eyes and saw a bright light. So this is it, she thought. I must be dying. Well, it's not that bad.

She opened her eyes in the emergency room. "She's coming to," said the doctor. Maeve heard the bleep, bleep, bleep of a heart monitor sound behind her. The doctor bent over her. "Mrs. Carey, can you hear me?"

Maeve fought the desire to close her eyes and drift off to sleep. "Yes," she replied sleepily and tried to smile.

"My name is Dr. Prichard. You were a very lucky lady this morning," he told her calmly. "Do you remember what happened?"

Maeve mouthed the word no.

"You had a car accident," he continued soothingly. "You have a concussion and will need some rest for a few weeks, but you should be fine after that. Your husband is here. Do you feel strong enough to see him?"

"Yes," she answered. What a nice young doctor, she thought as he left the room. I hope I didn't bother him too much. She heard footsteps approaching and smiled when she heard Jeremy's familiar voice.

"Hi, honey," he said nervously. "You sure gave us a scare." He turned towards the door and motioned with his hand. "Look who's here."

Clare stepped into the room and kissed Maeve on the forehead. She tried to hide the alarm that she felt when she saw Maeve's black and blue face. "Hi, Mom. How are you feeling?" she asked fearfully.

"My head hurts so much. I don't remember what happened." She turned to Jeremy. "Did you call Stephen at work? He will need to know I won't be in for a while. What about Mom and Dad? Someone will have to take care of them while I'm recuperating. Call Jack. He will have to watch over them," she said swiftly, her thoughts in a jumble.

Jeremy shifted his feet and rubbed the back of his head. "I'll call your boss and Jack as soon as I leave. Don't worry, Maeve. It will be taken care of," he assured her.

"What happened, Jeremy?" she pleaded uncertainly. She saw the sheepish look on his face.

He ran his hands through his hair and stammered, "I'm sorry. I guess I should have had the brakes replaced when I drove the car last week. I saw the warning light go on, but I didn't realize the brakes were that bad. Apparently you veered off the road into a ditch and flipped over. Guess you were avoiding something or the road was just slippery. The car is in the dealership right now being fixed. The police said that you were lucky that someone called 911 right away. If the paramedics hadn't arrived so fast, things might not have gone so well for you."

Maeve tried to sit up but felt too tired and drained. "Who called 911?" she asked, her head starting to hurt badly.

"He didn't give his name and he called from a blocked phone number. He just said to send an ambulance right away. No one was at the site of the accident when the paramedics arrived," he finished. "Honey, we have to go now. The doctor said that you need your rest." He kissed Maeve on the cheek.

Clare reached down and held Maeve's hand. "We'll see you tomorrow," Clare whispered. "Love you, Mom."

Maeve fell asleep before they left the room.

Chapter 20
The Requests For Help

Maeve's doctor discharged her two days later. At home, she spent each morning resting in bed, then moved to the family room in the afternoon to read and watch television. By the fourth day, she was bored and anxious to start work. She put on her robe and walked outside to the mailbox at the end of the driveway. There was little mail, just a few bills and junk mail and two get well cards. One was from Stephen and the other was not signed. All it said was, Get well soon. I am waiting for you. She didn't recognize the handwriting and there was no return address, so she just placed the card on the pile of the other get well cards she had received and reached for her cell phone and called her brother.

"Jack, how are things going with Mom and Dad?" she asked hesitantly. Jack O'Connor was a dentist on the North Shore. He made good money, but his wife, Susan spent it as soon as it came in. In the past year they had bought two new cars and built a new home.

"I bought them groceries the day after your accident," Jack responded crankily. "It's really hard dealing with them, Maeve. "He is so negative and she whines all the time. I have work to do and don't have time to look after them. It takes me thirty minutes each way to drive to and from their house. I've done enough for them and can't do any more. Call Annie. She can shop for them till you get better," he concluded abruptly.

Maeve sighed and looked out at the trees. The leaves were turning to gold and orange. Time was passing. And she felt a dull pain begin to form in the back of her head. "Jack, you just have to buy them groceries for two weeks. But I'll call Annie and see if she can help out next week. Then I'll take over," she replied with resignation. "The doctor said I could get back to a normal routine in three weeks, but I'll push it up a bit." She disconnected the call and called her sister, Annie Gordon.

Annie answered the phone on the fourth ring. "What do you want, Maeve?" she asked crossly. "Whenever you call, you always want something from me," she added, raising her voice.

"Annie, Jack can't help out with Mom and Dad while I'm recuperating. Do you think you could buy them groceries and take them to their doctor's appointment next week?"

"Maeve, I would love to, but I have a full calendar that week with school and Peter. I'm sorry, but I just can't," Annie spoke crisply. She puffed on a marijuana cigarette and blew the smoke circles into the air. "The school is holding conferences next week and of course, I must attend and Peter needs his home cooked meals. You understand, don't you?" she continued hopefully.

Maeve took a long breath and counted to ten before she answered. "All right. I'll take over again." It was all she could do to control her disappointment in her sister. Something must be wrong with me, Maeve thought. Why do I keep letting this happen to me? Then she had a thought and asked, "Annie, would you happen to know of any good women psychologists?"

Maeve found it difficult to admit to her younger sister that she needed help. Maeve had always been the strong one to whom others turned to for advice and help. But she knew her younger sister had connections in the psychiatric community from her work as a school teacher in the Evanston school district.

"It's funny you should mention it," Annie replied thoughtfully. "Just today, one of the counselors in school spoke highly about a woman psychologist in Highland Park. Her name is Ruth Stein and from what I've heard, she really is attuned to women's issues. It's about time you started to take care of yourself, Maeve. You put everyone ahead of yourself, especially Jeremy. I hope you call Ruth Stein. Goodbye," she concluded briskly and ended the call. Then she said a prayer to the spirits for Maeve and placed a crystal angel on her kitchen shelf in honor of Maeve's spirit and finished her marijuana cigarette.

Chapter 21
The Psychologist

Three days later, Maeve arrived for her one o'clock appointment with the psychologist, Ruth Stein. She leafed through a magazine in the empty waiting room of the small two room office above a beauty parlor on Center Avenue in Highland Park. At 12:57 P.M. she glanced at her watch. Please let her be on time, Maeve prayed softly. I don't have the energy to get upset about tardiness this afternoon.

A door opened and a small, stout woman with a shock of long, black curly hair rushed out and stood before Maeve. "You are Maeve Carey, correct?" said Ruth Stein with an accent as she extended her hand to Maeve. Maeve remembered that she had forgotten to put on her hand lotion that morning and realized that her hands were chapped, but said to herself, who cares, and she shook hands with Ruth Stein.

"Yes," Maeve answered biting her lip. She stared at Ruth Stein. She looks to be about sixty years of age, she thought, but her curly hair is so black she must dye it. And that red lipstick she has plastered across her mouth with that pink blush that covers her cheeks makes her look like a female clown. Give her a chance said a little voice in her head. Dr. Stein's voice interrupted Maeve's thoughts.

"Please come into my office. I am Dr. Ruth Stein," she said as she opened the door to the other room. Maeve followed her slowly. "Please sit down,

Mrs. Carey," Ruth spoke quickly. "Now tell me about yourself and why you are here."

Maeve took a deep breath. "Well, I'm a housewife who stayed home to take care of my daughter, Clare, as she was growing up. Now that she is an adult, I am my parents' caretaker," Maeve answered uncomfortably. "I recently applied for my first job in twenty years and to my surprise was hired, but I just had a car accident in which I had a concussion and I'm recovering from that now. I need some guidance on asserting myself. I feel as if I'm being taken advantage by everyone." She glanced down at her hands which were damp with perspiration and rubbed them on her pants.

Ruth Stein smiled and analyzed Maeve's appearance. Well dressed in black slacks and a crisp, white blouse. Clean, stylish. Short brown hair flecked with traces of gray. Bright green eyes, just a hint of crow's feet at the ends. Sad eyes, though, Ruth thought as she leaned forward in her chair. "Do you resent your parents?" she asked directly.

Maeve was taken aback and realized she was slouching. She pulled her shoulders back and sat up straight. "No, of course not," she protested immediately. "It's just that I've had a life altering experience, a car accident in which I could have died, and well, it's time to make some changes," she finished resolutely. Maeve crossed her legs and shifted in her seat. God, it was getting hot in here, she thought uncomfortably. A flash was coming on. Her face turned red as the flush spread across it and beads of sweat broke across her forehead. She grabbed a magazine from the coffee table in front of her and fanned herself.   "Excuse me," she apologized. "I'm very hot in here."

"Maeve, you don't have to apologize for anything. Especially for having a flash. I have them myself.   It's natural for women our age."   Ruth reached into her desk and brought out a small bottle of pills and offered one to Maeve. "Here, take one," she said cheerfully. "It will help."

"What is it?" Maeve asked skeptically.   She stared at the pill in Ruth's hand.

"A natural herb, made from the sap of a tree in Africa. You won't find it in any drug store, but I have a friend who brings them back when he visits Kenya," she replied as she handed the pill to Maeve. "I take them and swear by them. I've given them to all of my clients, too. Of course, if you prefer to suffer the side effects of menopause, I understand.   However, you came to me for help, and it seems to me that the first thing we can do is help you physically." Ruth walked to the water cooler in the corner of the office, filled a paper cup with cold water and handed it to Maeve.

Maeve looked uncertainly at the pill and then popped it into her mouth, took a sip of water and swallowed the pill.   Within minutes, she felt cooler. "Thank you," she said gratefully. "They actually seem to work."

Ruth handed the bottle of pills to Maeve. "Here, they are gratis for my new clients. Take one pill each evening at bedtime. So now tell me about your new job. Are you happy with it?"

"I can't answer that because the accident happened just as I was driving to my first day at work. Stephen sent me a message that he would hold the job for me until I am better. It should be in a week or so."

"That is good," Ruth commented thoughtfully, "Where will you be working? Your boss certainly sounds understanding."

"It's called the O'Mara Law Firm in Lake Forest. Stephen O'Mara is the owner."

Deep furrows appeared on Ruth's forehead. "That is a coincidence," she murmured strangely. "I recently referred my brother, Rubin to Stephen's firm. Stephen handled the closing of the sale of my home."

"Is your brother selling his home?" Maeve asked slowly.

"No, it's a personal injury case. Rubin tripped on the footings of a metal fence in front of Le Paris restaurant in downtown Deerfield. He fell head first into the fence, injured his head and sprained his ankle. An ambulance transported him to the the Deerfield Hospital where he blacked out. He remained unconscious for a few minutes, but eventually regained consciousness. The doctors ran some tests and determined that he sustained a serious head injury which may impair his ability to work in the future. Rubin could barely talk and didn't recognize me when I walked into the emergency room. He hasn't been the same since the fall. He lost his job as a school bus driver, sleeps a lot and is depressed. I feel so sorry for him." Ruth pulled a tissue from the tissue box on the coffee table and dabbed at her eyes and blew her nose.

"I'm so sorry," Maeve said comfortingly.

Ruth nodded her head and continued, "Thank you. In my opinion, the accident traumatized him. He sleeps most of the day because he's afraid to sleep at night. He even has become delusional. He assures me that everyone is out to get him." She shifted in her seat and stared at Maeve. "But enough of my brother. I'm sure he is in great hands with Stephen. Stephen is a jack-of-all trades, who handles all sorts of legal problems. I was friends with Stephen's wife. We met at an art show in Highland Park and found we had common interests in art. It's funny. You resemble her so much. You are around the same height, coloring, even your mannerisms. It's such a pity about her."

Maeve thought of her interview with Stephen and wondered if her resemblance to his deceased wife had anything to do with his quick offer of a job. "What happened to her?" Maeve asked quickly.

"She was in a car accident. She was driving on a rainy day and she plowed into a ravine near their home in Lake Bluff."

"What kind of a car was she driving?" Maeve said

"It was a BMW. The police said she must have had a blackout because the brakes were working The only thing that came up on the autopsy report, according to Stephen, was that she had been drinking heavily before the accident. She did have a drinking problem. When we went out to lunch, she usually drank three or more glasses of wine. Who knows? Perhaps she was using her cell phone at just the wrong moment. You know how distracting they can be. Anyway, Stephen hasn't been the same since. He now acts much more serious, quiet and reserved."

"Well, he certainly was kind to me by keeping my job open for me for a few weeks till I recover. I'm very grateful to him," Maeve stated forcefully.

Ruth looked at her watch and said tersely, "Now back to you, Maeve. What are your goals for this therapy? What do you want to achieve?"

Maeve crossed her arms over her chest. "Assertiveness," she answered emphatically. "I want to be able to say no when I don't want to do something."

"That's reasonable," Ruth replied. "We'll start working on that the next session." Ruth rose and walked to the exit door and held it open. "Our first session is over. Please come back the same day and time next week," she said quickly as she motioned Maeve to the door.

"But we've hardly talked," Maeve protested.

"Initial visits always last thirty minutes," Ruth replied firmly with a forced smile on her face.

Outside the office, Maeve realized she had spent less than thirty minutes in Ruth Stein's office. "She better not bill me for an hour," Maeve mumbled to herself. "My assertiveness should have started with Dr. Stein."

On the way home, she drove slowly, enjoying the feel of being behind the wheel of a car again. Coming to her appointment with Ruth Stein was the first time she had driven since the accident. Jeremy had protested, but she had insisted she could handle the rental car. At a stoplight, she glanced in the rear view mirror. Her eyes looked very bright. She stretched higher and and looked at the rest of her face in the mirror. The lines around her eyes seemed to have diminished and her hair looked darker, more brown. A blaring horn brought her eyes back to the green light. "All right, I'm moving," she shouted crossly as she pulled away.

When she arrived at her street, she stopped at the mailbox at the end of the driveway. She opened the box and sorted through the usual pile of bills and junk mail. A post card lay on the bottom. It read, You are getting better. I am happy for you. The address line was blank, but It looked as though a glass of water had fallen on the post card because of the smeared writing. Who could have sent it? Maeve thought bewildered. She pulled her rental car into the garage and entered the house.

"Hi, Maeve," Jeremy said. "How was the drive?" he asked with concern. He was just coming up from the basement.

"Not bad, sweetie," Maeve replied as she kissed him on the cheek. "Thank you for asking, though. I just wanted to get the feel of being behind the wheel of a car again." She had decided it was better to keep her visits to Ruth Stein a secret from Jeremy. He would think she was crazy to see a psychologist. After all, Jeremy provided her with everything a woman could want.

"You look different. Did you do something to your hair?" Jeremy asked.

"You're just trying to make me feel good," Maeve quipped playfully. She tossed the mail onto the counter, walked to the guest bath off the kitchen and peered into the mirror. Yes, Jeremy was right, she observed. The face glancing back at her did look younger, more vibrant and her hair shone in the light.

"I guess I'm just happy to be alive," she said to herself.

She and Jeremy ate in silence that evening. She cooked barbecued chicken breasts, baked potatoes, corn on the cob and a green salad with blue cheese dressing. Preoccupied, Jeremy cleared his dishes and walked down the stairs to his basement office. "I'm sorry, Maeve. I have work to do," he murmured.

Maeve finished eating her meal, washed her hands, put on her rubber gloves, rinsed the dishes and placed them into the dishwasher. As she wiped the counter, she came across the mail she had set aside earlier that day. Again, she examined the post card with the strange message. She started to descend the basement stairs to show it to Jeremy, but decided not to bother him and placed the postcard on her desk next to the other get well cards she received. Then she sat down and wrote thank you notes to each of the well wishers who had sent her flowers during her recovery.

Chapter 22
The First Day At Work

Maeve showed up for work the following Monday at 8:00 A.M. sharp. She pushed on the front door to the law office, but it was locked. She rang the doorbell and heard footsteps inside and the door lock turning. Damien opened the door. His uncombed hair hung over his red and glassy eyes and his wrinkled shirt spilled over his pants, which appeared dirty and damp in spots. He sniffled constantly.

Good morning, Damien," Maeve greeted him. She averted her eyes and acted as if she didn't notice his appearance. She started to enter the office, but Damien held up an open palm to stop her.

"Give me a few minutes, Maeve. Just wait here." He closed the door and left Maeve waiting on the front stairs.

What was that all about? Maeve asked herself as she sat on the wide stoop to the side of the stairs. She pulled out her cell phone and searched for the latest news. The Lake Forest e-News reported that the Coast Guard discovered a stash of heroin in a speed boat that was found floating on Lake Michigan off the Lake Forest beach. The boat's side was damaged and the boat was taking on water. The Coast Guard reported that no one was in the boat and that they had begun searching for any survivors who might still be in the water. The Lake Forest Police Department was also investigating the matter.

Maeve looked up as the front door to the law firm opened. "I hope you will forgive my appearance," Damien bemoaned. "I am catching a cold and spent the night reviewing the books of some of the classes that started this week. I just wanted to clean up. I spilled a glass of water on my shirt and pants while I was studying this morning. Stephen sent me a message that he'll be in around nine o"clock this morning and asked if I would show you around and get you started."

"That sounds good," Maeve responded calmly. "Did you stay on longer with Stephen because I was injured and could not come to work, Damien?" she asked.

"Yes. Stephen talked me into staying a bit longer, so I've been catching up on my schoolwork in the office." Damien smiled and stepped aside to let Maeve in. "Well, let's get started," he continued briskly. He showed Maeve how to use the phone and computer systems. Then he pointed to a small cabinet next to the reception desk. "The active real estate files are in this cabinet." He pulled out the middle drawer of the cabinet.

"That's it?" she asked as she stared at the half full drawer of files.

"I'm afraid so," Damien answered slowly.

"Are there files in the other drawers?" she questioned with a frown on her face.

"Just the closed real estate files," he answered hastily.

"I take it business hasn't been good lately," she remarked.

"With the economy the way it is, not many people are buying or selling their homes. Stephen has a new personal injury case he's working on. He can tell you all about it. He keeps the file locked in his office along with some other files that I haven't seen. I only answer the phones for him."

"You don't want to continue to work here while you are in school?" Maeve asked apprehensively.

"No," he replied. "Would you please excuse me a minute?" Damien interrupted quickly. "I want to bring my books and notes out to my car." He picked up a banker's box from under the desk and carried it out.

Chapter 23
The Stepson

Maeve sat at the reception desk and glanced through the file drawer that contained ten current real estate transactions. The phone rang. "O'Mara Law Office," Maeve answered crisply.

"Is Stephen there?" came the gravely voice at the other end of the phone.

"He's not in yet," Maeve replied. "May I take a message?" She noted the dangerous undercurrent in the man's voice and was determined to remain calm and professional.

"Just tell the prick to call Rubin as soon as he gets in," ordered the man. Maeve heard the sound of the click as the man slammed down the phone.

Just as Maeve hung up the phone, Damien walked in. "Who was on the phone?" he asked anxiously. She noticed that his right eye twitched and his voice sounded strained.

"Someone by the name of Rubin. Who is he?" she answered casually.

Damien let out a sigh. "Oh, he's the client with a personal injury case that Stephen is working on. He calls every morning and every afternoon of every day. Just take the message and give it to Stephen. Don't talk to the guy. He's got a few screws loose."

"Okay," said Maeve. "How did you meet Stephen, if you don't mind my asking?" She looked directly into Damien's face.

"I'm Stephen's stepson. My mother Sherri was married to him until she died last year."

"I'm so sorry about your mother. Stephen told me she died in a car accident. He seemed really broken up about it."

Damien smiled. "Thank you for your sympathy. But as to Stephen being broken up about her accident, I don't know. She was going to divorce him. She couldn't stand his drinking and flirting with other women any longer," he mentioned casually.

Is he joking? Maeve thought. He certainly is acting strangely this morning. "Did you live with Stephen and your mother?" she inquired nonchalantly.

"Yes, but not since she died. My Dad died five years ago. He left a small insurance policy naming my mother as beneficiary. Now that she's gone, I inherited the money. It's enough to keep me in a small coach apartment in Lake Forest until I graduate and get a job."

"Then why are you working here?" she continued.

"It will look good on my resume when I graduate. Stephen was okay that way. He let me intern here; no money, but he said I could bulk up my resume and he'd give me a good recommendation. Anyway, I just worked here this past month," he told her.

"What happened to his last assistant?" Maeve probed further.

"She quit. Guess she got tired of Stephen coming on to her," he replied offhandedly.

Maeve stared at Damien and couldn't tell whether he was telling her the truth or lying to her.

"Damien, you don't mean that, do you?" she blurted out.

"I saw it with my own eyes when I came over here to work with Stephen on another matter. He's a grabber. Guess she just got sick of it and left. That's when Stephen asked if I would help him out till he hired another assistant." Damien noticed the look of fear in Maeve's eyes. "Don't worry, Maeve. Stephen will behave with you. You're the opposite of his last assistant. She was a beautiful young blonde with a high school diploma who didn't know her way around a race track."

Maeve laughed. "I don't know whether to be insulted or flattered by your description," she smiled.

Damien laughed too. "I didn't mean to be rude to you. I was just trying to let you know what you may encounter. But you look like you can handle yourself."

"Now, that is a compliment, Damien," she responded happily. "I think I can defend myself, but I hope I never have to find out."

"I doubt that you will. I'll turn the phones over to you now. If you have any questions, just let me know. I'll be in the conference room. I have some calls to make. Just knock and I'll let you in." He got up and left the reception area.

Maeve sat at the desk and thought about what Damien had said. Either he was pulling her leg or he was telling the truth. She decided to withhold her judgment about Stephen and see how things worked out. It was possible that Damien was just upset that she was taking over his job and that he wanted to get rid of her. She pulled out the real estate files from the file cabinet and spent the next hour reading them to get some background on the cases.

Chapter 24
The Sinking Boat

Stephen arrived at the office at 10:30 A.M. "Morning, Maeve," he greeted her in a booming voice. "Welcome to your first day here!"

"Thank you," Maeve replied spontaneously. She thought he looked tired with dark circles that rimmed his brown eyes and made his oracles appear to recede into his forehead. His tan skin glowed under his freshly starched shirt with blue stripes and white collar and cuffs. She noticed his initials, SOM, monogrammed onto the cuffs of his shirt.

He flung off his suit jacket and flipped it over his arm. "How do you feel?" he asked with concern.

"I am so much better, Stephen. I can't thank you enough for holding this job for me," she replied gratefully.

"No problem. Damien agreed to stay a little longer. By the way, has Damien showed you the ropes yet?" he asked as he peered at the files on her desk.

"Yes," she answered. She pointed to the files and explained, "I was just reading these real estate files to familiarize myself with what you do."

"That's what I like," he commented as he looked about the room. "By the way, do you know where Damien is?" he asked.

"He's in the conference room. He said he had some calls to make. Do you want me to get him?" She started to get up.

"No, that's okay.   I'll buzz him."   Stephen headed towards his office.

Maeve started to follow Stephen. "Oh, I almost forgot, I left a message for you on your desk. A man by the name of Rubin called and wants to talk to you."

"Thanks," Stephen said. He entered his office and threw his jacket on a side chair. His desk was piled high with stacks of papers. "I have some work to do, Maeve. Damien will answer any questions you have, but if you need me for anything, just buzz me." He closed the door to his office. He then picked up the phone and pressed the intercom for the conference room. "Damien, get in here now!" he shouted angrily.

"Sure thing," replied Damien. He slammed down the phone and nodded quickly to Maeve as he passed her before entering Stephen's office.

Stephen sat at his desk with his fists clenched. "Have you got the money?" Stephen growled.

Damien shifted back and forth.   "I had an incident this morning. I used a boat to pick up the delivery in Monroe Harbor and then drove the boat to the Lake Forest beach harbor to make the drop off to my contact here. The weather became stormy and the boat started to take in water before I could make it to the harbor. I bailed and left the stash on the boat and swam to shore."

"You idiot," Stephen said through clenched teeth. "Can anyone trace the boat to you?" His face and neck flushed red in anger.

"No, a friend of mine stole the boat from a lake in Wisconsin at the beginning of the summer. It's an old speed boat that he fixed up and sold to me. All cash. No messy paper trail. I leave it stored at the garage at my coach house when I'm not using it. I felt like a ride this morning and decided to mix business with pleasure. Unfortunately, things didn't work out as planned." His heart was beating fast.

Stephen took a long breath. "When will you get more of the stuff?" he asked brusquely.

"I'm driving downtown tonight. I'll have a fresh load tomorrow and I'll sell it off by later afternoon. My usual customers are clamoring for more."

"Well, I need my share of that money. If you don't get it to me by tomorrow night, I'll report you to the police and you'll spend the next twenty years in jail," Stephen threatened.

Damien started backing out of the room. "I'll get it for you," he reassured Stephen.

"Be sure that you do, and use your head. Be careful. And don't bring any of the goods here. I don't want anything to be traced to me," he warned Damien.

"Whatever you say," Damien murmured as he left the office.

Maeve looked through the drawers to her desk as she waited for Damien. When she saw him leave Stephen's office with a scowl on his face, she stared at him with a quizzical look. Damien smiled at the confused look on Maeve's face. "He's just having his morning snort of liquor and then he'll sit on the phone schmoozing Rubin. Trial is set in a few months, so he's got to keep his client happy. Now, let's go through the active files together," he said as he sat down next to Maeve.

Chapter 25
The Backpack

It was Thursday, the end of Maeve's first week at work and Stephen had taken the afternoon off. She turned off her computer and picked up the closed files Stephen had left for her to file. She smiled at Damien and said, "Thank you for all of your help. You've been invaluable this week. Who knows, maybe when you graduate, you'll come back here to work for Stephen."

Damien laughed. "I've got bigger fish to fry, Maeve," he chuckled under his breath. He stood up and strolled to the bathroom. "I'll be right back."

While he was away, Maeve tried to open the bottom file drawer, but found Damien's backpack in the way on the floor. She picked up the backpack and placed it on his chair. It tilted to the side and fell off the chair back onto the floor. The top zipper had not been secured, so the contents of the backpack scattered at Maeve's feet. She reach down and to her surprise, found five plastic packets neatly wrapped and tied with drawstring. "I wonder what these could be, she thought to herself as she placed them back into the backpack. Five more plastic packets lay in the backpack.

Then it hit her. Could these be what I think they are? Impossible, she said to herself. She turned her computer back on and googled the word, heroin. She clicked on a website describing heroin and its effects. The website also displayed a packet of heroin that looked very similar to the packets she found in Damien's backpack.

Suddenly she heard the bathroom door open and Damien's footsteps shuffling towards the reception area. She quickly shut down her computer and lugged Damien's backpack onto his chair. Just as Damien returned, she picked up a file and filed it in the file cabinet.

Damien noticed that his backpack was on his chair. He peered at Maeve and said quietly, "Oh, I'm sorry my backpack was in the way of the file cabinet." He lifted it off the chair and observed that the zipper was unzipped and the plastic packets lay in full view. He zipped it up and flung it across his shoulder. "I have to get going, Maeve. Could you please hurry up? I'll wait till you finish your filing."

"I just have a few more to do," she replied uneasily. She quickly finished the filing and picked up her purse and put on her jacket.

Damien accompanied her to the front door. "Have a great weekend, Maeve. See you on Monday."

"Bye, Damien. You have a great weekend too," she mumbled. Once out, she hurried to her car. She sat in it for a moment to gather her composure. Then, she thought about the past week at the firm. It had flown by and she loved working there. Her days were filled with answering the phones, keeping Stephen's calendar and making files. She loved the satisfaction of doing a good job and earning money.

She was happy that she had disregarded Damien's warnings about Stephen and decided to take a wait and see approach, because Stephen had behaved like a gentleman since she arrived. Just that afternoon, she and Stephen and Damien had gone out to lunch and had a good time.

But what about that backpack and those packets? She found it hard to believe that this young, clean-cut, handsome young man was taking heroin. But there were so many packets. Even worse was the thought that he might be selling the packets. She shook her head, started the car and drove home while wrestling with whether or not to discuss this matter with Stephen.

Once Maeve left the office, Damien closed the door and walked back to his desk to make a phone call. "My backpack fell with the heroin and Maeve saw the packets inside of it. I don't know if she realized what they were, but I just wanted you to know."

"I told you not to bring the stash to the office, you idiot," Stephen shouted loudly. "Don't ever do that again, or you won't live to see another day. Another thing, I read an article in the Lake Forest newspaper about a Lake Forest teenager dying due to a heroin overdose a few weeks ago. Did you see the article?"

"Yes," Damien admitted slowly. He started to sweat and felt the beads form on his face.

"Was the kid one of your customers?'

Damien hesitated. "Yes," he confessed.

"Well, get yourself a new supplier," Stephen shrieked. "I don't want any more deaths!" He ended the call, slammed the phone down and considered his options.

Chapter 26
The Middle Lane

When Maeve arrived home, she received a text message from Jeremy stating that he was going out to dinner with a client and would be home later. That was unfortunate, because she wanted to talk with Jeremy about Damien. The following morning, she heard Jeremy's snores coming from the other side of the bed. Jeremy must have gotten home very late, Maeve thought, because he usually gets up much earlier.

Maeve decided to let Jeremy continue sleeping. It was Friday and she had to get to her parents' home, so she showered, dressed and left. She slipped into her car and secured the safety belt into the lock. Then she drove through the side streets until she turned onto Highway 41. Thank God it isn't crowded yet, she thought. She drove till she reached the first stoplight at Route 22. It had turned red. She stopped and checked the car's clock. It was exactly 9:10 A.M. She estimated she would arrive at her parents' home on the north side of Chicago at 9:40 A.M., exactly thirty minutes away in good traffic. The light turned green. She pressed the gas pedal until the car reached sixty-five miles per hour, exactly the speed limit.

Then she glanced into her rear view mirror and when the middle lane became free, she flicked on her turn signal and moved into it. She always drove in the middle lane. She didn't have to worry about cars pulling onto the highway from the right nor did she have to worry about faster cars beeping at her to go faster in the far left lane, which was the passing lane. So she always stayed in the middle lane, the safe lane where she went exactly the speed limit and let the cars on the left fly by and the cars on the right merge and exit the highway.

All she had to do was cruise ahead and listen to the radio. She had two stations programmed on the radio. One was an all news station and the other was a soft music station. When she wasn't listening to one, she had the other turned on. She pressed the soft music station and checked her speedometer. It clocked sixty-four miles per hour. That would do. She stared straight ahead and drove carefully with both hands on the wheel.

She thought of all the Fridays she had shopped for her parents, all the bills she had paid for them, all the times she had taken them to their doctor appointments, cooked for them, taken them out to eat, listened to their concerns. What else could she do? she asked herself. She had always been their caretaker, but it was becoming increasingly difficult. Her father had always held the purse strings in the family and even now, wanted to make all the financial decisions.

But now her parents were elderly and infirm. Her mother's memory was rapidly failing and her father found it difficult to walk after his stroke. He could walk a short distance with a cane and used his left arm to get dressed and prepare simple foods. Thank goodness his mind was still sharp. It was her mother's progressive memory loss now that caused the most concern for Maeve. She feared for her mother's future since the signs of dementia were becoming more apparent week by week.

Chapter 27
The Shopping Trip

Maeve turned onto the Foster street exit of the highway and drove west towards her parents' house. She parked her car on the street in front of their home, put a smile on her face, trudged up the driveway to their home and rang the doorbell. Therese O'Connor, her elderly mother, answered the door. Her face looked grim.

"Hi, Mom," Maeve said with a tight smile. "How are things?" She regretted asking the question even as she said it.

"Not good," answered her mother sadly. She looked haggard and her shoulders slumped. Then she whispered, "He's been mean today."

Maeve kissed her on the cheek and followed her into the living room. Straight ahead she could see her father seated in the kitchen. "Hi, Dad," she called out.

"Hello," he answered, raising his eyes from the newspaper on the table.

Maeve walked into the kitchen. "How are things?"

"Okay," her father mumbled. He pointed towards Maeve's mother and whispered, "She's not having a good day today."

Maeve looked at her mother who was standing in the doorway, shaking her head, then back to her father who was drumming his fingers on the table. "Do you have the shopping list, Dad?"

Her father looked up and pushed a piece of powder blue paper across the table. "It's here," he remarked gruffly. "Just buy what I wrote. We only need six yogurts. No more yogurts than six," he continued impatiently. "You bought more than we needed last week."

Maeve scanned the list. One milk, one orange juice, four bananas, two diet cokes, one loaf of bread, six yogurts. She opened the refrigerator door and peered in. It was practically empty. She started writing. Cold cuts, peanut butter, fruit, butter, meat, chicken. "What do you think you are doing writing more on the list?" her father growled at her. "I told you to buy just what I put on the list."

"Well, Dad, I want to make sure you haven't forgotten anything. I can't come back here in the middle of the week to shop for more food. I didn't tell you, but I am working now."

That caught her father's attention. He shifted in his chair and coughed. "Where are you working?" he asked shocked.

"At a law firm."

"Where is it?" he snapped.

"In Lake Forest."

"Why didn't you tell me you were looking for a job?" He coughed again and stared at her intently.

"Dad, I wanted to surprise you," she explained calmly.

"Did you have to take off of work to come here today?" he probed.

"No, I have Fridays off," she continued with a smile. "You don't think I would neglect you and Mom, do you?"

He sighed in relief.   "Well, that's good. Congratulations on your job. I'm proud of you." Paul slowly rose from his chair, pushing himself up with great effort until he stood at his full height of five feet eight inches and reached for his cane. "The money is on the table. Make sure you bring home the change. Don't lose any of it."

He hobbled into the living room and settled in the white chair facing the front picture window, picked up his rosary from the side table and started to say his prayers. A streak of sunlight from the front window reflected on him and illuminated the cream sheer drapes, cream walls and the cream wall to wall carpeting. A cream wood coffee table with gold leaf trim sat in front of the white sofa. Two oriental lamps perched on the cream and gold end tables. On the opposite side of the room, two powder blue upholstered side chairs faced the sofa. A two foot high lamp with a Chinese dragon motif stood on a small table in the middle of the powder blue chairs.

A large crystal chandelier hung over the mahogany dining room set in the adjoining dining room. Paul and Therese considered the chandelier and dining room set their pride and joy for they were the setting for many happy family holiday celebrations in the past.

Maeve took the $20.00 bill Paul left on the table and placed it into her purse. Then she took her parents' car keys off the hook in the kitchen and placed them into her purse.

Therese rolled her eyes as if to say, See what I mean. Then she put on her coat and zipped up her purse. It contained a rosary, an old lipstick that was smudged on the outside, a powder compact, a few used tissues, some bobby pins and a few loose pennies and nickels.

"Yes, Mother," I do," Maeve answered softly. "Let's go. I have a surprise for you today."

Chapter 28
The Driving Test

Maeve had decided to test her mother's driving skills to see if it was still safe for her to drive their car. "Let's take your car today, Mom," she suggested to Therese.

"Oh, that sounds like fun," Therese responded happily. They walked into the side door of the garage and got into the car. It was an old Buick that had seen better days.

Inside the car, Therese complained, "I can't take it any more. You don't know what he is like. When you're around he's nice, but when you are gone, he starts yelling at me. Saying terrible things, like I don't know what I'm doing. I told him I am going to get a job. I have to get away from him. Maybe I can get a job. That would be good. It would get me out of the house."

Maeve stared straight ahead. She heard the same thing every Friday. Her mother, now eighty-one years old, had never held a job in her life. She complained incessantly about Maeve's father, Paul, but they were inseparable and had been so throughout their marriage. So this is what it all boils down to, Maeve thought. "Yes, Mom," replied Maeve. She took Paul and Therese's car keys out of her purse, gave them to her mother and said, "You are driving today."

Therese smiled. "I like to drive. Where are we going?"

"We're going to the store to buy food," Maeve responded calmly.

Therese took the keys and started the car.

Maeve pressed the garage door opener and the garage door lifted up. "Now back out, Mom." Maeve turned around to make sure that the street was clear of oncoming cars.

Therese frowned and stared at the dashboard. "Where are we going?" she asked again.

"We are going to the store to buy food, Mom. Now back the car up," she sighed.

Therese sat still and looked bewildered. "I forgot how to make the car go backwards," she said apologetically

Maeve put the shift into reverse. "Now press the gas pedal softly so we go slowly into the street," she said calmly as she pressed the garage door remote to close the garage door.

Therese pressed the gas pedal and backed up slowly and pulled onto the street. "Oh, I remember," she said as she put the car into drive.

"Now let's go to the food store," Maeve said encouragingly.

"But I don't know where it is," Therese said in a quivering voice.

"Just pull ahead to the next street and turn left," Maeve directed. "I'll show you how to get there."

Therese stepped on the gas pedal and the car lurched forward.

"Slow down," Maeve said a bit too loudly. "Put your foot on the pedal more softly."

Therese pressed the gas pedal lightly and the car slowly inched ahead.

"A little harder, Mom," Maeve said impatiently. Therese pushed the pedal harder and they moved ahead at about twenty miles per hour. "Now turn left," said Maeve when they reached the cross street.

Therese turned toward Maeve. "Which way is left?" she asked in a bewildered voice.

Maeve pointed left.   Therese turned left, crossed into the left lane of traffic and hit the curb. Maeve grabbed the steering wheel and pulled the car into the right side of the street. Luckily, they were on a side street with no traffic, but Maeve had enough. "Mom, press the brakes," she ordered in a rising voice. Therese pressed down on the brake pedal and the car came to an abrupt stop.

Maeve put the shift into park, opened the passenger door and walked around to the driver's door. "Mom, get out of the car. I think I'll drive today."

Therese's face looked crestfallen. "But I like to drive. Dad and I drive every day."

Maeve's heart skipped a beat.   "Well, can I drive today?" she asked diplomatically. "I need some practice."

Therese's face softened.   "Of course," she replied and she got out of the car. Maeve helped her into the passenger seat and then got into the driver's seat. With a sigh, Maeve realized that she would have to take away her parents' car keys today so they would no longer be able to drive any more. It was one of the hardest things she would have to do because she realized that she was taking away the last shred of independence that they had and that her father would not give up the keys without a fight. But it had to be done. The thought of her parents driving alone made her blood turn to ice. They could get killed or injure themselves or someone else.

Therese was quiet for the rest of the drive. She looked inside her purse and found a tissue which she used to wipe her nose.

Chapter 29
The Tasks

Inside the grocery store, Therese perked up. She and Maeve made the rounds of the aisles and finally arrived at the milk section. "Mother, you get the yogurt while I get the milk," Maeve said as she lifted a gallon of milk from the refrigerated milk rack. She pointed to the yogurt section a few feet away.

Therese stared at the rows of yogurt. She seemed mesmerized by the variety of assortments. Maeve came over. "Here Mother, let's get the ones on sale. See, they are two for a dollar." She placed five in the cart and waited till Therese chose five more.

"Are we finished?" Therese asked exhaustedly.

"All done," Maeve answered cheerily. She emptied the cart at the check out aisle.

The young check out girl smiled at her mother. "You look so pretty today, Mrs. O'Connor. How are you?"

Therese's face brightened at the friendly voice. "Why I'm fine. How are you?"

"I'm having a good day," the girl continued in a happy voice. She placed the groceries in bags. "The sun is shining and the weekend is here. See you next week," she said pleasantly as she finished bagging the food. "That will be $75.00 please."

Maeve handed the check out girl $80.00 and accepted the change. On the way home, Therese seemed deep in thought. When they pulled into the driveway, and Maeve parked the car in the garage, Therese zipped open her purse and began searching.

"What are you looking for, Mother?" Maeve inquired softly. She knew the answer, but she couldn't stop herself from asking anyway. Her nerves were beginning to get frazzled.

"I can't find the money," her mother cried. "Do you have it?"

"No, Mother. We used it to pay for the groceries. I have the change. Now let's carry the groceries into the house."

Maeve opened the trunk of the car. She grabbed five plastic bags and handed the lightest one to her mother. She lay the bags on the front steps to her parents' home and unlocked the door. Then she and Therese carried the bags into the house.

When they entered the house, Paul was still sitting in his white chair and watching television. "Hi, Dad," she said cheerfully. He remained silent as she crossed the living room with the bags.

"Mom, put your bag on the kitchen table," Maeve told Therese. "Let's put the groceries away."

They began to unload the bags. Maeve heard her father getting up from his chair in the living room. He reached for his cane and slowly inched into the kitchen. "Why did you buy more bananas than I put on the list?" he shouted, his face contorted in anger when he saw the batch of bananas on the kitchen table. "When I put something on the list, just buy that, do you understand?" He stared at Maeve.

"Because I did," she replied calmly. What she wanted to say was, Why don't you just go back into the living room and leave us alone. I am keeping this house and the two of you going. Just leave me alone. But she didn't. She swallowed and said, "I bought what you needed." Then she continued to unpack the bags. He shook his head and moved slowly back into the living room.

Now it was time to give them lunch. She pulled out two dishes and made him a peanut butter sandwich and poured a glass of skim milk for him. He ate the same thing every day. Then Maeve made her mother a ham sandwich with lettuce and tomato, a fruit salad of bananas and apples and poured a soft drink for her. "Come and eat," she called to them. They followed each other into the kitchen, sat at the table and her mother started to eat.

Paul took the sandwich off the dish and handed the dish to Maeve "You know I don't eat my peanut butter sandwich on a dish. A napkin is fine for it. Put this dish away," he ordered.

Maeve shoved the dish back at him and placed the sandwich on it again. He swiped the sandwich off the dish, pushed the dish to the side and finished eating his sandwich off the napkin. Therese sat and ate as if nothing unusual had happened. Maeve cleared the table when they were finished and thought of the next task to be done.

The bills. It was the task she most dreaded. She usually tried to quietly sneak the bills into the kitchen and to get them done quickly without interference. But somehow he would know and sit down at the table. "Why don't you both go into the living room while I clean up the kitchen," Maeve suggested calmly. Paul and Therese shuffled back into the living room and he turned on the television.

Maeve put the dishes into the dishwasher, then snuck into the bedroom and placed the shoebox of bills under her sweater and slipped into the kitchen. She sat down and pulled the outstanding bills from under the rubber band holding them on the top of the box and opened the first one. It was the electric bill. With a sinking feeling, she heard her father inch out of his chair and walked haltingly into the kitchen.

Paul slid into the kitchen table chair, careful to not lose his balance, took the electric bill from Maeve and demanded, "Call the electric company. There must be a mistake. This bill is too big. I keep the lights out in the house and this cannot be right. Call them and have them come out here and retake their reading."

"I am not going to call the electric company, Dad," she responded in an annoyed voice. "I think $58.00 seems reasonable for a house of your size. I don't have time to call." She took the bill from him and started to write the check to pay it.

He grabbed the bill and shouted, "I said call the electric company. Do you hear me?" His face turned red and he pounded the table.

As usual, the commotion was starting. Therese edged into the kitchen cautiously and looked in pain. "What is happening?" she asked slowly as she sat at the table. "Why are you doing the bills without me?" She started to cry.

Maeve felt herself stiffen and the blood rush to her head, which started to pound. Every Friday was the same, the same and the same. "You can put the stamps on the envelopes, Mother," she suggested quickly. Her mother shook her head up and down and waited. Maeve moved the book of stamps across the table to her and then wrote the check for the electric bill. "Give me the bill, Dad," she asked irritably

He clutched it in his left hand and growled, "Not until you promise to call the electric company and complain about their billing system and have them come out and check the meter. Don't mail that bill and check until they come out here."

Maeve felt a burning sensation in her stomach, another rush of blood that made her face flush. She swallowed and reached for the bill in his hand. "I'll call them after we finish the rest of the bills today." He smiled that smile that said he had won, had gotten his way. "Why don't you go back into the living room so Mom and I can get these done quickly," she asked in despair as she looked at the stack before her.

"You want to get rid of me?" He looked at her as if she were an ant. "This is my house and I won't move anywhere."

"Fine," Maeve retorted with a sigh. She placed the check and bill into the envelope and pushed it across the table to her mother who placed the stamp on it. Only seven more bills to go, Maeve thought tiredly. I'll make it through this without killing myself.

They had a sort of assembly line going. Maeve wrote the checks, her father examined each bill and complained about each one, her mother placed the stamp on the envelopes and her father checked each one again to make sure the return address was correct, that the envelope had been licked and closed and that there was a stamp on it. It was a labor intensive, long, drawn out process. When they were finished, Maeve said, "Now I am going to do the medicines. Would you both go into the living room?"

Her mother and father got up and left the kitchen.   Even her father realized that she needed some quiet and space in order to get their weekly pills correct. Maeve found their pill containers and laid out her mother's pill bottles.   Her mother took ten medicines and some had to be cut.   Maeve took a knife and cut the pills in half and then laid them in the little plastic pill dispenser for each day of the week. She then did the same for her father. Finally, she was finished with the medicine.

She roasted a chicken, potatoes and carrots for one dinner.   That would last them a few days. Then she boiled some spaghetti and heated some tomato sauce and poured it over the pasta.   That should last at least three days, she thought.   She heated some creamed corn and then she placed the food in small plastic packets that they could pull from the freezer and reheat each night.   All done, she congratulated herself. Now I have to talk to Mom and Dad about the thing I fear the most.

Chapter 30
The Car

Maeve stood at the kitchen sink and took a deep breath. Oh, my God, Maeve thought. I cannot believe that I have to talk to them about selling their car. It's the last vestige of freedom they have. She steeled her shoulders back and entered the living room. "Mom and Dad, I want to talk with you about something," she stated softly.

Paul sat in his white chair and Maeve and Therese sat on the cream sofa. Everyone remained quiet until she spoke. "I want to talk to you about your car," she started hesitantly. Her father's pale blue eyes flashed like a lightning bolt searing a branch off a tree. He started to rise from his chair.

"Dad, sit down, please. We have to talk. This is about your safety and Mom's safety and the safety of others," she explained quickly Therese just stared at her.

"There's nothing to talk about," Paul interrupted loudly. "The car is staying. When Mom and I go out, I sit in the passenger side and tell her where to go and how to get there," he continued angrily. He pointed his left hand index finger at her, his voice rising in fury.

"Dad, I went out with Mom today. She drove and her driving is not safe."

Therese started to cry. "Now look at what you've done," Paul said sharply. "She's crying. It's all right, Therese, my dear. I'll take care of this." Therese smiled at him and wiped away her tears and blew her nose.

Maeve put her arm over her mother's shoulder and stated,"I know this is very difficult, but I don't want to get a call from the police department that you've been involved in a car accident and have been taken to the hospital."

"That won't happen," Paul interjected. "We are fine when we go out. Mom is the driver and I am, what do you call it, the GPS system," Paul explained proudly.

"The problem is that Mom's reflexes aren't what they used to be when she was younger. Believe me, I wish I didn't have to do this, but I have to. You know I'll take you wherever you want. Just trust me when I say that this is in your best interest. I want you both to stay healthy and safe," Maeve finished soothingly.

Paul's head dropped and he closed his eyes. A few tears fell onto his cheeks. He wiped them away, sighed and sat up straight. "Therese, my dear, it looks like we'll be having Maeve take us out from now on. I'm getting older, you know, and it's becoming harder for me to find the places we like to drive to."

Therese smiled at him. "Whatever you say dear." She rose and went into the kitchen and poured a glass of water for each of them and brought the glasses to them. "Here are some refreshments for you," she offered politely. She placed a glass in front of Paul and Maeve. She looked like a fragile bird feeding her babies in the nest.

"Thank you, Mom," said Maeve gratefully.

Paul took a sip of the glass of water and turned on the television. "Look, the Cubs are winning, ten to eight. Ninth inning," he said happily. Therese sat down on the sofa and reached over to hold Paul's hand while they watched the game.

Maeve finished her water, brought the glass into the kitchen, put it into the dishwasher and returned to the living room. "Want to go out for dinner tomorrow?" she asked hopefully.

"Yes," Therese answered excitedly.

"Then that's what we will do," Maeve replied happily. "I am leaving now. I'll call you tonight." Maeve put on her coat.

Her mother called out, "Bye, and thank you for everything. I don't know what we would do without you."

"Thanks," Paul said as he continued to watch the baseball game on television.

Maeve pulled away from their house and headed for the highway. It was seven o'clock and she would arrive home in time to make supper. The weekend had begun.

When she got home, she called Elderly SOS, an emergency notification system for people confined to their homes. She authorized them to install the system in her parents' home. That's a conversation for tomorrow night at dinner with Mom and Dad, she thought. I hope he doesn't protest too much.

Chapter 31
The Strange Mail

A t home, Maeve placed a whole chicken into the oven and went out to get the mail. The mailbox was full. Please let it all be junk mail so I can throw it all out, she thought. She flipped the mail onto the kitchen counter, leafed through it and tossed each envelope of junk mail into the garbage until she spotted an envelope with Maeve Carey scrawled across the top. There was no address below her name.

Someone must have manually placed it in the mailbox, she said to herself. She looked at the back of the envelope. It had not been sealed, but the flap was neatly tucked into the body. She pulled out a piece of paper and her heart began to pound. Her picture was superimposed on the paper, the same picture that had appeared in the local paper after her accident. Across the top of the paper appeared the words, I am going to protect you.

Maeve lost her breath. She felt weak and sat down and stared at her picture and the words above it again. What was going on and who could possibly be doing this? she thought. Maybe it is a joke, just some neighborhood kid who has too much time on his or her hands. But then again, maybe this is for real.

She heard a car pull into the driveway and the garage door open. Jeremy was home. As soon as he walked into the house, she shouted breathlessly, "Jeremy, please come into the kitchen and look at this."

"What is it, Maeve?" Jeremy asked in a tired voice. He stopped in the dining room and laid his keys and papers from work on the table. It was a habit that Maeve hated. She had told him at least every other day to put his personal effects on the dresser in their bedroom. Maeve bit her tongue and waited for him. Her legs went slack and she felt like vomiting.

Finally, Jeremy entered the kitchen. "I have work to do, so this had better be important," he stated impatiently. He stood in front of her like a soldier ready to go to battle.

She shoved the paper and envelope at him. He looked at them and said," I think we should call the police. This could be serious." He reached for his cell phone.

Maeve put her hand over his phone. "You really think this could be serious?" she asked incredulously.

"The print almost looks childish," Jeremy continued, "but it's better to be safe about this. There are a lot of crazies out there."

"Then call," Maeve said with determination.

An hour later, a young police officer sat across the table from Maeve and Jeremy. He slipped on latex gloves and inserted the envelope and paper into a plastic folder. "We'll see if there are any fingerprints on these," he said. He removed his latex gloves and stood up. "This is very unusual for a neighborhood like this. If you receive anything else, please call us. Also, if you want us to drive by the house to check on you, we will."

"That's not necessary," Maeve replied swiftly. "I work during the day and Jeremy is home almost every evening. I will be just fine, but thank you for the offer. If I receive anything else, I will call."

After the policeman left the house, Jeremy said, "I'll be in the basement if you need me."

"Jeremy, I need to talk with you now," Maeve said urgently.

"What now, Maeve?" he said impatiently.

"I knocked over Damien's backpack at work and found some plastic bags with a white substance in them."

"Did you ask him about the bags?" Jeremy asked thoughtfully.

"No, I just pretended I didn't see them. Do you think he could be taking heroin or be a heroin dealer?"

Jeremy shrugged. "You know, the O'Mara Law Firm has a good reputation in town. If I were you, I would mention my concerns to Stephen O'Mara. There's no point in getting the police involved if there is an innocent explanation for the bags. That is my advice, but do as you please."

"Thank you, Jeremy. I was thinking about talking to Stephen, but I just needed to get your input. I'm tired now. I'm going to rest in our bedroom."

Maeve shuffled to the bedroom and lay down. When she woke up, it was three o'clock in the morning. Her bed was empty on the other side. She rose and tiptoed down the hallway to the stairs leading to the basement. It was dark. "Jeremy," she called out loudly. No response. The house was totally dark, except for small beams of moonlight that shot through the sides of the shades that covered the windows in the dining room. She flicked on the switch at the top of the basement stairs that turned on the lights.

The hardwood stairs creaked as she padded down them in her bare feet. She peeked around the door and looked into the basement. Jeremy was not sitting at his desk and the computer was off. Maeve rounded the turn and walked further in. No Jeremy. She rushed upstairs and opened the door to the garage. Jeremy sat in his car talking on his cell phone.

When he saw her, he clicked the phone off and exited the car. "My God, woman, what are you doing up at this time of the morning?" he asked brusquely.

"That's a good one, Jeremy. But the real question is what are you doing up at this time of the morning?" she retorted angrily.

"I couldn't get any reception in the basement, so I went into the garage," he hissed.

"And who are you calling at three o'clock this morning?" She pulled her robe closer around her. It was cold in the garage.

"I was talking to a client in Rome. They are six hours ahead of us and I have business to conduct." He exited the car and put his arms about her. "Let's go inside where it is warm and I'll make you a cup of hot cocoa. I know you've been under a lot of stress what with the accident and now the note. Just relax and know that I'm here for you." He kissed her on the cheek and they walked into the kitchen.

Chapter 32
The Conversation

Maeve waited expectantly for Stephen to arrive in his office the following Monday to discuss the contents of Damien's backpack. When Stephen arrived, she followed him into his office. "Stephen, I need to talk with you," she said urgently.

Stephen sat at this desk and motioned for her to sit down. "What is it, Maeve?" he asked slowly.

"Last Thursday, there was an incident when Damien went to the bathroom."

"Well, there's nothing wrong with that, is there, Maeve?" Stephen laughed.

"No, but I had to move Damien's backpack in order to get into the file cabinet. I placed it on a chair and it fell to the floor. When I went to pick it up, the zipper was unzipped and some plastic bags with a white substance fell out of the bags. I placed them back in the backpack and saw five more bags inside it. I placed the backpack on top of the chair again before Damien returned from the bathroom. When he came back, I acted as if nothing had happened. I'm worried. Do you think Damien may be a heroin addict or dealer?"

Stephen laughed again. "Maeve, your imagination is getting the best of you. Damien has a hobby. He collects fossils and the habitat in which he finds them. He has been doing this for years. I bet he spends most of his weekends at the lakes and woods around Illinois looking for interesting fossils and their habitat. He places the fossils in a display case and encases the habitat in plastic bags. The next time you see him, ask him about his hobby. You probably won't be able to get him to stop talking about it."

Maeve's mouth fell and her face turned red. "I am so sorry, Stephen. I'm so happy we had this talk."

"No problem. I'm glad that you came to me to clarify the situation. If you have any other questions or concerns, please let me know." Stephen stood and gave Maeve a hug. "I have some work to do now," he said warmly.

"Of course, Stephen. Thank you." Maeve returned to her desk and thought about what he had said. Thank God I didn't go to the police and ruin Damien's reputation, she thought. He is such a clean cut boy. I'm happy Jeremy told me to talk to Stephen.

By Thursday of the week, it was all Maeve could do to stay focused on her work at the law firm. She still couldn't reconcile her suspicions about Damien. She hadn't slept well the previous nights and by noon, she was exhausted from her lack of sleep. She slipped out to get a breath of fresh air. In the distance, thunder echoed. The wind began to blow and the clouds darkened.

Maeve loved storms. She loved the feeling of the change in the air from warm to cool, the rush of the power of nature. As a child, when a storm approached, she used to lie on a small bed in her grandmother's back porch and open the windows. Then she would wait expectantly for the drops of rain to brush her face as the wind whipped them through the screens. Her grandmother would call out to her to come into the kitchen, but she would rest on the bed enjoying the thrill of the wind, thunder, lightening and torrents of rain.

Now she stood in the front of the law office and closed her eyes as the wind slapped at her face. It was only when the rain dropped in sheets that she rushed inside and brushed herself off.

"You don't look well, Maeve," Stephen told her soothingly. "Would you like a water or anything?"

Maeve shook her head. "Stephen, could I go home a bit early today? I'm just feeling a bit weak."

He frowned, but said, "You probably shouldn't have come to work so soon after your accident." He put his arms over her shoulders and hugged her to him.

Feeling uncomfortable, she pulled away from him. "Thank you, Stephen," she responded uneasily. She picked up her purse and headed for the door. "Will you need me tomorrow?" she asked hesitantly.

"No," he answered slowly. "Take as much time as you need. I can get a temp in to answer the phones. Just let me know if you cannot make it on Monday."

"I will. Hopefully, I'll see you on Monday."

"Maeve, if you need any help, let me know. I'll be there for you. Will Jeremy be home this weekend?" he asked casually.

She felt her heart start to pound and she began to perspire. Jeremy would be out of town this weekend. She stopped at the door and turned towards him. "Yes, Stephen. He's usually home every weekend," she answered with a smile, trying not to show her fear. "Why do you ask?"

He approached her slowly. "Just want to make sure you are safe," he reassured her.

"I'm safe, Stephen. Don't worry." With that she left the office.

Chapter 33
The Money Crunch

Maeve arrived home and immediately crawled into bed and lay her head on the soft pillow. After a few hours, she heard a tapping sound and sat up in bed. She realized the tapping sound was the wind whipping the branches of the trees against the bedroom window. The weather forecast reported there was to be a large storm this evening.

She slid out of bed and padded into the kitchen to get a bottle of water from the refrigerator. Jeremy's snores echoed from the family room. It was nine o'clock and Jeremy was sound asleep on the leather sofa as the television blared the sounds of the Bears football game and the crowd cheering as a touchdown was made. Maeve left the television on. If she turned it off, Jeremy would wake up. Somehow, he always managed to sleep while football sounded from the wide screen television set they had recently bought.

If he wasn't in the basement working, he watched sports on television. Football was his program of choice and the type didn't matter, professional, college, high school, as long as it was football. And when football season ended, he watched baseball, basketball or hockey. Maeve didn't mind. She enjoyed her evenings curled in bed under the covers reading a good book. She took the bottle of water out of the fridge and headed back into the bedroom and crawled into bed.

She placed her reading glasses on and looked at the assortment of books on the nightstand: *The*

Steve Jobs Biography, Instant Analysis, Pulling Your Own Strings, and *Boundaries and Relationships.* None of them interested her now.

She reached for the remote and flicked through the television channels like a woodpecker needling a tree. Click, click, click, not more than a few seconds on each channel, just enough time to decide if the program was worth watching. Jeremy hated it when she controlled the remote. He groused that he couldn't watch anything because she changed the channels so fast.

Her dexterity with the remote came because she hated most of the programs on television and only stopped for a few of her favorites, such as Downton Abbey on PBS, House Hunters on HGTV or Chopped on the Food Channel. She used to like the Housewives of Chicago, but had lost interest in it lately. Maybe her attention span was just becoming shorter with her advancing years. Good grief, now she was even thinking like an older person.

Maeve saw an advertisement for AARP on television and laughed to herself. Jeremy had joined AARP. He said it was for the discounts, not that he used any of them. He always found a way to spend money. She scrimped and he always seemed to end up with the big ticket items. He had once won a motorcycle in a contest. He had taken a class in motorcycle safety and had gotten a license to ride. Before he went out to ride, though, he wanted to dress properly so he had shopped for every motorcycle accessory known to mankind.

He bought a black leather jacket, black helmet and gloves, and installed gold trim all over the bright orange Harley. But after a year, he had sold the motorcycle, saying that he barely rode it on the weekends. She felt happy that the motorcycle was gone, but realized that Jeremy missed it. He works so hard that he hardly has any time for himself or her. Oh, well, she thought, Jeremy needs something to keep his life interesting. Maybe we can plan a trip to Europe next year.

Maeve pressed the remote again, but found nothing good on, so she clicked the television off and curled up in bed. So this was the life she lived. Slowly, she drifted off to sleep.

Jeremy woke up groggily, shifted off the sofa, stepped down to his basement office and sat at his computer. Just another night trying to make a success of this dam advertising company I started, he thought. Twenty years of this and what do I have to show for It? The economy is in the tank and I am barely getting by. At this rate, we might be in real trouble if the economy doesn't improve. I am going to need an influx of cash to keep this albatross going, he thought, as he turned back to the computer and continued entering the company's sales data. Unfortunately, I have bad news for Clare. He tore up the monthly rent check he had written to Clare and sent her a text message: Things are tight with my business. Can't send you the check right now. Would you consider moving back with us till you get on your feet?

Clare texted back: I'd rather not, but I'm in a bind. Maybe for just a few months till I find another job.

Jeremy texted: Great. I'll talk to Mom about your moving back with us. I'm sure she'll be delighted. She misses you a lot.

Clare texted: Thank you, Dad. Let me know what she says.

Chapter 34
Confiding in Stephen

Stephen was already in his office when Maeve arrived at work Monday morning. Maeve walked to his open door and said cheerily, "Good morning!"

Stephen glanced up from the large stack of papers on his desk and gestured for her to come in. "How are you feeling?" he asked warmly.

"I'm fine, Stephen. Thank you for asking. I can't talk now though. I have some work to catch up on."

She sat down at her desk and thought about Stephen. He was so kind. With his curly brown hair, crinkling brown eyes and quick smile, he looked like a big teddy bear. She would be eternally grateful to him for giving her a job. If it hadn't been for Stephen, she might still be an unemployed middle age woman making a nuisance of herself by hounding the landscapers and all the other service people that she and Jeremy used. Now she worked at a job she could call her own where she made her own money.

Though she was grateful to Stephen, she still wrestled these past days with Stephen's explanation about Damien and the suspicious letters that she had found in her mailbox. Finally, Maeve stood up and marched into Stephen's office. First, she told him about the strange letters she had received.

"Why didn't you tell me about them before? Bring them to the office so I can see them," he said with a worried look on his face.

"The police have them now. They are checking them for fingerprints and cross checking the printing," she explained rapidly.

"Do they have any suspects, yet?" Stephen asked tensely. His brow furled with lines. "I don't think you should spend any time alone. Will Jeremy be home this week or is he traveling?"

"Jeremy is traveling this week," she decided to tell him. "He is leaving after I get home tonight." She hesitated. "Stephen, I need to talk with you again about Damien."

"Yes, what is it?" Stephen said quietly. He leaned back in his chair and put his shoes on the desk.

"She took a deep breath. Just then, the phone rang and Stephen answered it and picked up a pen and pad of paper. "Hello, Rubin," he said in a loud, friendly voice. He waved goodbye to Maeve.

Maeve eased out of the room when she heard him say hello to Rubin, the client that had been injured in a car accident. The stakes in the suit were high, millions of dollars if Stephen won. He represented Rubin on a contingency basis and stood to collect thirty percent of the settlement if he won the case. This would make Stephen a very wealthy man.

Maeve had prepared a variety of files for the case and Stephen even let her sit in with him as he interviewed a witness in preparation for the trial. However, Stephen had seemed possessed, even erratic at times as he struggled to keep up with the myriad tasks to be completed before the trial started. He had a few months to go and the pace had only quickened each day.

Suddenly, Stephen rushed by her and shouted,"I have a last minute meeting in downtown Chicago. Hold down the fort."

Maeve looked up in surprise. "When will you be back?" she sputtered as he ran out the front door and slammed it behind him. She shook her head and wondered what meeting Stephen meant.

Chapter 35
Lack of Communication

W hen Maeve drove home after work that evening, she stopped at the entrance to her driveway to allow a black car to back out of the driveway.   She didn't recognize the car or the driver, but a man was behind the wheel. He passed her without acknowledging her.   When she entered the house, she found a life insurance policy on the dining room table.   She examined it closely.   It was her policy and the benefit amount had been raised to two million dollars.   She saw the light on in the basement and marched downstairs carrying the policy. Jeremy was working on the computer. "What is this all about?" she asked waving the policy in her hand.

Jeremy continued working on the computer for a moment and then turned to her.   "I just upped the payout amount of your policy. I did the same for mine too.   We're not getting any younger and I thought it important that Clare be taken care of if something happened to one or both of us.   Do you have a problem with the change?"

"I just wish you had consulted me about it," she answered crossly. "After all, it is my policy. I wouldn't have gone ahead and done the same thing to your policy without your knowledge."

"You're right," Jeremy said apologetically.   "I'll consult with you in the future, but now it is done. Right now I have to get the orders entered for the company. I'll see you in an hour or so and then I have to leave for the week."

A few hours later, after Jeremy left, the doorbell rang. When Maeve answered the door, she found Clare standing in the doorway sobbing uncontrollably. "What is it, honey?" Maeve asked in a worried voice. "Come on in." They walked to the family room, where Maeve sat down next to Clare and hugged her.

"Mother, I lost my job," Clare sobbed loudly. "Didn't Dad tell you?"

Maeve's mouth opened in astonishment." "No, he didn't. How could you lose your job when you were one of the up and coming advertising consultants in the company?"

"Mother, haven't you been reading the paper? Advertising sales are down. Companies aren't spending as much money as before. Businesses are going under and people are losing their jobs. They handed me my pink slip. They said there was no money to keep the company afloat. We all walked out with nothing, not even the last two weeks salary." Clare's shoulders shuddered and tears ran down her face. "I even asked Dad for a check to pay my next month's rent on the apartment, but he told me he couldn't give me the check because his business is in the tank too. Why didn't you tell me things are bad here too?"

"What!" exclaimed Maeve, her voice rising in horror. "I can't believe what you just said!"

"Well, it's the truth, mother," Clare muttered miserably. She gave Maeve a hug. "Mother, I have a favor to ask of you. I feel like I'm groveling, but can I come back to live here until I find another job? Dad said that he was going to talk to you about my moving back home, but he hasn't been answering my texts or phone mail messages."

Maeve stood up in shock. What in heaven was going on? she thought in a panic. She composed herself and said firmly, "Actually, I'd rather you didn't move in here." She told Clare about the strange letters she had received. "Why don't you stay with Aunt Annie and Uncle Peter?" she suggested.

Shocked at her mother's bad news, Clare stood up and stomped her foot on the floor. "I'm not hearing about anything that goes on here. Why didn't you tell me about the letters?"

"It just didn't seem important, dear. I didn't want to bother you with the matter," Maeve said sadly.

"Mother, from now on, I insist that you and Dad keep me informed about your lives. And I don't want to stay with Aunt Annie and Uncle Peter. They are weird," she stated firmly.

"She's just eccentric and he's an artist, that's all. Actually, yes, they are a bit different, but they still are family. For now it will be better that you live with them, just for a few weeks. You'll be safe with them. I'll call Annie now."

Annie sat in the lotus position praying in front of the crystals in her kitchen. She stared at the lighted candle in front of the crystals and took a long puff of the marijuana cigarette she held in her hand. Her braided black hair hung down her back. Dirty dishes filled the kitchen sink and her cats ate out of the cereal bowls on the table. Annie spent one hour every day meditating in front of the crystals and treating herself to a joint of marijuana during her meditations. She saw Maeve's number on caller ID on her cell phone and almost didn't pick up the phone. When it continued to ring, however, she relented and picked it up.

"Hello," Annie said with a sigh.

"Annie, it's Maeve. I have a favor to ask of you."

""Now what?" Annie asked crossly. "It's not Mom and Dad again, is it?" She took a long drag of her marijuana cigarette and hoped the smoke would calm her nerves during this call.

"No. Can Clare come to stay with you and Peter for a few weeks? She's lost her job and I am getting headaches and need the rest. Just for a few weeks, Annie," she pleaded softly.

Annie took another puff of the marijuana cigarette and blew the smoke into the air, watching it float to the ceiling. "Maeve, I'd love to have Clare stay here, but with my job and Peter's art work and the cats, we really don't have the time or the room for her," she stated indifferently.

Maeve clenched her teeth. "Ah, Annie. You always come through when I need you," she said sarcastically.   Before Annie could reply, Maeve disconnected the call. Maeve turned to Clare. "Looks like you're coming home," she said matter of factly. "Annie said she doesn't have room for you. Do you want me to help you move?"

Clare hugged Maeve. "Thank God I don't have to stay with them. Thank you, Mom. Dad said he knew you would say okay.   I'm paid up on the apartment till the end of the month, so I don't have to move till then. I'll get Sean to help me." Then Clare left the house, got into her car and drove back to River North.

Chapter 36
The Intruder

Maeve's head was truly splitting now so she plodded upstairs to the master bedroom and lay down. One hour later she woke up to darkness in the bedroom. She was sure she had left the lights on in the hallway and downstairs, but when she got out of bed, the hallway was black. She felt an eerie presence near her and then heard the sound of breathing. She reached for the light switch, but felt a gloved hand cover her mouth and heard a voice whispering into her ear. "Shut up and move," said the man's voice.

She pried the hand loose, but the intruder's other arm wrapped around her and pinned her to him. He held a knife to her throat. "Just keep your mouth shut and come with me," said the man's voice. "If you do what I say, you'll be okay." He moved the knife from her throat to her back and led her toward the door.

At first, Maeve thought she would comply with the man and try to make a break for it when they reached the outside of the house. Then, with a sinking feeling, she realized he might not take her out of the house, that he was just leading her on so he could kill her. She nodded and the man tightened his grip on her arms.

"You can have anything you want," Maeve cried imploringly. "There are jewels in the dresser drawer and I have money in my purse. Take the silverware, the car, anything." She felt her heart pounding in terror.

The man snickered. "But that's not what I came for," he said calmly.

"Then what do you want?" she pled in a quivering voice.

"You'll find out. Now walk with me. We're going into the basement." She took a quick glance at his face but all she could see was the black ski mask that covered his hair and face and the brown piercing eyes behind it. He was dressed in a black jacket and jeans. She pulled loose from him, jabbed him with her elbow, turned and kicked him in the groin. As he groaned in pain, she ran for the bedroom door, making it just in time to slam it behind her. She whizzed down the stairs and lurched out the front door to the house across the street. Looking behind her to see if the masked man was following her, she pounded on her neighbor's door.

"Hey, who's there?" asked David Ryan, her good natured Irish neighbor. He opened the door and stared at her. "What's wrong, Maeve? You look as though you've seen a ghost," he asked in a worried voice.

"Just let me in, Dave," she screamed loudly. "There's an intruder in our house and he threatened me with a knife." She pushed her way into the house.

David stepped aside and looked across and up and down the street. Then he slammed the door. "I don't see anyone now. Come on into the kitchen. I'll call the police. Dorothy should be home any moment now. She just went to the store to buy some medicine."

He pulled out his cell phone and dialed 911. After explaining the situation to the police dispatcher, he said to Maeve, "The police are on their way. Sit at the kitchen table and I'll make some tea." He then held a metal tea kettle under the faucet and filled it with water, placed it on the stove and turned on the gas. "There now," he said soothingly, "Just tell me what happened."

When Maeve finished the story, David paused and asked, "Where is Jeremy? I thought he was usually home in the evening."

"He's traveling this week and won't be home until Friday night," she explained,

Just then, the door opened and Dorothy walked in. She was a tall woman, with short gray hair and a friendly, open air about her. When she saw Maeve in the kitchen, she smiled and asked, "Well, kid, what are you doing here at eleven o'clock at night?'

David offered Maeve the tea and responded, "She's had a bad time of it this evening Dorothy. I called the police. They should be here in a minute. I'll fill you in on the details afterwards."

Chapter 37
The Police

Two policemen searched Maeve's house while she waited at the Ryan's home. After the search, the older of the officers said, "Sorry, Mrs. Carey, we didn't find anyone in the house. We searched the basement, the upstairs and the backyard, but whoever it was is long gone. He probably escaped through the backyard and ran down to the beach. We'll escort you into your house to get your purse and some clothes. After that, we're going to check the house for anything suspicious we can find. Since your husband is traveling, we think it best that you stay with some relatives or friends for the next few days."

"He was wearing gloves," Maeve stated in a firm voice. "There probably won't be any fingerprints." She felt as though her world was spinning out of control.

"Even so, he may have put them on after he entered the house. We'll check the outside and inside of the house for fingerprints and any other physical evidence that we can find. By the way, there was no sign of forced entry. Did you leave your doors unlocked?"

"Never. We never leave the doors unlocked!" she stated firmly. "How did he get in?"

"The only doors we found unlocked were the side door that leads into the garage and the door that leads from the garage into the mud room. Did you check them before going to bed?" He looked at her reaction closely.

"No, I didn't," she answered trying to recall the night.

The officer continued, "And your alarm did not go off. Did you set it tonight?"

Maeve's face turned red. She realized that she had been so upset about Clare's news that she had forgotten to check the doors and turn on the security system. "I forgot," she explained with embarrassment. "My daughter came over to tell me she had lost her job and I was so upset after she left, I just went to bed without checking the doors or the security system."

"I'm sorry, Mrs. Carey. Can you stay with a relative or friend for tonight?"

"I'd rather stay in a hotel," she replied quickly. "I'll stay at the Deer View Inn."

"As you wish," the younger officer stated. "Just call us if you notice anything suspicious. We'll have a car on call nearby in case you need us."

The officers accompanied Maeve to her house where she gathered her clothes. She then drove to the Deer View Inn. It was a landmark in the area, a small hotel situated on a quiet lane in downtown Lake Forest. She checked into the hotel, settled in her room and promptly called Jeremy on her cell phone. He didn't answer the phone so she left him a message to call her. Then she fell asleep. At two o'clock in the morning, she awoke to the ring of her cell phone. It was Jeremy.

"What's going on at this time of morning?" he asked in a worried voice.

"Someone broke into our home and tried to kill me," she burst out crying.

"What!" Jeremy shouted into the phone. "Is this some sort of a joke?" he questioned sharply.

"I couldn't be more serious," she replied sadly. "I'm at the Deer View Inn right now. The police told me to go to a relative's house, but of course, that is impossible. They are going to give the house a thorough search and see if they can come up with any fingerprints or clues as to who the intruder was. They said I can return in a few days. Can you come home now?"

"I'll drive home at once," he promised.

"Thank you, honey," she said in relief.

"I'll meet you at the Deer View Inn. It will take me five hours to get home."

"I love you," Maeve spoke gratefully.

"I love you, too. See you in a few hours."

Relieved, Maeve disconnected the call and promptly fell asleep.

At six o'clock in the morning, Maeve's cell phone rang and awoke her. She recognized Stephen's cell phone number. "Hi, Stephen," she said sleepily. "Why are you calling me at this time of the morning?"

"Oh, Maeve," Stephen said in a surprised voice. "I'm so sorry to bother you at this time of day, but can you come to the office earlier today?"

Maeve hesitated a moment, and then answered, "Yes, but why?"

"I'll tell you about it later," he replied quickly. "See you at seven o'clock this morning."

Maeve tapped the end call button and heard a knock at the door. She looked through the keyhole and saw Jeremy standing outside the door. "Oh, my God, I'm so happy to see you," she cried as she opened the door.

Jeremy stepped into the room and gave Maeve a hug. "How are you doing?" he asked in a concerned voice. "Were you sleeping? I'm sorry if I woke you up."

"No, I was just talking to Stephen. He asked me to come into the office at seven o"clock."

"Why?" Jeremy asked suspiciously.

"I haven't the faintest idea. But I said I would go."

They both sat down on the sofa in the room. "Now tell me exactly what happened," said Jeremy holding her hands. He looked intently at her. "Were you harmed or injured at all?"

"No, but I'm frightened out of my wits," she stated in a shaky voice.

"Can you identify the man?" he continued.

"No, he had on a ski mask that hid his hair and face. I did notice that he had brown eyes."

"What did the police say?"

"Just what I told you on the phone. They are going to search the house for fingerprints and any other clues, but nothing of this sort has every happened in Lake Forest before. They suggested that I stay in a relative's house, but I opted for the Deer View Inn. You haven't told Clare, have you?"

"No, I just drove straight here." He stood up and removed a bottle of water out of the bar in the room and took a long gulp.

Maeve looked at her wristwatch. "It's six fifteen in the morning. You said it would take five hours to get here. How did you arrive so fast?"

"I just gunned it. Traffic was light. I needed to get here quickly to be with you." He place the water down and hugged her.

"There is something else," she continued cautiously. "There was no sign of a break in. The police said the side door that leads to the garage and the door from the garage into the mud room were unlocked. Also, the security system wasn't on. I must have forgotten to lock the doors and turn on the security system," said Maeve.

His face went pale and he started to stutter. "I was in such a hurry to get going, maybe I forgot to lock the doors. I'm sorry if that was the case. As to the security system, you are the one that usually checks that it is on."

"Yes, that is right," she stated with a shrug. Just then, Maeve remembered what Clare had told her. "By the way, why didn't you tell me that Clare has lost her job?" she asked accusingly.

He took another chug of his water and said, "I thought it best not to tell you."

"Why not?" she asked angrily.

"Because you get so emotional about everything. You're the helicopter parent who can't let go," he retorted loudly.

Maeve felt as though she had been slapped in the face. "That's a very nasty thing to say. I've spent my whole life taking care of Clare."

"That's just what I mean. She's an adult now and can make her own decisions."

"So that's why she didn't ask me to give her the money for her rent." Then Maeve remembered what Clare had said about Jeremy's company. "And why didn't you tell me about the financial problems you are having with the company?"

"How did you hear about that?" Jeremy asked coldly. His mouth hardened and he stared at Maeve.

"From Clare."

"It looks like Clare is our go between in communication. That has got to end," he stated determinedly.

"I agree. Also you told her you would talk to me about her moving back home, but she hasn't heard from you and not been able to contact you for the past few days."

"My phone hasn't been working," he explained vaguely.

"Then why was it working when I called you?"

"I had a new battery installed in it. The old battery just gave out."

"Look, Jeremy. We need to have a heart to heart talk about our lives. It seems as if we are growing apart."

"I know," he replied directly. "Let's have the talk in a few days. I need to get some sleep. I'm tired from the drive."

"That sounds reasonable," she answered in a resigned voice. "Right now, I have to get ready to go to Stephen's office."

Chapter 38
The Talk With Stephen

Stephen was sitting at his desk having a scotch and coffee when Maeve walked in at seven o'clock in the morning. His looks shocked her. His eyes were sunken with dark circles under them and he appeared tired and disheveled.

"Want some more coffee?" she asked as she entered his office. "Were you here all night? You look like death warmed over," she observed cautiously.

"Stephen pointed to the wastebasket, which held five discarded paper coffee cups. "It has been a long night," he replied defensively, "but I got a call late yesterday that the trial date has been pushed up. It seems that Rubin's counsel wants his day in court and that day is one month sooner. If I win this one, Maeve, I'll be out of debt. If not, things will be a little iffy around here. I took out a large bank loan to start the law firm and business hasn't been strong lately. So a lot is riding on this case," he explained in a shaky voice.

"I'm sorry, Stephen. I will help you in any way that I can." She paused and put her head down. "I don't want to burden you too much, but I need to tell you what happened to me last night."

"What is it?" Stephen asked rapidly.

"An intruder broke into our home last night. He had a knife. I know he was going to kill me. I bolted and made it out of the house before he could get me into the basement." She started to cry.

"Can you identify the man?" Stephen probed as he wrung his hands.

Maeve shook her head. "No, he had a ski mask over his face and head. And his voice was muffled. I was so afraid. It's by the grace of God that I was able to escape to my neighbor's home."

Stephen sat back in his chair. "How do you know he wanted you to go into the basement to kill you?" he questioned her.

"Because he told me to go down there with him and he had the knife in my back."

"I'm so sorry, Maeve. If there is anything I can do, just let me know. I realize you have enough worries going on in your life right now, but you need to know the truth. We'll need to be working longer hours. If you can't do that right now, I understand. I'll muddle through." He rose and poured himself another cup of coffee from the pot in his office. "Want one?" he offered.

Maeve showed him the paper cup she had in her hand. "I'm set with my tea, but thanks for asking anyway." She smiled. "So where do you want me to start?" she inquired in a strong voice. "We're going to win this case, Stephen. Mr. Stein was injured and has suffered medical bills and mental and physical trauma. He's a sixty-five year old man who may never work again. You're going to win this one for him, Stephen and I'll be here to help you," she stated positively.

Stephen sat up straight in his chair. "That gives me comfort, Maeve. Let's get to work then. The day I hired you was the smartest thing I've done since

Sherri died.   By the way, I am leaving early for a meeting. I'll see you in a few hours."

Chapter 39
The Tryst

The restaurant was dimly lit and almost empty. Stephen sat at a table sipping a glass of beer and glancing at the menu. A woman entered the restaurant and was shown to the table by the maitre d.

"It sure took you long enough to get here," he growled, his tone betraying an anger that took the woman by surprise. He slowly gave the woman a once over. No wonder she'd cost so much money, he thought. Her blonde hair flowed across her shoulders. Her hazel eyes sparkled as she smiled at him. She wore a black leather pantsuit that fit perfectly on her tall, slim frame. The top of the suit revealed a black lace camisole that stretched over her generous breasts. They invited him to look more. He couldn't take his eyes off them.

"Aren't I worth the wait?" she teased him . She took his hand in hers and ran it across her face and down to those creamy mounds.

He knew he would get his money's worth that afternoon.

Chapter 40
The Emergency

Stephen returned to the office later that day. "Hi, Maeve," he called as he passed her desk.

Maeve looked up and was shocked. Stephen looked even worse than that morning. He's been drinking, she thought. He can barely walk straight. "Can I get you some coffee, Stephen?" she offered as she pushed her chair back.

"No, thanks, Maeve. I'll get some in my office." He closed the door and reached for his bottle of scotch in his desk drawer and filled his coffee cup with it.

Maeve observed him close the door. Looks like he's going to spend the rest of the day drinking, she thought This isn't a great way for him to prepare for the lawsuit. Just then, Maeve's cell phone rang. Elderly SOS was at the other end. The man from Elderly SOS said the buzzer on her father's chain around his neck had gone off and no one was answering. "I'm on my way to their home," Maeve shouted with her heart racing. "I'll call the City of Chicago Fire Department and ask them to go to my parents' home." The man at Elderly SOS said he would continue to try to contact her father.

Maeve dialed the City of Chicago Fire Department and told them Elderly SOS could not reach her father. She explained that her mother had dementia and asked them to enter the house.

"If we cannot get in, do we have your permission to break open a window?" the fireman asked urgently.

"Yes," break open the side front window. I am leaving work right now. It will take me about thirty minutes to get to my parents' home Take down my phone number and call me when you assess the situation. Please let me know what you find." She shut her cell phone and ran into Stephen's office and told him the news.

"Go," he ordered hastily. "Call me and let me know how your Dad is." He put his arm around her and escorted her to the entrance to the firm. "If you don't think you can drive, I'll take you."

"Thank you, Stephen, but I'll be fine," she answered quickly.

On the highway, Maeve pressed hard on the gas pedal and prayed that her father was all right. She was so happy that she had insisted that he wear an Elderly SOS chain around his neck that he could press when he or Therese needed help. "I don't want to wear this thing," Paul had protested, but since he was vehemently against hiring a caretaker to stay in the house, Maeve stressed that the only way he and Therese could continue to remain the house was to have Elderly SOS installed and he had to wear the chain around his neck.

Little did she realize how soon it would be used. She thought of it as an insurance policy against an accident. Now she gunned the car down the left passing lane of the highway to find out the status of her father's health.

She dialed her parents' home phone number. No one answered. She stepped on the gas pedal and speeded up to seventy miles per hour. The traffic was heavy as it always was on the way to the city. She maneuvered in and out of the lanes till she came to a mile from her parents' home. Her cell phone rang.

"Mrs. Carey," the voice at the other end spoke. "This is the Chicago Fire Department paramedic at your parent's home. Your mother let us in and your father is sitting up in the living room. We found him lying on the floor by the side of the bed. We are going to take him to the hospital. What should we do with your mother?" he asked in a rushed voice.

"Please take her too. I will meet you at the hospital.   Thank you so much," she replied breathlessly.

Chapter 41
The Decision

Paul lay in bed in the emergency room of the hospital. He had regained consciousness. Therese sat beside him crying and wringing her hands.

Maeve rushed into the room. "How do you feel, Dad?" she asked in a worried voice. She patted him on the head.

"I don't know what happened," he explained tiredly. He wore a heart monitor. The emergency doctor walked in, a tall, thin man with a serious air.

"Are you his daughter?" he asked in a brusque voice.

"Yes," Maeve replied quickly.

"We're admitting your father," he stated briskly. "He's being sent to the cardiac floor for tests. We're not sure why he blacked out. Someone will be down shortly to bring him upstairs. Do you have any questions?" he asked tersely.

Maeve was speechless. The cardiac floor. To her knowledge, her father didn't have a heart problem. "Why are you sending him to cardiology?" she demanded.

"We need to rule the heart out," the doctor replied as he left the room.

The next few days passed quickly. There were tests, tests and more tests. Finally, after three days of tests, Maeve had had it. A doctor strolled into Paul's room, pushed a paper in front of her and stated,"Sign this."

Maeve examined the paper. It was an authorization to take a stress test. At the bottom, there was a section listing all the dangers that could happen when the test was given, such as heart attack, stroke, even death.

Maeve tossed the paper back on the table and drew an x through it. "We won't sign," she stated firmly. "My father can't take this test. He cannot even walk without a cane or haven't you read his history? When will my father be released from here? And what are the results of the tests you have already taken?" she pressed crossly.

The doctor remained impassive. "As you wish," he replied slowly. He pick up the paper and placed it in his pocket.

"Doctor," Maeve insisted, "you haven't answered my question."

"Your father has diabetes. It can be controlled through diet and exercise. He blacked out because of a sugar imbalance. I'll have a dietician come in to familiarize you with a nutrition and physical exercise program. We'll have a therapist come to your father's home twice a week to strengthen his legs."

"I said, when will my father be able to come home, doctor?" Maeve now was angry. She folded her arms in front of her and ground her teeth together.

"We will release him tomorrow," the doctor responded cooly. He turned and left the room.

Maeve looked at her parents. "Dad," she said softly, "you realize that it is time for your and Mom to come and live with Jeremy and me. You can't safely stay in your house anymore. You've repeatedly said that you don't want a caretaker in your home and right now, I can't think of any other options to keep you both safe."

Paul's shoulders sagged. He looked at Maeve and shook his head. "I know it's best we sell the house and move in with you, Maeve. I know that we can't handle living alone in our home anymore and I don't want a stranger living with us." A tear rolled down his face and he turned in the bed and faced the darkened window outside. She saw his body shake as he sobbed quietly into his pillow.

Chapter 42
The Gun Purchase

Jeremy sat quietly on the family room sofa while Maeve talked to him about her father and mother coming to live with them. "We can put them up in the guest bedroom here on the first floor," she explained thoroughly. "We'll just move the guest bedroom furniture into the basement and put Mom and Dad's bedroom set, a few of their chairs, their small side table and television set in the room. I'll get a caretaker to watch them in the day. What do you think about the plan, Jeremy?" she asked hopefully.

Jeremy stared at Maeve. It was a look she had never seen before. It was almost as if he was looking through her and didn't see her at all. "I won't throw your parents out on the street," he murmured slowly. He strolled to her and gave her a kiss on the cheek. "If it will make you happy, dear, I am all for it."

"I really appreciate this, Jeremy. I know it will cause some loss of privacy for us, but I truly feel that there is nothing else that I can do. Mom and Dad are helpless and he refuses to have a caretaker in their home." She reached out and put her hand over his.

He smiled and took her hand. "We'll get through this together," he assured her. "I have to go to the office for a few hours to review the books." He picked up his briefcase and trudged to his BMW.

Just as he shifted the car into reverse and started backing down the driveway, she ran outside waving her hands for him to stop. "What time will you be home? Perhaps we can go to a show or out to dinner? Would you like that?" she yelled loudly.

"I'll call you when I leave the office. We can make our plans then. Talk to you later," he replied softly as he backed the car to the street.

Maeve waved goodbye to him, but he stared straight ahead and did not look at her. She returned to the house and wondered how having her parents live in the house was going to work out. Only time would tell.

Jeremy drove towards the highway and headed north to Wisconsin. He had to clear his head. When would all this end? he thought. This business is sinking faster than I anticipated. And now we'll have the added expense of Maeve's parents living with us. I've got to think of a plan. He floored the gas pedal accelerating the car to eighty-five miles per hour and turned up the volume on the radio. When he reached High 178 near the border of Illinois, he veered west and kept driving until he spotted a sporting goods store with a big sign advertising guns for sale. He spun the wheel to the right and pulled into the sporting goods parking lot.

He entered the store and strode to the gun section. A burly man with a grey, wiry beard, long stringy mustache, thick, stubby fingers and a head as bare and shiny as a pink balloon stood behind the counter. "Looking for a gun, are you?" the salesman ventured with a smirk as he sized up this man before him. Must be a yuppie, he thought examining Jeremy's kaki pants and striped shirt.

"Yes, I need one right away," Jeremy answered nervously. He scanned the enclosed and locked glass case that was filled with a variety of guns.

"Let me see your FOID card," the burly salesman stated in a friendly manner.

Jeremy frowned. "I'm afraid that I don't have a FOID card," he declared nervously.

"Well then, I can't take a gun out of our display case. All I can do is let you look," the salesman explained in a thick drawl.

Jeremy stared at the case. "I need a gun right away. Someone broke into our house and attacked my wife. I need a gun in order to defend her if that someone should decide to come back," he pleaded solemnly.

The salesman scrutinized Jeremy. Nice clothes, clean cut, older man, maybe an executive in some company, he thought. "I know someone who sells guns privately. No FOID card need," he suggested quietly as he looked to the left and right.

Jeremy looked up from the case. "That sounds really good. Would you mind writing down his name and phone number?"

"No problem, man. Just tell him that Mitch sent you. He'll give you a nice discount." He then held out his hand to Jeremy.

Jeremy reached into his wallet and handed the man fifty dollars. "Will this do?" asked Jeremy hopefully.

The salesman smiled and took the money.

Jeremy entered his car and dialed the phone number on the piece of paper the burly salesman gave him. After a short conversation, he speeded to the gun owner's house and easily bought a gun and ammunition, no questions asked. The gun seller also gave him a quick one hour lesson on how to load, shoot and clean the gun. When the lesson was over, Jeremy hurried to his BMW, tucked the gun under a blanket in the trunk of his car and headed back to Lake Forest.

Chapter 43
The Hit

The man patiently sat in an abandoned car in North Chicago. He had driven through North Chicago a few weeks ago and noticed the car in the parking lot of a boarded up old factory. The car had been picked clean. Two tires were gone and the windows were broken. The inside of the car was putrid and dirty and the cloth seats slashed. He thought the car had possibilities, so he returned every few days to see if it had been towed. It was still there at the end of the week, so he decided to use it for the meeting. Now he sat and looked at his watch. Midnight. Black outside and the the street lights were broken. Perfect. No one around and no one to see him. A steady rain beat on the hood of the car. Soon he heard footsteps. The passenger door of the car opened and a younger man got in.

"Sorry about my foul up," the younger man apologized nervously. He closed the passenger door and lit a cigarette. "I didn't expect her to put up a fight. I thought she would be a mouse, easy to handle. It will be better next time." He took a drag of the cigarette and watched it curl into a circle and float out the broken window. Then he turned to look at the person in the driver's seat who was unusually quiet.

A gun exploded and the cigarette went flying. Blood splattered all over the car, but the driver had already opened the door and was bolting down the alley to the rented car that he had parked on the side street four blocks away.

Chapter 44
The Home Care Agency

Maeve munched on some toast and jelly at her kitchen counter as she called the home care agency that her neighbor, Dorothy had recommended. "Hello, I need a caretaker for my parents," she explained patiently. "I need someone right away, as my father is leaving the hospital Sunday and I need someone to start on Monday."

"I'll see what I can do," said Judy at the other end of the line. "I'll make some calls and get back to you."

Maeve hung up the phone and waited. She wondered if she was doing the right thing by taking her parents into her home. Jeremy seemed so understanding though. She couldn't put her parents into a nursing home. She had visited the nursing home her friend's mother had been placed into. Though it was rated one of the best on the North Shore, it seemed so cold and antiseptic, so full of old people with no place to go, just waiting for death. She was so grateful that she had such a wonderful support system with Jeremy at home and Stephen at work. Just then, the phone rang. It was Judy, the woman at the agency.

"I just spoke with one of our caretakers who finished her last job a week ago. Her hame is Sophia and she lives in Deerfield. Can we come to see you in a few hours?"

"Yes," answered Maeve excitedly. "I'll see you both at one o'clock."

Chapter 45
The Caretaker

Sophia sat on a straight chair across from Maeve in Maeve's family room. Sophia was a quiet, stocky woman in her early forties with short, curly brown hair and a ready smile. Judy, the woman from the home healthcare agency, sat on another chair facing Maeve who was sitting on the sofa.

"Sophia completed her last job just last week," Judy said efficiently.   "She remained in that assignment for a year and has been working for our agency for three years.   Her references are outstanding," she finished proudly. "Here they are." She handed the sheet of paper to Maeve. "Do you have any questions?" she asked Maeve.

"Yes, I do," Maeve responded after reading the references. She turned to Sophia. "What were your responsibilities in your last position?" she asked warmly.

Sophia looked directly at Maeve and sat up very straight. "I cooked for the lady of the house. I did laundry. I shopped for food. I helped her with bathing and dressing and gave out her medicines,"   she replied in a soft, accented voice.

"Where do you come from?" Maeve asked when she heard her accent.

"Lithuania," Sophia responded proudly.

"My husband's mother was born in Lithuania," Maeve stated excitedly. "What city are you from?"

"Vilnius," Sophia answered with a smile. "Where was your husband's mother born?"

"It was the capital of the country," Maeve answered.

"Why that is Vilnius," Sophia pronounced quickly with a broad grin.

Maeve took an instant liking to Sophia. She seemed so open and direct, so kind. Just then, Therese shuffled into the room. She had just gotten up from bed. "This is my mother, Therese O'Connor," Maeve said as she helped her mother onto the sofa. "Mother's memory is not very good."

Sophia smiled at Therese. "My name is Sophia. I am very happy to meet you."

Therese looked at Sophia and Judy and smiled back. "I am happy to meet you, too." She turned to Maeve and asked, "Who are they?"

Maeve put her arm around her mother's shoulder. "I am looking for someone to come here to take care of you and Dad while I work," she explained softly.

"Where is Dad?" Therese asked as she looked about the room.

"Dad is in the hospital," Maeve explained quietly. "He will be coming home tomorrow. Isn't that exciting?"

Therese shook her head yes.

"Do you have any other questions?" Judy inquired.

"Actually, I don't," responded Maeve. "Can you start on Monday, Sophia?" she asked quickly.

A smile broke across Sophia/s face and she shook her head yes. "I will be here on Monday," she responded happily.

"What hours will you need her?" Judy continued.

"Seven thirty to five Monday through Friday," Maeve declared swiftly.

Judy placed the contract in front of Maeve and told her the payment would be made automatically through her credit card. Maeve gave her the credit card number and signed the contract. Judy handed Maeve a copy of the contract with a brochure outlining the services of the agency and gathered up her belongings.

Maeve remembered something. "Oh, would you send me a copy of your insurance policy?"

"Of course," Judy replied as she reached for her pen. "What is your email? I will email it to you."

Maeve gave her email to Judy.

"To sum up our discussion today, Sophia will start on Monday at seven thirty in the morning. I will stop by the first few days to make sure things are going smoothly," Judy said firmly. "It was a pleasure meeting you, Maeve and you, Mrs. O'Connor," she finished politely. She and Sophia shook Maeve and Therese's hands.

Maeve led them to the front door and waved goodbye. "See you on Monday," she called out. Then she reconsidered. "Actually, can you come over on Sunday for a while? We will be picking up my father from the hospital and I would like him to meet you before Monday. Also, he is a diabetic and I want to show you how to take his blood sugar level."

"I will be happy to come over," Sophia replied. "What time shall I arrive?"

"Four o'clock," Maeve answered.   "That will give him some time to rest before meeting you."

When she returned to the kitchen, Therese said,"Who were those ladies? And where is Dad?"

Maeve foresaw some difficult days ahead.

Chapter 46
The Move

The movers removed the furniture from Maeve's first floor guest room and carried the pieces downstairs to the back room of the basement. They then transferred her parents' bed frame, box spring, dresser and armoire, as well as two white side chairs, a side table, lamp and a television set from the moving truck to the guest room.

Jeremy and Peter had gone to a mattress store in Vernon Hills to pick up two twin size mattresses he had ordered that day. "I appreciate your help, Peter," Jeremy said as he drove to the store.

"No problem, bro. Happy to help out. Annie said the old man is worth a lot of money. Do you know how much?" He pulled a cigarette from his shirt pocket and lit it.

Jeremy's face turned red. "Peter, I have no idea how much Paul and Therese are worth. All I know is that they are moving into our home and it was good of you to come to help me. Don't ask any more questions about money, understand?"

Peter took a drag on his cigarette. "Just curious, bro. Annie and I are in the dark about what's going on with the old man. Just want to be kept in the loop." He turned toward Jeremy. "You still doing well at your business?"

Now Jeremy was really mad. "None of your business, Peter. Just help me get these two mattresses onto the top of my car."

"Sure thing. Why don't we stop for some six packs of beer before going back to your house? I know I'm going to be parched after all this manual labor."

Jeremy felt his anger ease. "We'll stop as soon as we get the mattresses secured on the car roof."

"You're buying, right?" Peter asked cautiously. He took another drag on his cigarette and blew a puff of smoke forward.

"Peter, do me a favor and don't smoke in the car. I'm a former smoker and I can't stand the smell of cigarette smoke and I don't want my BMW smelling of smoke."

"Will do, bro." Peter took a deep drag and flicked it onto the parking lot.

With the mattresses secured to the top of his car, Jeremy drove up to his house just as the movers pulled out of the driveway. He and Peter pulled each mattress off the top of Jeremy's BMW and carried them into the guest room. Luckily, the movers had assembled Maeve's parents' bedroom set, so Jeremy and Peter washed the dust from the front and back of the king bed frame, headboard, dresser and armoire, plus the side chairs, side table and television set. They then eased the new twin mattresses on top of the box spring.

Maeve and Annie got to work making the bed. Maeve peered with satisfaction at the new flowered sheets and bedspread she had bought the day before. The room appeared very cozy.

"It looks really good, Maeve," Peter said hurriedly. "But I have to get home," he said as he looked at Jeremy. Jeremy followed him outside   and they moved a carton of beer from Jeremy's car into Peter's car. "Thank you, Peter," Jeremy said gratefully.

"No, problem, bro," Peter responded. "Thanks for the beer. Tell Annie I'll see her at home." He took a beer out of the carton and twisted the cap off. "That's not a good idea," Jeremy warned.

"No, problem, bro. Just tell Annie I'll be waiting for her at home."

Jeremy walked back to the house and said to Maeve and Annie, "Peter has left. He'll see you at home, Annie."

Maeve looked at her watch and realized that it was time to pick up her father. "Time to leave," she called quickly to Therese. "Dad is waiting. Annie is going to drive us to the hospital."

Chapter 47
The Trip Home

Paul sat in a chair in the hospital room with his tweed hat in hand waiting for Maeve to take him to her house. I can't wait to get out of here, he thought. He smiled at Therese who sat beside him. "I'm coming home, my dear. I have missed you very much." He patted her hand.

Therese smiled back. "I missed you too. Where have you been?"

"Just getting a little check up from the doctors. They say that I am fine. Look at me. Don't I look handsome?" He wore his tan jacket, a pale blue shirt, tan pants and gym shoes. His cane stood at attention beside him.

"You certainly do look handsome," Therese replied as she blew a kiss at him.

The nurse came in and gave Maeve the discharge orders and list of medications. An orderly arrived with Paul's wheelchair to take her father to the front doors of the hospital.

Annie Gordon strode along one side of her father's wheelchair. "I'll go to the parking lot to get the car and swing around," Annie said purposefully. She pulled in front of the hospital and placed Paul's belongings in the trunk of the car while Maeve helped Paul and Therese into the car and buckled their seat belts. When both were comfortably settled in the car, Maeve folded Paul's wheelchair, pushed it into the trunk of the car and got into the rear seat. Annie drove quickly up Lake Shore Drive and headed west to I 41.   "So, good news that you're out of the hospital," Annie said loudly as she turned to look at Paul and pressed hard on the gas pedal.

"Just take us to my home, Annie," Maeve whispered crossly.   "Can't you see he is falling asleep?" In the passenger seat, Paul's head rested on his chest and his eyes were closed. Therese sat quietly in the rear seat next to Maeve.

Once they reached the house, Maeve showed Paul and Therese their room. Paul look impassively at the room.   He looked very tired.   Therese just stared.   "Here, why don't you both go to bed for a while," Maeve suggested as she took off Paul's coat and placed it in the closet. "Mom, let me have your coat too." She pointed to the closet. "This is where we can hang it."

"Well, I have to get going," Annie stated with a sigh of relief. "Peter and I are going out this evening. There's a play in Evanston we want to see."   She headed towards the front door.   Maeve rose and walked her to the door.

"Goodbye, Annie.   Thank you for helping me today and taking us to the hospital and driving us home," Maeve said gratefully.

"No problem, Maeve. By the way, do you still have Power of Attorney for them?" she asked quickly.

Maeve was taken aback. "Yes," she answered grudgingly. "Why?"

"Just wondering. I want to make sure they are taken care of. How much money do they have in the bank?"

"That's something you'll have to ask Dad," Maeve responded irately. "Bye, Annie." She closed the door and stomped back into the kitchen where she made herself a cup of chamomile tea and rubbed her temples. Her head was throbbing. Maeve knew she was on her own now.

Jeremy walked into the kitchen with his briefcase. "I have to run into the office to do some work," he explained.

"Can you wait until I go to the drugstore to order and get my parents' medications?" she asked in an exasperated voice.

"Of course," Jeremy replied cooly. "But I need to be out of here soon and I won't be home till ten o'clock or so."

"I'll be back in a half hour or so," she stated tiredly.

When she returned, Jeremy left for the office.

Chapter 48
The Meeting

O n Sunday, at four o'clock promptly, Sophia arrived at the house. Paul O'Connor had just gotten up from his nap and sat at the kitchen table reading the newspaper.

"Dad, I would like you to meet Sophia, the new caretaker who will watch over you and Mom while I work," Maeve said as she brought Sophia into the kitchen. Sophia extended her hand to shake Paul's right hand.

"I can't shake hands with you with my right hand," Paul said apologetically. He forwarded his left hand and squeezed Sophia's hand strongly. "I'm afraid my right hand is impaired."

"That is no problem. I will take good care of you," Sophia said soothingly. She winced as her hand felt the strength of the shake from Paul's left hand.

I'll show her who is boss, Paul thought with satisfaction as he released her hand. I may have had a stroke, but I still can show people that I have my wits about me.

"I am going to show you how to take Dad's blood sugar level," Maeve interjected. She brought out the diabetes testing kit and laid out the monitor and injection pen. She wiped cotton soaked with rubbing alcohol on the forefinger of Paul's left hand, inserted a needle into the injection pen, pressed the button to activate the needle and pressed it into Paul's finger. A little drop of blood oozed out. She placed the monitor's testing strip under the drop of blood until a buzzer sounded, then watched as the monitor displayed Paul's blood sugar count.   It was one hundred twenty.

"Do you think you can do this?" Maeve asked Sophia.

"Of course," Sophia replied confidently.

"Then let me see you do it," Maeve stated hopefully.

Sophia followed the procedure that Maeve had just demonstrated perfectly.   "Good job," Maeve said approvingly.

"I have done this before in previous jobs," Sophia stated cooly.   She looked at Maeve with satisfaction, then turned to Paul. "Mr. O'Connor, I will take good care of you."

"I'll make sure of that," Paul answered with a laugh.

"Thank you for coming over today," Maeve commented.   She walked Sophia to the door.   "We'll see you tomorrow."

When she returned to the kitchen, she asked her father, "What do you think of her?"

"We'll see once she is here," he replied skeptically. "The proof will be in the pudding."

Maeve had planned a simple meal for dinner, a meal designed to be low in fat and sugar.   The instruction sheet the hospital had sent home with her father had suggestions on preparing diabetic meals and Maeve, perfectionist that she was, planned the evening meal carefully.   She prepared small portions of roasted chicken, carrots, and boiled potatoes.   This was going to be challenge, she thought, trying to keep Dad on his diet and keep Mom and Jeremy happy with the menus.   Talking about juggling different needs, she mused.

That evening, Maeve, Paul and Therese sat in the kitchen and ate.   There was little talking.   When they were finished, Maeve slipped on her rubber gloves and loaded the dishes in the dishwasher while Paul slowly shuffled into the family room and turned on the television.   Therese help clear the kitchen table.

Maeve handed Therese the kitchen sponge. "Will you wipe off the table please and the counter tops too?" she asked softly.

"Of course," Therese replied happily. She took the sponge and started wiping the counter tops in short strokes that missed the crumbs near the toaster and coffee pot. Maeve kept quiet. She knew Therese was doing the best she could.   Then Therese approached the kitchen table and started wiping.

"Mother, please shake out the place mats in the sink and then leave them over the back of the chairs while you wipe the table."   Therese pulled up each placemat and piled them on top of each other. Then she started wiping the table and put them back afterwards.

"No, Mom, shake each one separately and leave it draped across the chair while the table is drying. She saw the confusion in her mother's face and realized she was not processing what Maeve had just said.   Is it really important that she follow my instructions perfectly?" Maeve asked herself. At least she is doing something to help.

"Thank you, Mom," Maeve spoke warmly.

"No, thank you," Therese replied with a sad look on her face. "Thank you for taking us into your home. You are being very good to us."

Maeve was shocked that her mother was more fully aware of what was going on than Maeve had realized.   After the dishes were loaded in the dishwasher, Maeve and Therese walked into the family room where Paul was watching a basketball game on television.   Maeve decided that she would have the television set in her parent's bedroom hooked up to the cable as soon as possible so Paul could watch his sports games there and Maeve and Therese and Jeremy could watch whatever programs they wanted in the family room. She pulled out her to do list, and entered, Call cable company tomorrow.

Chapter 49
The Tour Of The House

Sophia arrived promptly at seven thirty in the morning on Monday.   Maeve laid out her parents' medicines in two small plates on the kitchen table and explained to Sophia how they were to be disbursed to her parents.   Then she showed Sophia the house.

"First, I'll take you to Mom and Dad's bedroom on the first floor.   They are still asleep," she whispered, "so be quiet." They poked their heads into Paul and Therese's bedroom quickly and saw them sleeping in their bed.   They exited the room and quietly closed the door.

"Follow me upstairs," Maeve gestured with her hand.   They climbed the circular staircase to the second floor. "There are four bedrooms up here," she explained. "My husband and I are the only ones who sleep up here now." She showed Sophia the exercise room. Sophia was astonished to see all the exercise machines that filled the workout room: an elliptical, stationary bike, step master, rower and treadmill faced a flat screen television that hung from the wall. They continued down the hallway to two other bedrooms.

"This room belongs to our daughter, Clare, who moved out a few months ago, but will be returning to live here for a while next month. The other bedroom now serves as a guest room. I won't show you our master bedroom because Jeremy is getting ready now and will be down shortly to leave for work."

They descended the stairs and proceeded through the large, airy living room, formal dining room, family room, library/den, kitchen and on to the laundry room. "This is our laundry room. It is located between the kitchen and the mud room." They entered the room. "Would you like me to show you how to use the washing machine and dryer?" she asked in a friendly manner.

Sophia shook her head no. "I am familiar with these things," she said firmly.

"Okay," Maeve replied. "Come with me." She gestured for Sophia to continue to follow her. "We have a mud room that serves as the entrance to the house from the garage and leads to the laundry room then the kitchen.

"You certainly have a large home," Sophia said with pursed lips.

Is she criticizing me or am I just imagining her displeasure? Maeve thought. She brushed off her observation and motioned for Sophia to follow her down the basement stairs.

"While Mom and Dad are still sleeping, I'll show you the basement," Maeve said as she descended the stairs. "Jeremy uses the main area of the basement for his home office." They moved through the carpeted and paneled room strewn with files and books. Papers, bills and receipts covered Jeremy's desk. His computer and printer sat on another table. Banker's boxes and papers concealed most of the wet bar in the basement. Sophia shook her head in disgust as she followed Maeve to the next room in the basement.

They walked through french doors to the room next to Jeremy's office. Maeve turned on the light in the back room that held a drum set, three mattresses, their guest bedroom furniture, books, a desk covered with banker's boxes and baskets, an ironing table and iron and old art supplies. There was barely any room to walk. Maeve smiled as she explained, "This is our catch all room." Sophia scanned the room and frowned.

"Now you've seen most of the house," Maeve commented politely. They proceeded upstairs to the kitchen where Maeve picked up a piece of paper on the kitchen counter and showed it to Sophia. "This is my parents' schedule. I'll leave it posted on the refrigerator door with my cell phone number and the police and fire departments numbers. It includes the instructions for my parents' medications. They are in top shelf of this cabinet," she explained as she pulled open the kitchen cabinet door and showed Sophia the medicines. "Please call me at any time. I work only ten minutes away in downtown Lake Forest. Do you have any questions?" Maeve asked.

"No," Sophia answered quickly. "Everything will be fine."

Just then, Jeremy entered the kitchen. "Good morning, Jeremy. I would like you to meet Sophia. Sophia this is my husband, Jeremy."

"Mr. Carey, it is so nice to meet you," Sophia spoke softly.

"The pleasure is mine, Sophia. Please call me Jeremy."

They shook hands and sized each other up. Handsome man, Sophia thought.   Distinguished looking, trim, well dressed.

She reminds me of my mother, Jeremy thought.   Round face, small stature, sound handshake, same accent.

"Now I have to leave for work," Jeremy said politely. He gave Maeve a kiss on the cheek and left.

"What a nice man," Sophia commented to Maeve. "I can see the Lithuanian in his face. He is so handsome."

"Thank you," Maeve replied with a smile. "Now I have to leave too." She pointed to the schedule she had posted on the refrigerator.   "Call me with any questions or concerns."

"Everything will be fine," Sophia said confidently.

Chapter 50
The Caretaker's First Day

Sophia peeked into Paul and Therese's bedroom when Maeve's car pulled out of the driveway. They were still fast asleep. It was now eight o'clock, so she emptied the dishwasher and threw yesterday's papers into the recycle bin in the garage. She descended the stairs into the basement again and looked around.

The man of this house is so messy, she thought. He keeps papers everywhere. She looked at the documents lying on his desk: invoices, unopened envelopes, contracts, files, pens. Little drawers were built into the back of the desk and these too were stuffed with papers. How does he get any work done? she thought. She moved over to his other desk on which a computer and printer stood. Papers lay strewn about this desk too, with computer books stacked to the side. Then she moved over to the wet bar at the other end of the office area of the basement. Banker's boxes crowded the countertop. Some were labeled Personal Taxes and some were labeled Carey Consulting Taxes ranging from 2004 to 2023.

Sophia shook her head and moved on. This basement is a mess, she thought. She again looked into the catch all room. She clicked her tongue four times against the top of her mouth and uttered in a disgusted voice, "What clutter." Suddenly, she looked at her watch. "Oh, no," she shouted. "It is eight fifteen.   I must see if Mr. and Mrs O'Connor are awake."

She hurried up the basement stairs and looked into their bedroom. Paul was already dressed.

"Good morning," she said in a cross voice. "Why did you not wait for me?   I will help you get dressed."

"I called for you, but no one answered," Paul replied gruffly.   "Where were you?   Maeve said you would be here at seven thirty this morning."

"Oh, I was just folding some laundry," she lied. "Here, let me help you to the bathroom."   She put an arm under his and steadied him.

Paul pulled his arm away from her.   "I don't need help.   I have my cane."   He shuffled to the bathroom and closed the door.   Inside, he washed his face and shaved with left hand.   His right arm hung at the side of his body.   He combed his hair and blew his nose into the clean linen handkerchief he kept in his pants pocket.   What a waste of money this caretaker is, he thought angrily.   I can take care of Therese and myself.   This Sophia couldn't even get here on time. I'll see to it that she is fired.

When he moved slowly into the kitchen, Sophia pulled out the chair to the table and waited for him to sit down.   Then she opened the diabetes testing kit and laid out the monitor and injection pen.   She wiped his forefinger on his left hand with rubbing alcohol and cotton as Maeve had demonstrated to her on Sunday, inserted a needle into the pen and pressed the button to activate the needle and pressed it into Paul's finger. A little drop of blood oozed out.   She placed the monitor's testing strip under the drop of blood until a buzzer sounded, then watched with Paul as the monitor displayed his blood sugar count. It was one hundred twenty.

"It's okay," Paul commented . "Maeve said it is normal as long as it is within ninety to one hundred thirty."

"I know that," Sophia responded in a condescending voice. She ejected the needle into a can and replaced the injection pen and monitor into the black holder for the kit. "Now I will make you breakfast."

Maeve had left Sophia instructions for exactly what to serve Paul based on the recommendations she had been given by the hospital in order to keep his blood sugar stable. Sophia reached into the refrigerator and poured a half glass of orange juice. Then she peeled a banana and placed it on Paul's plate.

Paul swallowed the pills Maeve had laid on his plate that morning with the orange juice and started cutting the banana with his fork.

Sophia placed a low carb yogurt in front of him and sprayed a no stick small frying pan with oil spray. Then she fried eggbeaters and toasted a piece of wheat bread and placed them on Paul's plate. Paul ate the food methodically. First he ate the bananas, then the eggbeaters and toast. He pushed the plate to the side and opened the yogurt container and pulled off the top. He touched the top to his lips and licked the remaining yogurt off of it. Then he took a spoon and ate the yogurt in the container. When he was finished eating, he pushed the container to the side and looked around for the morning newspaper.

"Where's the newspaper?" he asked in an annoyed tone of voice. "I always read the newspaper after eating breakfast."

Sophia saw the newspaper resting on the counter and placed it before him.

"Thank you," he muttered and began to read the sports section.

Sophia cleared the table. Just then Therese padded down the hall and entered the kitchen. She wore her robe and had applied lipstick to her lips.

"Good morning, my lovely," Paul said cheerfully. "And aren't you beautiful this day." A smile broke across his face as he gazed at her.

Therese walked around the table, the sound of her slippers brushing across the floor. "Good morning," she replied softly. A puzzled look came over her face when she saw Sophia.

Sophia held her chair out for her. "I am Sophia. I will be taking care of you and your husband while your daughter is at work."

Therese smiled. "Thank you," she said sweetly. She sat at the table and waited.

"Maeve said you like cereal for breakfast. Is that what you want?" Sophia asked as she stood next to Therese.

"Yes," Therese answered. She looked at Paul who now was reading the newspaper. "How are you this morning?" she asked brightly.

"Paul looked up and touched her hand. "I'm just fine, my sweet." Then he went back to reading the newspaper.

Sophia poured a glass of orange juice, filled Therese's bowl with cereal and poured two percent milk into it.

Therese ate a spoonful and asked, "Would you please heat this milk? It is very cold."

"Of course," Sophia answered. She took the bowl and placed it into the microwave for forty seconds. Then she placed it before Therese and poured her a cup of instant coffee.

Therese downed her pills with the orange juice and started eating the cereal. Thirty minutes later she was finished. "I think I'll go back to bed," Therese shared. "Is that all right with you?" she asked Sophia.

"Of course, let me help you into the bedroom," Sophia replied as she pulled out Therese's chair. She walked with Therese to the bedroom and tucked her into bed.

"She's tired," Paul explained when Sophia returned. "She always goes back to bed after breakfast."

"I will help her with her shower when she gets up," Sophia responded with a sigh. Then she sat with Paul at the kitchen table and read the paper too.

Chapter 51
Stephen's Diversions

Stephen sat at his office desk and dialed a number on his phone. "Put one thousand dollars on the Bulls," Stephen bellowed over the phone.

The voice at the other end snarled, "I'll book it, but you're already into us for one hundred thousand dollars. Have the money for me by the end of the week, you hear! No excuses or some of my guys will pay you a visit."

Stephen hung up the phone and poured himself a tall drink. The Bulls better pull through tonight, he thought.

That evening, he sat in his office and watched the Bulls lose. By the end of the game, he had consumed a bottle of scotch. I've got to come up with some fast money before the end of the week, he said to himself. But where am I going to get it?

Stephen bent over and reached into the right hand drawer of his desk and pulled out the extra bottle of scotch he kept in a paper bag in the back of the drawer. He tipped his head back and poured the scotch into his mouth, gulping the liquor down as quickly as he could. He started to gag and wiped his mouth with his hand. He realized his personal injury case might not have any merit. Now what? he thought. He had worked so hard since the death of Sherri, but it hadn't gotten him anywhere.

He thought of Sherri. She was the biggest nag of all time and all she did was hound him to make more money. The problem was she spent it like a drunken sailor. He had grown sick of her within the first year of their marriage with her constant complaining about everything. In short, he didn't like her most of the time.

So he had his diversions, the call girls, the gambling. Sherri had given him an ultimatum. Quit the girls and stop the gambling or she would leave him and take everything he had. He tried, he really did, but he couldn't control himself. So when Sherri looked at his cell phone and saw a message for a meeting with a hooker, she went berserk. She screamed at him and hit him. She threw a kitchen knife at him. It just missed him.

He lunged at her, but she tripped him. He fell like a beached whale. Before he was able get up, she ran outside and hopped into her car and sped off. He jumped into his car and gunned the gas pedal. It was late and dark. He followed her taillights till she reached the winding road to the Lake Bluff beach.

As she turned onto the road, he bumped her from behind so hard that her car missed the turn and careened over the ravine into the ditch below. When he reached her, she wasn't dead yet. He took a bottle of scotch that he kept in his car and poured it over her and made her swallow the rest. She died a few minutes later. The coroner said she died due to intoxication, which led to the accident. It was too bad, but he had to do it. Then he was free to gamble and see the call girls.

That is, until Maeve came into his life. When Maeve entered his office for her interview, he couldn't believe his eyes. Maeve looked so much like Sherri, with her sparkling green eyes, shoulder length brown hair and slim build. She was even as tall as Sherri. It was as though the Sherri he originally loved had come back to be with him.

He knew she would be good for him and he was right. She was an excellent legal assistant who made sure everything in the office ran well. She was so organized and reliable. She cleaned up his messy desk and created files for the stacks of papers he had strewn about his office. She color coded each file and numbered it so he could find each file easily.

She took the calls and scheduled his meetings and depositions. She typed his documents and researched the facts he needed for discovery in the personal injury case. He wondered how he had been able to work without her. Each day when she came into the office, he felt a happiness he had not felt in years.

But this past month, things have gotten too messy, he thought. First, Damien delivered the heroin to Lake Forest in a boat, crashed it and lost the stash. The he defied me by bringing packets of heroin to the office where Maeve saw them. Little did Maeve know that Damien and I were drug dealing partners and running a small drug dealing operation when she spoke to me about her suspicions about Damien. And the last straw was Damien screwing up trying to kill Maeve. He took another slug of his scotch, closed his eyes and rubbed his temples. What to do now? he asked himself.

Chapter 52
The Odd Client

Stephen sat at his desk and stared at the papers in front of him.   He owed more than one hundred thousand dollars to his bookie. It had started out so small. One of his clients told him about a bookie he used. He placed one bet, just a medium one on a football game and made a quick five thousand dollars. After that, he placed another and another, just small bets of one or two hundred dollars. After a month, he owed the bookie five thousand dollars, so he was even. He decided to go to the Outdoor Race Track to bet on the horses. It seemed an easy way to get some money to pay back the bookie. He lost one thousand dollars.

The betting relieved his stress at the office with this large case. He had been neglecting his other clients since he was putting all of his energy into this personal injury case. He remembered the day he first met Rubin Stein. Stein's sister, that quack Ruth Stein, had referred Rubin to him after he had handled the closing of her house.

What an odd client Rubin was. He remembered the first appointment he had with Stein. Stein carried in a banker's box and plopped it on Stephen's desk. Stein looked like an absent minded professor with his cardigan sweater stained with a mustard smear on the front, his loose beige pants which hung on his thin frame like a tent and wrinkled striped shirt with a frayed collar. His brown piercing eyes peered through his dark rimmed thick glasses that perched on his hawk like nose. He kept running his hand nervously through his greasy uncombed black hair.

"These are my medical records, all of them," Stein had stated heatedly.   "I fell in front of the restaurant. I tripped on the metal fence in front of the restaurant and hit my head and sprained my ankle. I've been having headaches since then and my vision has been affected," Stein continued anxiously.

"Have you seen any other lawyers about your case?" Stephen had asked.

"Three others," Stein shot back crossly. "They don't want to handle it."

"I received a call from your sister saying that you wanted to see me."

"Yes, Ruth used you for the closing of her house. She said you were the best lawyer she had every used. So I made the appointment with you."

Stephen remembered the woman. She was strange, but the closing had been uneventful. "Will you leave these records here?" Stephen had asked. "I want to go through them and will let you know if I will take the case."

"Sure, but I need them back in a few days," Stein retorted angrily.

"By the way, do you have any other medical symptoms?" Stephen probed further.

"I have anxiety attacks. I lost my job and my wife and kids left me."

"I'm sorry to hear about that," Stephen said cautiously. I'll get back to you about the case."

Stephen spent the next day reading the medical records. The case seemed promising. The doctors documented Stein's injury to his head and and reported that his headaches and impaired vision could have come from the injuries he sustained from the fall. It would be great if Stein could collect for pain and suffering.

This might be my big break, Stephen thought. After spending so many years working on the small stuff that's become my bread and butter, I'll take a chance and accept this case. God knows I need the cash it will provide if I'm successful in representing Rubin.

When Stein returned later in the week, he didn't seem very excited when Stephen told him he would take the case. There seemed to be an undercurrent about him as if he were a volcano ready to burst.

"How soon till you get some results?" Stein asked suspiciously. "Let's take those bastards for everything. I've got mine coming, you know." Stein removed his glasses and wiped them with the edge of his shirt which was hanging out over his pants. His eyes looked piercing and did not leave Stephen's eyes. He finished wiping his glasses and placed them on his head again.

"I'll contact the restaurant and see if they want to settle. I'll call you," Stephen finished quickly.

Stein reluctantly stood up. "You know, sometimes I just think it would be easier to take things into my own hands. There are a lot of people who have crossed me in the past. I'm a nice guy, but I have my limits," he smirked. He then left the office.

Stephen watched him leave and sat down. Was that a threat? he wondered. Or is Stein just a loose cannon?

Chapter 53
The Futility Of Stephen's Work

Stephen rose from his desk and tried to stop thinking about his initial meeting with Rubin. A shot of scotch will help he thought. He poured himself a scotch and swallowed it in one gulp. His nerves began to calm. He glanced through at all the unopened mail on his desk and stopped when he found an envelope from opposing counsel in the Stein case. He quickly tore open the envelope and stared at the letter from the restaurant's attorney.

Stephen eyes widened and his shoulders slumped. His mouth hung open in disbelief. His eyes sunk into his ashen face. He rung his hands in despair. Suddenly, he heard a knock at the door. "Who is it?" he shouted angrily.

"It's me, Maeve," came the reply. She tried opening the door, but it was locked.

Stephen pushed himself up from his chair, unlocked the door and let her in.

"My God, what have you been doing?" Maeve asked fearfully. "You look like you've been up all night!"

He reached for the letter on his desk and shoved it towards her. "Look at this," he moaned in a defeated voice.

Maeve stared at the letter, but before she could start reading it, Stephen interrupted angrily. "It states that the restaurant's attorney has filed a Summary Judgment motion because a tape from the gas station across the street from the restaurant shows that

Rubin did not trip and fall on the metal fence outside the restaurant. It proves that he looked around and sat down holding his head and started moaning.

Two people walked by and helped him into the restaurant. The owner of the restaurant called the police and the police issued a report. Rubin went to the Emergency Room at the hospital where the ER doctor found a gash on his forehead and a sprained ankle. They stitched up his gash and told him to see his primary doctor. The injuries he sustained are not consistent with the gas station's recorded tape. He must have fallen at his home and decided to try to cash in on the event."

Maeve sat down in disbelief. "How could this have happened?" she asked sadly. "You have put so many hours into this case."

"The gas station owner was reviewing his security camera tape because he had a burglary a few week ago. When he looked at the tape, he saw Rubin's incident across the street. He notified the police who called the restaurant. The restaurant owner called his attorney. It's a good bet Summary Judgment will be granted and our case will go down the drain. All that work for nothing."

"I am sorry, Stephen," Maeve said softly.

"There is something else," he continued. He looked at her and paused. "Damien is dead. His body was found in North Chicago."

Maeve gasped. "No!" she shouted. "How did he die? He was so young."

"He was shot. The police found him in an abandoned car. They think he was involved in a drug deal gone bad. There were drugs in the car." He dropped his head and started to cry.

Maeve put her arms around Stephen's shoulders. "Oh, Stephen. I am so sorry."

He picked up his head and held onto one of her arms. "You warned me," he said in a muffled voice.

"I wish I had gone to the police about the plastic packets in Damien's backpack," Maeve admitted regretfully. "I wondered what they were, but it was so hard to believe that Damien was a heroin dealer."

"No, he had both of us fooled. I believed him when he spoke about collecting fossils and keeping plastic bags of the areas where the fossils were found."

Stephen took his hand off of Maeve's arm. "It's like the world is coming crashing around me. First Damien. He was like a son to me. He had such a promising future. And then this Stein case I've been working on falling through.   What more could happen?"

"Maeve hugged Stephen. "Oh, Stephen, this is unbelievable," she stated sadly. "Please let me know if there is anything I can do for you."

Stephen shook his head. "Just let me be alone for a while," he asked in an annoyed voice.

"Of course," she replied quickly and left the room. She sat at her desk and thought about the fact that Stephen had been counting on the settlement to keep the office going. And now he had to deal with the death of his stepson, Damien.

Maeve also realized that although Stephen's case load had shrunk over the past year, he seemed preoccupied with something else. There were those phone calls when he closed the door to his office, the times he left work early. Even in the middle of this important case, Stephen seemed distant from the work. She wondered why.

She knew that he had no children and lived alone in a home in Lake Bluff near Lake Michigan, the home he had shared with his deceased wife, Sherri. He had told Maeve that when he won Rubin's settlement, he wanted to sell his home and start anew in a different place with no memories. Now it seemed a certainty that he would move. He would need the money from the sale of the home.

She stood up and returned to Stephen's office and knocked on the door. "What is it?" Stephen groaned.

Maeve opened the door and said, "Stephen, things will work out. They always do. By the way, I have a favor to ask of you   I am going to put my parents' home in Chicago up for sale. Will you take care of the legal details?"

He looked up at her and nodded. "Of course, I will handle the sale of your parents' home." He paused a moment while he stared at her. "You're right, Maeve. Things will work out. I'll make sure of that. Now if you don't mind, I have to call Rubin and let him know the news. Please close the door behind you."

As soon as the door closed, Stephen poured himself another scotch. After three drinks, he decided that the call to Rubin could wait for a while. He poured another scotch and fell asleep at his desk.

Chapter 54
The Real Estate Agent

Megan McCormack, a well known real estate agent in the northwest side of Chicago stood in front of the single story brick home on the well kept street in Edge Bay, an attractive neighborhood on the north side of Chicago. Megan had sold homes in this neighborhood for the past fifteen years, ever since her husband had died. She had four children she had raised on her own and she was successful because she was good at analyzing a home's value, marketing the home and dealing with the owners and buyers. Megan wasn't flustered easily. She had handled all sorts of situations and problems with a calm, steady manner.

Megan was a half-hour early for her initial appointment with Maeve Carey. She decided to use the time to review the exterior of the O'Connor home and determine her first impressions of it. She walked around the exterior of the home. She saw peeling white paint on the eaves and noticed that the roof needed replacement. She looked at her watch. Twenty minutes till Maeve would arrive.

She opened the gate to the small, well kept backyard with towering trees. A chain link fence surrounded the yard. The landscaping was a definite plus, she thought. The driveway on the side of the house provided a passageway to the one car garage. Just then, she heard the sound of a car pulling into the driveway and the car door open and shut. She walked back to the side entrance of the home. "Hello," she said with a wave. "You must be Maeve."

Maeve waved back and smiled. She initially had seen Megan's picture on the small pads of paper in her parents' home that Megan distributed as part of her marketing program. Maeve had used the pads to write grocery lists these past years and the marketing paid off in name recognition now.

Also, Maeve knew of Megan because Megan and Therese used to belong to the neighborhood garden club. Before her mother's memory started to decline, she often talked about Megan and what a great reputation she had as someone who sold a large volume of homes quickly each year. In taking a drive through the neighborhood streets, Maeve had found five of Megan's For Sale signs dotting lawns within a ten block perimeter of her parents' home.

Megan looked just like her picture, only a bit older. She wore her hair in a short bob, cut to the neck, much shorter and blonder than her picture. She wore a light tan suit and comfortable open toe shoes with a small sling back heel. She appeared the picture of professionalism, but it was Megan's easygoing manner that got Maeve's attention. She smiled all of the time and spoke in a raspy tone of voice, as if she had to clear her throat. She must be a smoker, Maeve thought. She pulled out the keys to the house.

"Lets go inside," Maeve said in a friendly voice. They walked through her parents' home. Megan said nothing as she looked at the combination living room and dining room with the worn cream carpeting, the nicked and fading paint and the cream valance and sheer drapes that covered the large picture window that looked onto the street. The furniture had been lovely in its time, but now it looked old fashioned with its ornate oriental lamps and faded sofa and chairs.

"Let's go into the kitchen," Megan suggested as she looked around. She stared at the white wood cabinets, cream formica countertops and flowered wallpaper.

"It's a bit small, but is usable," Maeve commented when she saw the frown on Megan's face.

"Let's go into the bedrooms," Megan remarked softly.

They walked into the master bedroom of the home. Worn cream shag carpeting covered the floor. Sheer cream drapes and a sheer valence hung on the two windows. Behind the drapes, faded shades were pulled halfway down the windows. Crystal wall sconces hung on the wall where the dresser used to be. Otherwise, the room was bare.

"It looks a bit tired," Megan said quietly.

They then moved to the second bedroom in the back of the house. It was painted in blue with cream shag carpeting. Wood shutters hung crookedly on the window. The middle bedroom was painted in peach with cream shag carpeting and peach sheer drapes. Stacks of clothing and boxes covered the single bed in the room. Boxes of family photos and old clothes and a vacuum cleaner cluttered the floor of the room.

They entered the master bath.   Two crystal chandeliers hung in front of a large mirror and over the pink sink that was shaped like a seashell. Pink and gray tile covered the walls and floor. The sink looked faded and scratched from years of scrubbing. When they strolled into the other half bathroom, Megan made note of the tan flocked wallpaper that was starting to peel off the walls. The fluorescent lights on each side of the vanity flickered.

"It all seems a bit tired," she said again as she followed Maeve into the front of the house. "But the house certainly is in a good neighborhood and the location near the church is wonderful," she added with an air of unmistakable diplomacy. "I do have some suggestions about fixing the home before we put it up for sale though," she added quickly. "Do you know if there are hardwood floors under the carpeting?" she asked.

"I think so," Maeve answered. "There is hardwood in the front closet and the closets in the bedrooms.

Megan pulled up a bit of the carpeting in the living room to reveal hardwood floors. "First thing I suggest is to pull up all the carpeting in the house. Then I think you should take down the wallpaper in the kitchen and half bathroom and paint it all white. Get rid of the clutter in the bedrooms, the boxes, clothes, vacuum cleaner and clean up the place. I'd take down the pictures in the hallway. They are lovely, but add to the feeling of clutter in the small space. Who painted them?" she asked.

"My mother," Maeve replied proudly. "She used to paint when she was younger. I'll take them down. Megan, I also think the outside of the house needs painting, don't you?" she asked.

Megan sighed in relief. This was going much easier than she had anticipated. The house had suffered years of neglect, but that was not unusual considering the circumstances of Maeve's parents' health.   She had seen much worse than this home. Megan thought of all the other homes she had sold. This one would go quickly once it had been cleaned up and the clutter removed.

"Yes, it certainly would help to spruce up the exterior of the home," she answered.   "Also, how old is the roof?"

"My father had it replaced about thirty years ago," Maeve recalled.

"I'd also like to see the basement," Megan continued.

As they walked down the basement stairs, Megan noted that they were covered in the same cream shag carpeting that was in the bedrooms. The basement was finished in pine and stacks of boxes, lawn furniture, tools and Christmas boxes lined the walls.   "This too, will need to be cleaned up and organized," Megan commented.

"I know," Maeve agreed.   She looked at the stacks of boxes and furniture and wondered how she was going to get the home in shape in order to sell it. They climbed the stairs to the first floor and sat at the dining room table.

"Now let's go over what has to be done," Megan stated.

Maeve reached for her pen and yellow legal pad. "Shoot," she said.

"Exterior painting, tear up all the carpeting and leave the hardwood floors bare, take down the valances in the living room and dining room, take down the wallpaper in the kitchen and half bathroom and paint them cream, clear the clutter out of the bedrooms, take down the window coverings in the bedrooms, clear out the basement," said Megan methodically.

Maeve numbered and wrote down each task. "I don't want it on the market for three weeks," she said to Megan. "That will give me time to get the house painted and cleaned up."

Megan smiled and said," Here's the name of a painter I use and you can call a cleaning service to spruce up the house. As to removing the clutter, I'm afraid that will just take some elbow grease."

After Megan left, Maeve sat in the house and reminisced about growing up there. She remembered the family dinners during the holidays, the times her parents and she and her sister and brother and their spouses and aunts and uncles and cousins had gathered around the dining room table to celebrate a birthday or graduation or holiday. The quiet echoed throughout the house now. Her mother's pictures would have to come down.

She decided to ask her parents if she could take their dining room set into her home and put it into the basement until they decided what they wanted to do with it. She planned on calling Jack that evening to see if he would help with clearing out the boxes in the house and basement. Maeve took her pen to the legal pad and updated the list of what needed to be done as she took another walk through the house.

That evening she mentioned the dining room set to her father. "Dad, would you like to keep your dining room set? It is so lovely. We can have it moved to our house and store it in the basement."

Paul's face glowed with happiness. "That's a wonderful idea, Maeve," he replied. "You can have the set if you want it."

"Let me think about that, Dad. I'll call some movers to get a quote on moving the dining room set."

She called three small local moving companies and asked each for a quote to move her parents' dining room set to her home. She booked the move with the last company she called. Their quote was reasonable and they happily provided her with a copy of their insurance.

Chapter 55
The Caretaker's Complaints

The following Thursday, when Maeve arrived home after work, she heard her parents laughing in the family room. "Hi, how is everyone?" she greeted them as she entered the family room.

"Hello, how are you?" Paul responded happily. "We are fine!"

"Hi," Therese said as a bright smile broke across her face.

Sophia got up and followed Maeve into the kitchen.

"How have they been today?" Maeve asked.

"Everything has been okay. I did your mother's hair and nails and washed their clothes and sheets and made their bed. She gathered up her purse and cell phone and said curtly, "I will see you tomorrow."

Maeve walked her to the front door. "Have a great evening and thank your for everything."

Sophia stood at the door and tears formed in her eyes.

"What is wrong?" asked Maeve in a concerned voice.

"I didn't want to tell you this, but today your father wanted to go out to lunch. I told him no. I did not want to go to a restaurant with him and your mother."

Maeve's eyes narrowed. "Why not?" she asked. "Is it because it is difficult to get them into your car?"

"No, it is not that," Sophia snapped.   "It is because he tells me that I don't work a full day, that he is paying me for nothing. He says I just sit and read in the afternoon and that I should only be paid for a half day." Sophia's face clouded over. "I take good care of them. I keep them clean and wash their clothes. I wash the linens for their bed and make their meals. I give them their medicines and go for walks with your mother.

Your father doesn't want to go outside, not even in his wheelchair. He just enjoys sitting and watching television. When I am finished with my work, I do sit with them in the afternoon and watch television or read, but I am still here taking care of them. I don't want to go out with him and have him tell me that I am being paid for not doing work."

Maeve could not believe what she was hearing. When Sophia started the job, the agency made it clear that her duties were to take care of her parents, not to do the housekeeping or any other chores that did not relate to her parents. Maeve could understand this. A caretaker could turn into a full time cleaning lady or housekeeper if the agency did not draw boundaries and state her specific duties. Sophia showed up for work at the same time every day. So far, she had not missed a day of work.

"I'll talk to my father," Maeve answered calmly.

"Thank you," Sophia replied. "I do want to talk with you about something else," she continued. "You are not giving me enough hours to work. I need more money."

Maeve caught her breath and shook her head. "But you are working from seven thirty to five Monday through Friday each week. That is what we agreed upon when I hired you."

Sophia straightened her shoulders and frowned. "I am a single woman who is supporting herself without help from anyone else. I have to take care of myself. I have applied for a job at a store in Skokie. It will be part time, in the evening, after I leave your home."

"How many hours will you work there each week?" Maeve asked.

"About thirteen hours," Sophia answered. "From five thirty to ten o'clock on Mondays, Wednesdays and Fridays. I will need to leave here at five o'clock on those days. I need to earn more money," she stated emphatically.

Maeve sighed. "That will be fine. I will be home in time to take care of Mom and Dad and if I'm not home at five o'clock sharp, you can leave. They will be all right for the short time they are alone."

Sophia stepped outside. "Thank you. See you tomorrow," she said as she left with a big grin on her face.

Maeve thought about a recent chat she had with her neighbor, who told her how lucky she was to have Sophia. Her neighbor complained that she had hired four caretakers in the past three months to take care of her mother who lives in a condo in Chicago. One caretaker wanted to bring her family to America to live in her mother's condo and another decided she didn't like the work and left without giving notice. It was only after visiting her mother did she find out that the caretaker had left.

Of course, those caretakers were hired without the benefit of an agency. Maeve was very happy she had used an agency. She wanted the security of hiring someone who had been pre-screened, had references and whose social security taxes would be paid by the agency. It cost more than hiring someone through a newspaper ad, but it was worth it to keep her parents in her home. Maeve decided that life was complicated enough without having to worry about replacing Sophia. If Sophia didn't work out, the agency would replace her with another caretaker.

Chapter 56
The Call For Help

A month later, Maeve sat at her kitchen table and breathed a sigh of relief. Her parents' home had sold in one day. Thank God, she thought. One less thing to worry about. Then she checked her calendar. She was scheduled to take her father and mother to their internist at Memorial Hospital for their checkup the coming week. She had taken off one-half day the previous week to take her mother to her geriatrician for a checkup for her dementia. She had also taken another half day off to take her father to the podiatrist to have his feet checked. Each time, the trip involved at least a one hour trip on the Edens Expressway to get downtown and another hour to return home.

Most of the time, she had to leave work early in order to get to her parents' home on time, help them into the car and maneuver through traffic on the highway in order to arrive at the doctor's office on time. Feeling exhausted, she decided to ask her brother, Jack, to take her parents to their upcoming doctor's appointments. She dialed his cell phone number.

"O'Connor here," he answered quickly from the leather sofa in his family room. He and Susan had moved into their new home just six months ago. Construction of the home had taken over one year to complete. The family room sported a white stone fireplace with french doors on each side that led to the grand brick patio and the large backyard. A spectacular kitchen with granite countertops and top grade stainless steel appliances flowed into the family room.

"Hi, Jack, it's Maeve," she said.

"What's happening?" he asked.

"Mom and Dad have an appointment with their internist next week. I've already taken Dad to his podiatrist and Mom to her geriatrician last week. Can you take them next week?" She heard a sigh at the other end of the line.

"Down to Memorial Hospital?" he asked in an exasperated voice.

"Yes," she responded.

"You know, you really should change doctors. Get a doctor in Lake Forest. It is too far to take them downtown," he finished.

Maeve continued, "You still haven't answered the question. Will you take them downtown to see Dr. Murphy?"

"There are good doctors in Lake Forest. I just don't have time to take them downtown. So, no, I won't."

Maeve took a long breath and tried one last time. "Won't you take some time to help me?"

"I have to get going. Bye." He quickly hung up the phone and turned to his wife, Susan, who was lounging on the sofa filing her nails.

""Can you believe her?" he asked pompously.

"What did she want?" Susan asked casually. She continued filing her nails without looking up.

"She wants me to take them down to Memorial Hospital for their checkups. If she thinks I'm going down there with them, she is nuts. You know she's got control of their money. We've got to do something about it."

Susan moved closer to him on the sofa and ran her fingers through his hair. "Jack, you've been supportive of Maeve throughout this ordeal with your parents. Maeve has always been a taker, not a giver. We could go to an attorney to get some advice about getting control of the money." She smiled at him.

"You're right," he replied. "I'll make the call tomorrow."

Chapter 57
The Sleepless Night

Maeve shrugged her shoulders. Same answer every time. Why did she even ask? What to do now? She dreaded her next move. She knew the response she would receive, but decided to make the call anyway. She dialed her sister, Annie.

Annie sat on an old upholstered second hand chair in the living room of her small wooden house in Evanston, staring at her favorite show on television, Guess the Price. When the phone rang, she became annoyed. Who was calling and interrupting her private time relaxing with her favorite program? She checked caller ID. She always screened her calls to keep from talking to the bill collectors who were hounding her lately. Oh, no. It's Maeve, she thought. What does she want now?

She bent over and answered the phone. "Hi, Maeve," she said. "What's going on?"

"Hi, Annie. Will you take Mom and Dad to Dr. Murphy for their checkup next week? I took them to the doctor two times last week and need a break."

"What day?"

"Wednesday."

"I'd like to, but I'm doing substitute teaching that day. Maybe you can change the appointment to a few weeks from now," she suggested.

"When are you free?" Maeve asked.

"Well, I don't have my appointment book in front of me, so I'll have to call you back, but I'm pretty sure I'll be free in a month or so."

"Forget it," Maeve said in disgust.   "I'll take them to the doctor."

"Hey, I said I would take them," Annie murmured slowly. "Just give me a month or so. I'll call you back when I check my calendar."

"Goodbye, Annie." Maeve hung up the phone and walked into the bedroom. All she wanted was some peace and quiet, some time out from taking care of her parents. She changed into her pajamas and lay on the bed. Her parents were watching television in their bedroom. Their door was closed as they knew she went to bed early. Her father always watched the ten o'clock news in the evening and didn't want to wake her up.

Maeve pulled up the comforter and lay her head onto the soft pillow. Before she knew it, she was asleep. She awoke at two o'clock in the morning to the sound of footsteps in the hall. She turned towards Jeremy's side of the bed and saw that it was empty. Maeve got up and peeked around the corner of the door into the hallway. No one was there. She heard another sound of footsteps. She walked down the hall, then down the stairs and heard someone going down to the basement.

Maeve called out, "Jeremy, is that you?"

"Go back to bed," he shouted in a frustrated voice. "I've got some work to do."

Maeve descended the basement stairs and saw Jeremy at the computer. "What kind of work are you doing at this time of the morning?" she asked.

Jeremy shook his head. "Leave me alone. I can't sleep, so I'll do the payroll." He turned towards the computer and pressed the start button.

Maeve climbed the stairs to the first floor where she heard a padding sound in the hallway. She made out the outline of Therese as she shuffled to the bathroom. Then she heard the toilet flushing. Therese returned to her bedroom and started coughing as she did every night.

Maeve decided to monitor her mother that evening. She stayed up and watched as Therese got up after an hour or so. Therese entered the kitchen and swallowed a capful of cough syrup. She then returned to her bedroom, started coughing again and got up and tried to take another dose of the cough syrup. Maeve grabbed the cough syrup from her mother and hid it so her mother wouldn't take it again.

Maeve found this exhausting. Her sleep began to suffer as she lay on full alert for her parents. Thank God for Sophia, she thought as she lay in bed awake. If we hadn't hired her, I don't know what I would have done. Quit my job. No, that was not an option, although with the situation at work, Stephen's office might not be in existence soon.

She decided to talk with Stephen soon to see how dire things had gotten. She rolled over and looked at the clock on the side table. It glowed three thirty in the morning and Jeremy was still in the basement. She spent the rest of the night falling in and out of sleep. She had a dream. In it, she was swimming in a dark, murky pool of water which surrounded a castle. The water appeared to be a moat and she swam faster and faster, but could not make any progress. She couldn't get out of the water nor could she break free of the current which was running against her. It was all she could do to keep

swimming around the castle in the middle of the
water.

Chapter 58
Visit To The Doctor

Paul, Therese and Maeve sat in Dr. Murphy's office waiting for him to enter. Maeve felt a dread she had not felt before. Paul's diabetes necessitated that Maeve check his feet every day. The previous day, she had checked his feet for sores or cracks and noticed a small sore between his fourth and fifth toe. The sore appeared white. She knew that it was imperative that she mention this sore to Dr. Murphy. This morning the sore had taken on a dark red color.

Dr. Murphy entered the examination room and took her father's and mother's blood pressure. "Your mother's blood pressure is normal," he said. He took the cuff off her arm and wrapped it around her father's left arm. "Hmm, his blood pressure is a bit high," he stated seriously. He placed the stethoscope on his father's back and listened. "His lungs seem clear and he has no fever. I think your father is fine," he said after he moved the stethoscope around Paul's back and chest.

"I noticed a sore on his toe yesterday, doctor. Would you please look at it?" Maeve asked in a worried voice.

Dr. Murphy took off her father's shoe and placed a small light on it. He turned off the lights in the room. "Tell me what color do you see when this light is on the foot," he said.

Maeve got up and looked at the foot. "It looks red to me."

"That's what I thought too," he continued. "I am going to give you a prescription for an antibiotic lotion to put on the sore. It should be gone within a few weeks."

Maeve took the prescription and helped her parents out of the doctor's office. Driving home, Maeve took Lake Shore Drive to avoid the traffic on the Kennedy Expressway. Her mother sat quietly in the back seat while her father fell asleep in the passenger seat. Maeve thought about the appointment they just had with Dr. Murphy. She was developing an uneasy feeling about her father's foot. When they got home, she decided to take her father to his podiatrist for a second opinion. She made an appointment with him for the following Friday.

Chapter 59
The Afternoon In The Park

Maeve sat in Ruth Stein's office for her weekly appointment. She had been seeing Stein for over a month now and felt she was not making good progress. It annoyed her that Stein kept trying to push those pills on her, even after Maeve said that she didn't want to take them. Lately, Stein had started reminiscing about her life and how her husband had left her. Maeve felt as though she were the analyst and Stein was the client. Maeve sat up straight and said in a calm voice, "I am discontinuing my visits with you."

Stein seemed very upset. "I need more time to help you," she growled. "I've just started working with you. And you are just finding yourself."

Maeve shifted in her seat. She didn't like the pressure, but decided to give Stein another chance. "I'll continue my therapy for another month or so, but if I don't feel better then, I'm not coming back," she warned.

She left the office and breathed in the fresh air. Shades of pink and blue colored the sky and fluffy white clouds floated by. Birds chirped in the branches of the trees. The weather was glorious. Instead of walking to her car, Maeve decided to take a walk through the small park near Stein's office. She sat on a bench near the children's playground.

She needed some time to clear her head. What did Stein mean by finding herself? Was she so lost? She examined her life so far. She had remained at home until she married.   It was a decision she regretted.   She had always wanted to get an apartment after she graduated from college, but her parents objected to a woman living alone and in deference to them, she remained at home and paid them a monthly sum for her room and board.

No, she thought, actually I stayed at home because I just didn't have the guts to go out and make it on my own and live alone. All talk and no action; that is me. She had always wanted to be a writer and had called the editor of the Midwest Daily newspaper after graduating from college. Miraculously, he gave her a job as a copy girl. She worked in that job a week until they offered her a job assisting the editor of the Help Column. Readers wrote into the newspaper asking for help with solving their problems with various businesses. The editor of the column allowed Maeve to write some of the answers to the questions.

However, her father was pressuring her to teach school. So she applied to the public school system and was hired to teach first grade. Two weeks before she was to leave the newspaper, the editor of the newspaper's magazine offered her a position writing features for the magazine. She turned him down. It was a decision she regretted to this day. But there was no looking back. Since then, her life had been uneventful and placid.

She had known Jeremy since high school. They had drifted apart in college, but when he returned from service in Vietnam, they started dating again and became engaged and were married. Two years later, Clare was born. The principal at the school where Maeve taught first grade said she would hold her job open for her if she decided to continue teaching after having Clare. Maeve thanked her, but made the decision to forgo the extra money and stay home and raise Clare. Jeremy agreed with her decision. He was working in sales at the time and spent a few days each week on the road traveling. When he was home, he treated Clare like a doll and adored her.

Now, unfortunately every day has become the same, she thought. I go to work, come home, get the mail, give my parents their pills, make supper for them, sit in the family room with my Mother while Dad watches the new or sports in the bedroom. I take her for walks when the weather permits, but usually she tires easily. Jeremy usually watches television in the basement or works in the basement.

Around eight o'clock each evening, I help my parents change into their pajamas. I bring them their favorite diabetic pudding and whipped cream around eight thirty in the evening and then give them their pills at nine o'clock before they watch TV and go to sleep, she thought.

There had not been any strange mail since she had taken in her parents. And the police said that they had not found any prints in their search of Maeve's house that could be identified in their criminal database, nor any fingerprints on the mail they had examined. Whoever entered the house had worn gloves. She had the locks on the house changed and a new security system installed. Jeremy rarely traveled now, so he was home most evenings. Maeve felt more safe having Jeremy and her parents in the house. Not that her parents would be able to help in an emergency, but at least there were some other   people around.

Unfortunately, Jeremy said he was going on another trip, his usual trip to Las Vegas for a trade show. This trip would last a week and he was going to take it the following week. The only people she had told about Jeremy's trip were her parents, Clare and Ruth Stein.

The sound of thunder in the distance jolted Maeve out of her thoughts. She left the park and headed toward her car which was parked in the indoor parking lot in town.

Chapter 60
The Homeless Man

Maeve looked at the sky and saw lightening flash in the distance. The wind whirled and blew from the west, dropping the temperature from the seventies to the fifties in a few minutes. This is going to be a big storm, she thought. Maeve quickened her step as the rain began to fall. At first the drops licked her face softly, then a gust of air blew through the spiderweb branches of the trees and slashed at her face. As she hurried along the sidewalk, she noticed mothers pulling their children close as they raced inside stores to hide from the storm's fury.

She rushed into the vestibule of the nearby parking lot just as a clap of thunder echoed through the blackened, furious sky, She pressed the buzzer for the elevator and waited impatiently while the illuminated number above the bronze doors dropped from eight to seven to six to five to four to three to two and finally to ground level. Now the storm had broken in all of its ferocity. It was dark as night outside. She entered the elevator and pressed the sixth floor, where she had parked her car. Slowly the elevator ascended. It stopped on the fourth floor and a man entered it.

Maeve tried not to stare. His brown stringy hair hung in greasy clumps to his shoulders and his black framed glasses perched on his straight nose. He may have been a handsome man at one time, Maeve thought, but he looks like a homeless person with his unshaven face and stubbly brown hairs needling through his red blotchy skin. He smelled of stale liquor, perhaps beer and leaned against the side wall of the elevator. When he didn't press a button for a floor, Maeve realized that he was going to get off at her floor. She remembered that the sixth floor had been vacant except for a few cars parked near the door to the elevator. She prayed that those cars were still there and perhaps someone would be leaving or drive down from the top two floors on the way to the exit.

The man coughed and cleared his throat, a loud, raspy cough which sounded as though it pulled his phlegm from the bottom of his bowels. He spat upon the floor of the elevator and cleared his throat again. When Maeve glanced at him, he smiled at her and peered at her through the thick glasses which emphasized the glassy blueness of his eyes. There is something familiar about him, Maeve thought.

She raced forward as the elevator doors opened onto the sixth floor and quickly bounded for her car. She heard his footsteps close behind her. As she reached her car, she fished into her purse and pulled out the car keys. His footsteps were gaining on her. With trembling hands, she pushed the key into the lock of her car. Suddenly, she felt a hand on her arm.

Maeve screamed just as another bolt of lightening slashed across the sky and the echo of a thunderous boom permeated the air, boom, boom, boom, drowning out her cries. "Leave me alone," she screamed. She struggled to open the car door.

"Lady, all I want is some money," the voice behind her cried. He tightened his grip on her arm. "Just give me a few bucks. You look like you can do without a five or so. Look at this great BMW you have. I have nothing and I am hungry. Please have mercy on a poor man."

Maeve reached into her purse and withdrew a ten dollar bill and handed it to him. "Here, take this and leave me alone," she said in a trembling voice.

The man took the money and stepped back. "You won't regret this lady. Some day you'll be happy you took pity on a hungry old man." He smiled that strange smile and retreated away leaving the smell of musk and booze behind him.

She opened the door to her car, jumped into the front seat, locked the doors and placed the key into the ignition. Her heat beat like the sound of a drum thumping in a wild frenzied dance. She rubbed her cold clammy hands against each other to bring some warmth to them. Her teeth chattered and the chill in her soul brought goose bumps to her skin. She realized that she was so terrified that she had forgotten to start the car, so she twisted the key again and with relief heard the engine turn over.

Why was I so stupid to stay in the elevator with that man? she thought. Why didn't I press the alarm or run down the stairs when I exited the elevator or scream for help? Why did I try to get into my car when I heard him so close behind me? Why do I block out anything that is unpleasant and pretend that it doesn't exist? Why have I put up with so much crap from so many people all these years? She felt her adrenaline roar through her veins. She had much to accomplish in the years to come and it was time to take control of her life.

Chapter 61
Jack's House

Jack O'Connor heard the doorbell ring and opened the front door to his home. "Hi, Annie," he said.

Annie Gordon walked in and uttered in surprise, "My God, you told me you were building a new house, but you didn't say it was so large." She looked in amazement at the two story foyer with marble floors and a circular staircase that led to the second floor. A massive modern crystal chandelier hung from the ceiling.

"Construction took a year, but we finally have our new home," Jack said with a grin on his face. "Susan loves white as you can tell."

Annie gazed at the all white living room's floor to ceiling windows that covered one wall. White hardwood floors gleamed under the white sofas and side chairs in the room. Sleek glass tables dotted the room. The only splashes of color came from the modern paintings that hung from the walls.

"Come into the kitchen," Jack said proudly. He led her into the ballroom size kitchen that flowed into the family room. Annie stood at the center island and looked about at the shiny stainless steel refrigerator, stove, dishwasher and microwave. She ran her hand across the smooth black granite countertops and marveled at the white oak cabinets with backdrop lightening. She walked into the large butler's pantry that was filled with crystal goblets and fine china.

"This is outstanding," Annie said in astonishment.

"You haven't seen it all yet," Jack responded. "Come into the family room."

She followed him to the all white family room with a large screen television that covered the center of the main wall. She had never seen a television that big. Sunlight flooded he room from all angles through the windows on three walls. Sliding glass doors opened to the bluestone patio with new white lawn furniture. Pots of flowers lined the perimeter in a bold display of powder blue and gold colors.

"Jack, you and Susan have outdone yourselves," Annie exclaimed loudly.

"Wait till I show you the rest of the house," Jack continued. He motioned for her to follow him. "Let's go to the master bedroom."

They climbed the winding staircase to the upper floor of the house. As they entered the master bedroom, Annie gasped in amazement. The room was larger than her whole house. The ceiling was nine feet tall and again, sunlight streamed through the custom floor to ceiling windows that covered each wall.

"This is spectacular," Annie proclaimed.

"Wait till you see these," Jack said as he opened the door to his master closet. The walls were lined with mahogany and mounds of casual shirts and shorts lay neatly in row upon row on the mahogany shelves. Business suits, organized according to colors from black to gray and brown, and dress shirts hung from the brass poles. Five row of shoes bordered one wall.

Jack then opened the door to Susan's walk-in closet.   One wall was mirrored.   Casual dresses, skirts, tops and slacks fill one section of the closet. Formal dresses hung from the mirrored poles in another section and ten rows of shoes filled up a wall.

"You have got to be kidding," Annie exclaimed in surprise.

"Now come with me," Jack said as he led her to the his and her master bathrooms.   Each room boasted a whirlpool bathtub, marble counters, floors and walls, and a glass enclosed shower with upscale fixtures. The toilet area was recessed and separated by walls for privacy.

"We're not finished," Jack bragged. He led the way down the hall again. "We had the laundry room built next to our bedroom.   You can't believe how convenient it is."

"You and Susan must be doing really well," Annie murmured as she thought about her small frame home in Evanston. She and Peter had lived in the home for the past twenty-five years. They bought it a year after they married and she started working as a substitute schoolteacher. Peter had tried a few jobs selling clothing and working in an insurance company, but he chafed at working for others and the hours he was required to keep.

Peter was an artist and a free spirit. That was what Annie loved about him best. So he turned the third bedroom of their home into a studio in which he painted landscapes. They lived on Annie's income because Peter's work was erratic at best. They never had children but loved each other in the way that couples do after being married for so many years.

"We're doing fine," Jack explained, "but first things first. Let's go downstairs and I'll make you your favorite drink."

Chapter 62
The Seed Is Planted

Jack stood at the bar in the family room, mixed a martini and handed it to Annie. "It has four olives," he said. "I remembered what you like."

Annie sat on the plush white leather sofa in the family room. It felt like a soft pillow under her weight. She twirled the olive pick and waited. She could tell that Jack was nervous.

"Susan is out of town," he said tensely. "She went to a spa in California to get rid of the stress in her life." He laughed and filled a tall glass with ice and poured gin to the middle of it. "Some stress," he continued. "She spends her days shopping, lunching with her friends and getting her hair and nails done." He poured tonic to the brim of the glass and looked straight at Annie. "If you must know, I'm barely working any more. The economy has been in the toilet lately and I just wasn't pulling in enough dental patients to pay all the bills we have." He gestured towards a stack of bills on the built-in desk in the room.

Annie almost choked on her drink. "What about this grandiose house?"

"Yeah, we have a problem. But you know Susan. She doesn't want to think about things like that. She just wants life to go on as always and leave the headaches to me." He took a large gulp of his drink.

Annie ate the four olives and took a sip of her martini as she listened to him in shock and could not believe what he said. "So what are you going to do?" she asked pensively.

"Well, you know the bank accounts that Mom and Dad have from the sale of their home and what they have saved?"

"No. What about them?"

"I was over at Maeve's house last week for a quick visit with Mom and Dad. That caretaker they have, Sophia, had taken Mom out for a walk. Dad brought out his checkbook and guess what?"

Annie looked at him with interest. "What?" she asked.

"He's loaded. He's got $125,000 just in his checking account. He told me he's got the rest stashed in $100,000 CD's in banks all over the city."

"So?", Annie commented suspiciously.

"So, Maeve's got Power of Attorney. Guess who is in line to take control if something happens to her?"

"Who?" Annie asked quickly.

"Dad said that you are. Didn't you ever ask Maeve about what she did with the proceeds of the sale of their home or their savings?"

"I didn't even bother. You and I both know that she's always been tight lipped about Mom and Dad's financial affairs. Maybe she knows us too well," she snarled sarcastically.

Jack poured himself another gin and tonic. "You want another drink?" he asked. Annie nodded yes, polished off the rest of her martini and held her glass out to him for a refill.

He took it and peered at her. "How's Peter doing? Has he sold any paintings lately?"

"You really know how to stick that knife in, don't you," she retorted angrily. "Peter is doing okay. He just needs a little more time and he'll get his big break." Annie knew she was lying, but she wasn't about to give Jack the satisfaction of knowing they were living paycheck to paycheck on her earnings as a substitute teacher.

Jack smiled and gave her the second martini. "I know," he murmured. "Peter will get that break when he gets off the booze."

Annie stood up and shouted. "Who do you think you are showing me this monstrosity of a house and throwing it in my face that we aren't doing as well as you and that wench you married. What do you want Jack?"

"Just think about it," he whispered with a grin.

"Think about what?"

"You having control over Mom and Dad's finances. Just think about how good it would be for us both."

Annie stormed out of the house, but the seed had been planted.

Chapter 63
The Argument

When she arrived home, Annie found Peter drinking at the kitchen table. She grabbed his glass and threw it into the sink. "How many times do I have to tell you to stop drinking?" she shouted. "Why don't you get a job like a normal man? Get out and make some money! I've carried you on my back long enough." She placed her hands on her hips and hovered over him.

Peter looked at her and laughed. "So you've carried me along all these years? What a crock. You wouldn't know what to do without me. Little miss perfect. Little miss teacher. Little miss nothing. You can't make any decisions without me. You couldn't even pick a plumber for the kitchen pipes without me. I'm the one who takes care of everything in this house. I pay the bills. I keep the house clean. I do the gardening and mow the lawn and shovel the snow. And for what? All I get from you is for me to go out and get a job. Well, if that's what you want, I'll leave you and go out and get one. Will that make you happy?" he yelled at her as he stomped out the room.

Annie felt a sense of panic creeping into her body. She started shivering and her heart started pounding quickly. Her legs felt wobbly so she collapsed on a chair at the table and started to sob. Her shoulders shuddered as the tears fell from her eyes. She knew that Peter was right. She was nothing without him. He provided moral support for her. What a joke. Everyone thought she was the one in charge in her home. If only they knew it was Peter who was the strong one in the family. Yes, he had a drinking problem, but he was working on it. He was attending Alcoholics Anonymous and going to meetings almost every night. His behavior was changing slowly.

Annie felt the queasiness begin to decline and walked to the sink. She picked up Peter's empty glass and smelled it. Apple juice. He was drinking apple juice. She looked into the refrigerator and there it was, a gallon jug of apple juice.

She slinked into the bedroom where she found Peter painting on a canvas that was perched on an easel. "Peter, I'm sorry," she apologized as she entered the room. "It's just that I went to see Jack today and he told me some things that upset me."

Peter put down his paint brush and turned towards her. "What things?"

She told him about her conversation with Jack.

Peter laughed. "Your brother, Jack, has lost his mind. Does he really think you can take control of your parents' finances and will give him some of the money to tide him over until the economy improves or he finds another line of work?"

"I know. It sounds ridiculous," Annie answered sheepishly.

"How does he expect you to take over the reins from Maeve?"

"He didn't say anything about that. Just offered it as a solution to his problems and ours. Do you have any ideas?" she finished.

Chapter 64
The Therapy Session

Maeve shifted in her seat at Ruth Stein's office. "Would you like a bottle of water?" Ruth asked.

"No," Maeve replied. She folded her arms in front of her chest.

"So tell me what's going on," Ruth said distractedly. Then she started to cry. "Really, Maeve, I'm so upset. Why don't you tell me?"

"Tell you what?" Maeve asked in an annoyed tone of voice. She sat straight in the chair.

"Tell me about Rubin's case. My poor brother is counting on a settlement from the restaurant."

Now Maeve was angry. "It isn't my duty to tell you about confidential cases that Stephen handles."

"You know that you can trust me to keep confidential information. If not, why would you still be coming to me?" Ruth asked. "Actually, I am insulted that you don't tell me about Rubin's case."

"I am not here to defend my behavior in not revealing confidential legal information to you. I'm here to get help for myself." Maeve bit her lip. "Are we going to talk about my problems or shall I just listen to yours? My time is valuable, you know."

Ruth took a deep breath and set her jaw. "All right. What's happening with you now?"

"I'm giving Thanksgiving dinner again this year."

"What do you mean by again? Do you usually prepare the meal every year?"

"Yes."

"Why?"

"Because my brother and sister never offer to do it." She shifted again in her seat.

"Why don't you ask them to cook for Thanksgiving?"

"Because it seems useless. If they don't come to our home, they go to their relatives on Susan or Peter's side of the family."

"So why don't you just not invite them? Tell them you are tired of being the one who is the keeper of the holidays, so to speak?"

"Because I think family is important and it is better to have them over than exclude them and have friction in the family."

"So you would rather continue to be the enabler and not express your true feelings, is that right?"

"I didn't say that. All I said is that it is nice to have a family gathering. It would just be nice if once in a while, they had a holiday dinner and took the load off of me."

"Well, how are they going to know this if you don't tell them?"

Maeve's face turned red. "What good would it do? They always have an excuse like, we can't handle the stress. It just seems easier to give in and have them at our house."

"So why are you sitting here talking about this?" Ruth started to get up.

"Just complaining, I suppose." Maeve looked at her watch. She had been there for thirty minutes.

Ruth saw Maeve glance at her watch. She sat down again and continued, "And what will that get you?"

"The satisfaction of complaining."

"I think there must be more to it." Ruth swiveled her chair from side to side. She looked very bored.

Maeve felt her blood begin to boil. "Like what?" she asked forcefully.

"Like you tell me."

"I have no idea about what you are talking about."

"Then tell me what you would consider an ideal Thanksgiving dinner."

"One in which I held it once every three years, one in which others would pull their weight for once." Maeve crossed her legs and felt her blood pressure rise. Her face and neck started to turn red.

"Are you going to keep this a secret?" Ruth uttered with a long sigh. "Secrets will not get you anywhere, you know."

"I told you, they won't do it anyway."

"Then what other options do you have?"

"I suppose I could just not invite them when they call to see if I am having Thanksgiving dinner."

"Go on." Ruth now stood up and walked to the door.

"I could just tell them we are going to spend Thanksgiving, actually any holiday, with Clare and our parents alone until they decide to invite us over."

"How do you fell about that?"

"Right now it seems like a good idea. When the time comes, I don't know that I'll feel the same way.   Maybe I'll just revert back to my old spineless self."

Ruth looked at her watch. "As you wish. The hour is over," she spoke dismissively. "See you next week."

Chapter 65
The Overdose

Maeve got into her car and pulled onto the Eden's expressway going north. The rush hour had begun and traffic was heavy. She eased into the middle lane where she was most comfortable. Then she turned on the radio and listened to the news reports about corruption in the Illinois state government, the unrest in the Middle East, various robberies and killings and the growing heroin trade on the North Shore. Another day, another story, she thought. All this drama going on in the world and it all starts with each person. She pondered about the session she had just had with Ruth Stein. So what did she have to lose by talking frankly with her brother and sister? She thought long and hard about making other changes in her life.

Maeve drove into her driveway and pulled her car into the garage. She walked into her home, but no one was there. Sophia's car was gone and her parents weren't in the family room. She saw the lights on in the basement and hurried downstairs. Jeremy was sitting at his computer.

"Hi, Jeremy," she said anxiously. "Where are my parents and Sophia?"

"When I got home, I told Sophia she could leave. She doesn't need to hang around here when I am here. Your parents are watching television in their bedroom."

"Didn't Sophia start cooking dinner? She usually makes potatoes or a vegetable."

"I don't think so. I got home at three o'clock and told her she could go."

"So now I have to start cooking. It's a little late and you know how important it is to keep my parents on a regular schedule."

"Sorry, honey. I'll be up in a while to help you." He turned back to his computer and continued working

Maeve found her parents in the bedroom watching the evening news. Every night her parents watched the news and then came into the kitchen to eat at six o'clock. She knew she had only half an hour to prepare something nourishing for them to eat. She tried to make sure the evening meal consisted of chicken or fish, a starch such as a potatoes, a vegetable and a salad. It was important to portion control her father's meals in order to keep his diabetes under control.

She looked into the refrigerator and pulled out the catfish she had taken out of the freezer the night before. It was still a little frozen, but it would be okay. She pulled out a cookbook for a favorite recipe she had for baked catfish. It called for oil spray on a baking pan, then dipping the catfish in flour seasoned with salt, pepper, paprika and cayenne. She sprayed the baking pan with the oil spray, placed the seasoned catfish on the pan and sprayed the catfish. Then she turned on the oven to 350 degrees.

Her mother walked into the kitchen. "Mom, it's time to take your medicine," Maeve said. Maeve opened the kitchen cabinet and stretched her arm high to open the door where she kept her mother's medication pill dispenser.

Maeve had hidden Therese's medicine on the top shelf of the kitchen cabinet after an incident a few months before when she had laid out her mother's pills on a plate to cut them before she placed them in her mother's weekly pill dispenser. Before she had a chance to cut the pills, Jeremy had called to her from the basement. She had left the room for a moment to see what he wanted.

As fate would have it, her mother wandered into the kitchen and saw the pills on the plate on the table and sat down and put them all in her mouth and swallowed them thinking they were her morning pills that Maeve usually set out. Her father was sitting at the table too, but he was reading the newspaper and barely noticed that Therese was there. When Maeve returned to the kitchen, her heart stopped when she noticed that all the pills were gone. She called the doctor's office and they urged her to take her mother to the emergency room.

Maeve had explained the situation to Jeremy and asked him to keep an eye on Paul while she drove Therese to the hospital. It was barely a ten minute ride. Therese seemed a little sleepy, but showed no other symptoms of pill overdose. Maeve turned onto the winding road to the Park Frontage Hospital and slowed the car to a twenty mile per hour pace per the traffic signs.

Trees stood tall and green on each side of the road. Maeve parked her car and helped Therese out of it. They walked into the emergency department where a receptionist greeted them and took her mother's initial information.

The triage nurse took her mother's history and blood pressure and admitted her to the emergency room where a female doctor decided to keep Therese for observation. They spent the next seven hours in the emergency room while Therese was hooked up to a heart monitor and her blood pressure slowly dropped.

Maeve could not believe she was so stupid as to the leave the medicine out. She had never done that before and would not do that again she vowed to herself. As she sat and watched her mother close her eyes, Maeve promised to herself that she would hide the pills on the top shelf of her cabinet and never leave them out again unless she or Sophia were there to supervise her mother and father.

After a while, Therese began to come out of the drowsiness which resembled a foggy stupor. As the drugs continued to wear off, Therese became agitated and pushed off the covers and wanted to get out of the bed. The bed rails kept her contained in the bed and she again dozed off to sleep. Finally, after seven hours, Therese woke up and the doctor said that Maeve could take her home. When they arrived home, Maeve helped Therese into her bed where she promptly fell asleep.

Maeve finished cutting Therese's pills and dispensed them into Therese's pillbox and hid them in the back of the top kitchen cabinet behind the closed cabinet drawer. This has been an experience I never want to repeat, she had thought.

Chapter 66
The Deadly Screams

The sound of Paul's voice shook Maeve out of her reverie. "Are we eating now?" he asked as he walked into the kitchen. He slid into his seat and picked up his fork.

"Sorry, Dad I was just thinking about something," Maeve responded. "I'll have the food on the table in a half hour or so. In the meantime, have some cheese and crackers." She pulled some cheddar cheese spread out of the refrigerator and took some crackers out of the pantry. She spread the cheese on the crackers, placed them on a dish and handed the dish to Paul.

"Thank you, Maeve," Paul said gratefully.

Just then, Therese padded into the kitchen. "Therese, my love, sit down and have some cheese and crackers too. We won't be eating for a while and this will tide us over till we do eat."

"Why, thank you," Therese replied happily. She smiled as he held out a cheese and cracker to her.

Maeve served the meal a half hour later, but by then, her parents had filled up on the cheese and crackers and were not that hungry. "Jeremy, in the future, please don't tell Sophia to leave earlier than her scheduled time. This has thrown the whole schedule off," she complained after Paul and Therese left the kitchen and walked to their bedroom.

"Must everything go according to your schedule, Maeve?" Jeremy said in an annoyed tone of voice. "Can't there be any leeway at all?"

"But I'm the one who has to deal with it when things are off schedule. Do you want to give Dad his blood sugar test tomorrow morning and see if his blood sugar is high because of tonight?"

Jeremy shook his head and walked down the stairs to the basement. A few hours later, Maeve gave her parents their pudding and she went to bed. She was exhausted. At four o'clock in the morning, she awoke to the sound of blood curdling screams coming from the backyard. She jumped up and pulled the bedroom drapes aside to look into the darkness, but the blackness outside prevented her from seeing anything. She turned and shook Jeremy until he awoke.

"What is it, Maeve?" he murmured sleepily.

"Get up," she answered anxiously. "Listen." Just then, the screaming sounds started again. "Did you hear that?"

He jumped out of bed and looked through the parted drapes, but he too saw nothing in the morning darkness. "Let's go downstairs and turn on the outside lights," he declared.

They put on their robes and hurried down the stairs. Maeve peeked into her parents' bedroom, and was relieved to see that they were sound asleep. Jeremy flicked the switch to the backyard lights, but when he and Maeve looked outside, there was nothing out of the ordinary. They moved outside and looked about. Everything looked the same as always.

"It sounded like an animal being attacked by another animal," Maeve whispered as she pulled her robe closer to herself. "Those were blood curdling screams, the screams of something facing death. I hope we never hear that again. I fully expected to see the body of some animal lying on the ground after being killed by a coyote. I saw a coyote in the backyard the other day. It strolled by and looked at me as I watched it from the kitchen window. It was thin and moved quickly. Maybe it found some small animal to eat, like a squirrel or chipmunk."

""Let's go back in," said Jeremy quickly. "I don't hear anything any more and I don't see a body or blood anywhere. Maybe the sounds were coming from the beach below. The noise we heard certainly didn't sound human. Probably just a prey finding its food. The natural order of the wild." He put his arm about Maeve and they returned to the house.

"I'm tired," Jeremy said. "I'm going back to bed."

"I'm going to make a cup of tea," said Maeve. "I need something to calm my nerves." She pulled out a cup, held it under the spout of the refrigerator and placed it in the microwave. She pressed the timer to one minute and waited while the water boiled in the cup. Then she took it out of the microwave and took a Chamomile tea bag from her pantry and dunked the bag ten times so the tea bag infused its flavor into the water. She took a long sip of the hot tea and felt the soothing liquid flow down her throat. She closed her eyes and tried to relax, but her nerves were stretched thin. She brought the tea cup into the family room, lay down on the sofa and pulled a blanket that was always draped on the side of the sofa over her. Within minutes, she fell asleep, but the sound of the deadly screams filled her dreams.

Chapter 67
The Aura Of Success

Jack O'Connor leaned back into his kitchen chair and took a sip of freshly brewed coffee. Susan strolled into the room. She looked splendid as usual in her white jogging suit and white gym shoes.

Her blonde hair was pulled back into a pony tail and her freshly washed face gleamed with the radiance of the weekly facials she had in the expensive beauty salon where she had a standing appointment for her hair, face, nails and a massage. Jack admired the way Susan worked out every day. She made it to the gym for at least an hour per day and then came home, took a shower and if it wasn't her day at the beauty salon, she went shopping or out to lunch with the women from the country club they had joined.

"Jack, I have an idea that I want to talk to you about," Susan said as she stood next to the kitchen table.

"Yes, what is it now?" he replied, bracing himself for a request for more money.

"Well, you mentioned that your business has slowed down. I think that you should call Maeve and tell her to send Paul and Therese to a nursing home and cash in their bank accounts."

Jack stared at her. How could such a beautiful woman be such a bitch, he thought. He took another sip of his coffee and decided it was time to take a stand. "No way," he hollered loudly. He waited for her response.

"You're a coward and a pushover," she screamed. "I don't know why I married you." She grabbed her gym bag and headed for the door.

He took another gulp of coffee and ran his hand across the prickly night's growth of hair on his face. He stood up and hurried to the front of the house where he saw Susan gun the car out of the garage. She sure is a beautiful woman, he thought. It's a pity that she is such a spoiled brat. He realized his marriage was over if he didn't find a job or come into some money soon. Susan was high maintenance and she wouldn't remain in the marriage if their standard of living diminished.

Susan came from a family of modest means. Her father had been a barber and her mother worked as a saleswoman in a small dress store on the south side of Chicago. She was their only child, a stunning beauty who had parlayed her good looks and substantial drive into a successful career as a model. She had gone to college for a year, but when her modeling career took off, she quit school and opted for the lifestyle her career could afford her.

She and Jack had met at a charity function for abused children. Funny, he thought, how they had clicked from the first time they met. He was a successful dentist and she was the well known beauty who had appeared on magazine covers and in fashion shows. At the time, his income was substantial, in the high six figure range. An attorney friend of his had introduced them and it was lust at first sight.

It was only later that he discovered his friend had briefed her on his income and the fact that he had just broken up with his last girlfriend. He knew he wasn't much to look at. He carried extra weight around his middle and was out of shape. He hoped that the custom made suits he wore and the Ferrari he drove would make up for his appearance.

He knew it was important to impress his patients. It was all about the look, the aura of success he created. And it had worked. Susan had accepted his proposal after their fifth date. He wanted her on his arm, a trophy to compliment his other trophies of success.

They had a huge wedding at the Gold Horizon room of the Dearborn Hotel. They honeymooned in the south of France and returned to live in a large penthouse condo on Lake Shore Drive. That was when his dental practice was booming, when people didn't blink at spending large sums of money for homes, clothes, cars, vacations and wanted to look their best too. He had capped more teeth than he could remember.

Interest rates were low and the economy flourished. His high end dental practice was booming so much that he hired two other dentists to keep up the the patient demand. Because of his high income, Susan had cut back on her modeling career. Well the economy has gone bust and so has my business, he thought. The first thing he had done to raise some money was to sell the condo on Lake Shore Drive.

He explained to his friends and business associates that he and Susan were moving to the suburbs because they wanted to start a family and realized that the city wasn't a good place to raise children. He thought that his friends had believed him. Susan had objected, but when he assured her that she could continue to spend freely and they would join a country club in Deerfield, she acquiesced. The economy improved for a while and during that time, he and Susan decided to build their present home.

But as the economy again started to falter, he realized that he was in dire straights. Once he told Susan they no longer could afford the country club, he knew it would all be over. He didn't deceive himself into thinking she really loved him. No, she married him for his money and the things he could provide for her.

Funny, how he had turned out this way. As a kid, the other kids had picked on him. He had always been underweight and brainy. He never ran with the in crowd and compensated for it by trying harder at everything he did. He studied hard in high school and was accepted at Boston College. Paul and Therese acknowledged his success at being admitted to the school, but the price of the tuition was too much. It was Maeve who came to his rescue. She gave him the money she had saved to pay for part of his tuition at the college. He could always count on Maeve.

When they were kids, they used to sleep in the same room of their small house on the north side of Chicago. They were six years apart in age, but it could easily have been twenty years by the way that Maeve protected him. Before they went to bed, Maeve always started praying the rosary aloud and at her urging, he would finish the Hail Marys and Our Fathers with her. Why was he remembering that now? he thought.

Funny how he felt good after telling Susan that he wouldn't talk to Maeve about moving their parents to a nursing home and cashing in their bank accounts. He then realized that if Susan left him, he would survive.

Chapter 68
The Diagnoses

Maeve and Paul arrived at Dr. Turner's office. Dr. Turner, a podiatrist, had been recommended by Maeve's neighbor. The sore on the inside of Paul's foot had been there for one week so far and Maeve wanted a second opinion after visiting Paul's internist, who recommended using antibiotic ointment on the sore.

Maeve put Paul into one of the wheelchairs available in the reception area of the medical office. The receptionist in Dr. Turner's office handed Maeve the initial forms and asked her to fill them out. She completed the forms and returned them to the receptionist. At this time, she noticed a sign on the wall that stated that the office could not assure that Medicare would cover any procedures. The receptionist asked Maeve to sign a statement that her father would be responsible for payment if Medicare did not pay.

Then an office nurse dressed in a flowered uniform escorted Maeve and Paul into the doctor's examining room. Maeve pushed her father in his wheelchair and helped him get out of it and onto the tall examining table in the room. She took off her father's socks and shoes and the nurse removed the wheelchair from the room. After a ten minute wait, Dr. Turner appeared. He was portly and jovial. He took the gauze off her father's foot and looked. "You have foot ulcers," he diagnosed. "You have diabetes, don't you?"

"Yes," answered Paul.

"How long have you had the foot ulcers?"

"A week now," Maeve answered.   "Dad's internist said to continue using an antibiotic ointment on the sore, but it seems to have changed in the last few days. It has gotten darker.

Dr. Turner pulled a card out of his pocket. "Here is the name of a vascular surgeon. I suggest that you try him.   He has had much success in treating diabetic patients and will have some suggestions as to how to get the circulation moving in your leg," he said to Paul. "You probably have no circulation in the right leg and this may be why the sore on your toe is not healing. Keep exercising your leg each day to improve the circulation. Also, here are some pads to put between your toes. These will let the air get at them." He pulled a drawer open and took out a small package with little round pads and handed them to Maeve.

"Well, it was very nice to have met you. Just put the pads between your toes and keep doing what you are doing with the foot and see the vascular surgeon I recommend." Then he shook Paul's hand and left the room.

Paul and Maeve looked at each other in surprise. "Well, that took five minutes," Paul said crossly.

"Not even five minutes," Maeve responded. She put on his socks and shoes and helped him off the examining table. The nurse opened the door and brought in the wheelchair and assisted him into it.

"Just stop at the nurse's station to check out," she said briskly.

The nurse at the nurse's station handed Maeve three packages of toe pads. "The doctor asked me to give you these," she said.   "That will be $10.00. Medicare does not cover them."

Maeve pulled a ten dollar bill out of her purse and handed it to the girl. Then she wheeled Paul out to the car and they drove home.   That evening, as always, Maeve cleaned her father's feet. She filled a plastic tub with water and washed his feet with soap. Then she dried the feet and applied the antibiotic ointment to the sore on the right foot. They sore had become darker, almost black.   I don't have a good feeling about this sore, she thought as she waited for the medicine to dry. I think I'll make an appointment with that vascular surgeon and see what he thinks. She applied the gauze and placed the small elastic bandage over the gauze in order to keep it in place.

"Thank you," Paul said as he always did when she cleaned his feet. "This is very important to me."

"You're welcome, Dad.   But you know what, I think we will go to see the vascular surgeon, Dr. Peters, to see what he says about your foot."

Maeve was able to get an appointment with the vascular surgeon in three days. She would have to take another day off of work in order to keep the appointment, but felt that this was a priority.

Three days later, Paul and Maeve drove to the vascular surgeon's office. Maeve helped Paul into a hospital wheelchair and he and Maeve took an elevator up to the doctor's office.   Once in the examination room of Dr. Peters, Maeve helped Paul into a chair. The young doctor came into the room. His white coat hung perfectly on his tall, thin frame.

He projected an air of complete sterility and cleanliness. He kept his hands in the pockets of his coat when he entered the room. His hazel eyes were guarded and his manner cold and impersonal.

He pulled up a stool and gently removed the gauze off Paul's toe. He looked closely at the small black sore the size of the eraser on a pencil on the inside of the toe. "It's gangrene," Dr. Peters said at once.

Maeve's mouth hung open. "How could that be?" she asked incredulously. "We just went to see his internist and a podiatrist who mentioned nothing about gangrene."

"Well, I deal with his all the time and it is gangrene. I am not going to clean it out or scrape it because it is too risky. We can operate, but I cannot guarantee success. If we operate and the incision does not heal because of your circulation, Mr. O'Connor, complications may set in and we will have to amputate your leg. At your age, the risk factor rises. I think we have a fifty fifty chance of success, which is much lower that I would prefer. However, if you want me to operate, I will do it. What do you want to do, Mr. O'Connor?"

"Well, doctor, at my age, I think I have lived a good, long life. I don't want to lose a leg and end up in nursing home in a wheelchair without a leg. What would I do to go to the bathroom? I would be dependent upon others. Right now I can walk, though slowly and with effort, with my cane, but at least I am mobile and can get up and walk about. I don't want to be an imposition upon my daughter and be confined to a wheelchair in her home. So, I think I will just wait doctor. And if the foot starts to go, well, so be it. I have lived a good life."

The doctor's face perceptibly softened. He put fresh gauze and and a fresh elastic bandage back on Paul's foot. "I understand and respect your decision," he spoke softly. "I want you to come back every week from now on so we can monitor your foot." Then he put his hands back in the pockets of his white coat and started to leave the room. "See you next week. My assistant will set up a meeting with you," he said as he left the room.

"Are you comfortable with your decision?" Maeve asked gently.

"Yes, that is what I want," Paul said decisively. He pulled himself up from the chair and leaned onto his cane. He then slowly made his way to the waiting wheelchair from the hospital and they left. As she drove home with Paul, she noticed tears falling down Paul's face as he stared straight ahead. He remained quiet and closed his eyes to rest. It had been an emotional day.

Chapter 69
The Bill

A week later, Maeve picked up the mail from the mailbox at the end of their driveway. In it, a statement arrived from Medicare. It stated that Paul's visit to Dr. Turner had been denied and that Paul would be responsible for the entire bill, which came to hundreds of dollars. When Maeve examined the bill, she noticed that it documented that the podiatrist had performed a surgical procedure on Paul. She examined the bill again. What is this all about? she thought. He didn't perform any procedure on Dad. He just looked at the foot and gave us some pads to put between Dad's toes. She called Dr. Turner's office.

"I would like to speak with the person who does the billing," she said forcefully.

The receptionist transferred Maeve to the woman who handled Dr. Turner's accounting.

"Hello, this is Nancy from Dr. Turner's office," the woman said.

"My name is Maeve Carey and I am calling about my father's bill," Maeve stated.

"What is your father's name?" Nancy asked.

"Paul O'Connor. He and I had an initial visit with the doctor last week. We just received his denial of payment from Medicare. I want to know why it was denied and also why the statement says that Dr. Turner performed surgery on my father's foot. Dr. Turner did not perform any surgical procedure on my father and I would like the bill corrected."

"Oh, that is not a problem" Nancy replied. "I will simply resubmit the bill. Often Medicare will not pay a bill the first time we submit it, so we submit it again and they pay. As to your father's surgical procedure, I will have to talk to Dr. Turner about that and he is on vacation now. I will ask him about it when he returns next week."

Maeve hung up the phone and marked on a sheet of paper the date that she had talked to this Nancy. It was the strangest thing, she thought. This was the first medical bill that Medicare had denied and she became suspicious about Dr. Turner. Why would he charge for a procedure, a very expensive procedure, that he had not performed? Was it an honest mistake? Was it something more sinister? She decided to wait to hear from Nancy.

No one returned her call, so the following week, Maeve picked up the phone again and call Nancy at Dr. Turner's office. The receptionist said that Nancy was sick and would return her call in a few days. When Maeve didn't hear from Nancy for the next four days, she again called her. This time, Nancy answered the phone.

"I haven't had time to talk to the doctor," she said in a gruff tone.

"Well, I have had to call you three times now to try to get an answer," Maeve responded politely. "I would appreciate it if you would take the time to talk to him and get back to me."

"You don't have to get rude with me," Nancy shouted.

"I am not getting rude, but I do want an answer. If I don't hear from you by the end of this day, I am going to call Medicare to dispute the bill. I will tell them that the doctor did not perform this procedure." Maeve hung up the phone. There definitely was something wrong here.

A few minutes later, the phone rang. It was Nancy at the other end. "I just spoke with the doctor. He said he did perform that procedure, that he remembered your father well, but he is willing to delete it from the bill. However, you will owe for the initial visit and examination. I will resubmit the bill to Medicare. Is that all right with you?"

"Well he did not perform any surgery on my father. However, if he will delete that from the bill, that will be fine and then you can resubmit the bill for the initial visit to Medicare," Maeve replied cooly. "That is only fair."

Chapter 70
The Blood Test

Saturday morning Paul moved slowly into the kitchen from the bathroom. He pulled out the chair to the kitchen table and eased himself into it. Maeve noticed that he was perceptibly slowing down. It seemed an effort to take even a few steps now and he tired easily when he walked from the family room to the bathroom, a distance of just twenty feet. He had just washed his face, shaved and combed his hair and he looked fresh and clean in his dark green long sleeved cotton top. His tan pants hung loosely from his once portly frame.

He had lost weight on his diabetic diet in which Maeve carefully monitored the amount of food that he ate. Maeve could gage his blood count by the size of the portion she gave him to eat for supper. If he ate a larger portion, his blood count was higher. If he ate a smaller portion, his blood count was lower. She decided to ask Sophia to move the button on his pants so they would fit him better.

"Can you get me my sweater, Maeve?" he asked cheerfully.

"Of course, Maeve replied. She tiptoed into the bedroom and glanced at her mother who was still sleeping in bed. Therese lay curled under the comforter that was pulled up to her nose. Maeve removed the sweater off the chair next to the bed and brought it back to the kitchen. She pulled the left arm of his sweater over Paul's left arm, draped it across his back and pulled his right arm through the other sleeve. She started to zip it up, but Paul took the two sides of the zipper in his hands and zipped it up with his left hand.

"See, I can still dress myself," he remarked proudly. "I even dressed myself this morning!"

"Yes, you can," Maeve responded happily. She placed the Medicare bill in front of Paul. "I have been speaking to the podiatrist's billing person about this," she explained. "This bill states that he performed a surgical procedure on you and of course, he did not. I disputed the bill and finally, after going back and forth for a few days, the billing woman has agreed to remove the surgical procedure from the bill, although she said the doctor insists he performed the surgery. It is very fishy. If they had not adjusted the bill, I would have contested it with Medicare. I wonder if he has done this to his other patients?"

"Well, good for you," Paul said as he nodded in agreement. "That Medicare is running out of money as it is. If there are mistakes on the bill, they should be corrected."

Paul then turned the palm of his hand over so Maeve could prick his finger and take his blood count. She swabbed his finger with rubbing alcohol and inserted the small needle into the pen. She pressed the side button on the pen to activate the needle. Then she placed the pen on Paul's clean finger and pressed. She removed the pen and applied pressure to his finger near the spot of the pricking. A small drop of blood appeared. Then she placed the paper swab against the blood until the buzzer sounded that the test was complete.

Maeve handed Paul the cotton that had been doused in rubbing alcohol. "Here, put this over your finger," she directed him. They waited expectantly for his blood count to appear on the face of the testing machine. After five seconds, the number one hundred ten showed on the monitor. Paul smiled as he looked at the count. It was well within the normal range.

"Looks good," he commented in a delighted voice. He smiled at Maeve and picked up each of his pills and swallowed them with his glass of orange juice. Then he started to read the sports section of the morning newspaper.

"How's about some breakfast?" Maeve asked.

"That sounds wonderful," Paul replied gratefully.

Maeve scrambled some eggbeaters and toasted a piece of whole wheat bread, then she cut a half banana into small pieces and laid it all on his plate with a pat of butter. Finally, she removed a small low carb yogurt from the refrigerator and placed it in front of Paul.

"How are the Bulls doing?" she asked as she sat at the table.

"They won last night. I think that they have a chance of going all the way," he answered.

"And the Cubs?" she continued.

"They lost, but they are still in the running. Their pitchers have been injured, but they have a solid team."

"And the White Sox?" she inquired.

"They won. They might be the best of all," he boasted.

"You sure love your sports, don't you?" she laughed.

"Well, what else do I have to do all day except read the paper and sit in front of the television set and watch sports. Sports and Judge Judy. That is what I do." He turned back to his paper and continued to read.

Maeve placed a cup under the refrigerator spout and filled it with water. Then she set it in the microwave and pressed a minute. When the buzzer sounded, she placed a tea bag in the boiling water and poured another glass of juice. Then she took her vitamins out of their container and laid them on the clean cutting board on the counter. She placed a paper towel over the pills and held a meat cleaver over them and came down on the pills with a few thuds until the pills were pulverized. She scooped the squashed pills onto a spatula and sprinkled them into her half container of low fat strawberry yogurt. She too ate the same breakfast each morning and found that pulverizing the pills made them more palatable to take.

While they were eating, Therese got out of bed. She went to the bathroom and then shuffled into the kitchen. She wore red lipstick and her hair was combed. Even at eighty-one years old, she still took pride in her appearance and wanted to look good. She was a lovely woman whose blonde hair framed her sparkling brown eyes. She sat down at the table and Maeve handed her morning pills to her. Then she waited while Maeve poured cereal and milk into her bowl and warmed it in the microwave. After she finished the cereal, she stood up.

"I am tired," she said quietly. "I am going back to bed." She then shuffled back to her bedroom and got into bed.

"Have a wonderful rest, my dear," Paul called out to her. He blew her a kiss and then continued to read the paper while Maeve cleared the table and placed the dishes int he dishwasher. Maeve picked up the phone and called Sophia.

"Hello," Sophia answered the phone.

"Sophia, this is Maeve. Can you come here tomorrow, Sunday morning from eight o'clock till noon?"

"Of course," said Sophia. "I will be there at eight o'clock.

Chapter 71
A Very Lucky Woman

Sophia arrived at the house on Sunday at eight fifteen in the morning. Maeve drove down the winding road on the steep hill that led to the Lake Forest beach. She navigated her BMW slowly in the event that a car should suddenly appear on the other side of the road. Though she usually trekked down the wood stairs behind her home that led to the Lake Forest beach, she decided to take her car because it had rained the night before and the stairs behind her home appeared muddy and slippery.

The parking lot was empty and the beach was deserted. The lifeguards no longer manned their posts, but the beach still remained open. Maeve marveled at the churning lake water and sand and grassy areas. The twenty-nine acre beach resembled a European sun spot with its sheltered pavilions, grills, a fishing pier, boat launching ramp and storage area, walking paths and a concession stand that remained open until late fall.

Today, however, the weather was blustery. The dark clouds slathered the sky like chocolate frosting on a cake. The wind whipped and whirled over the lake, forming frothy waves that plunged in vain against the stone breakfronts that protected the white sandy beach. Maeve parked her car at the north end of the parking lot near the snack shop and bathrooms. She got out of the car and put on a sweater to ward off the chill air. She estimated the temperature to be about fifty degrees but the dampness went through her and caused her to shiver. The wool sweater felt good against the wind.

She loved coming to the beach. She strolled along the walkway that separated the sandy beach to the east and the grassy green park grounds and hill to the west. The city of Lake Forest had built steep steps that led to the top of the hill and the street above. She stopped just before the pier at the south end of the beach and looked at the waves that pounded against the rocks that formed a barrier between the water and the sand.

She hadn't been to the beach since late summer when she and Jeremy had strolled from the north end to the south end. The beach had bustled with the noise of children playing in the sand while bronzed lifeguards sat in their high perches standing guard over mothers, fathers and their children as they frolicked in the water. Elderly people sat on the wood benches that lined the walkway and gazed as the parade of humanity strolled by. The smell of barbecue and smoke wafted from the barbecue pavilion next to the snack shop where families ate their lunch or dinner.

But now the beach was deserted. A mist hung over the lake and a damp chill permeated the air. Maeve pulled her sweater tightly around herself and wrapped her arms in front of herself. She walked along the path to the pier at the south end of the beach and climbed the rocks that formed a breakfront along the angry lake. She sat at the edge of the rocks and watched as the seagulls swooped and turned in the sky as the heavy gray clouds moved swiftly from west to east over the lake. Being near the water was her favorite place.   As a child, she had dreamed of living near the water.

And now her dream had been fulfilled, since she and Jeremy had their home adjacent to the lake. She felt the spray from the waves splash across the rocks and the mist caress her cheeks.   She used to come here often, before her parents moved in with her and Jeremy. It was a place where she could be by herself and think about things away from the demands of home.   She watched the clouds pass over her and enjoyed the sun that peeked out for a few moments from behind a large dark cloud.

She decided that she was invisible, the shrinking, invisible woman. And if she was invisible to herself, she was invisible to others.   She led an invisible life, invisible to Jeremy, invisible to her daughter, Clare, invisible to her brother and sister, invisible to her parents, she thought. She was a shell and the inside of the shell was desolate and empty. She saw herself as a token, someone to be used by others, but then she remembered the   inspirational quote in a book that she had read that morning.   It stated: 'A happy woman is someone who does not blame others.'   So who was there to blame for the way that she felt?

Of course, she blamed herself. She allowed all this to happen to her.   Jeremy in the basement, her brother and sister not helping with her parents, Clare rarely calling or wanting to go out with her, her father taking for granted all she was doing for him and her mother.

A cloud covered the sun and the sky turned dark again. The wind whipped in strong gusts.   She felt cold even with her sweater on and decided to leave the beach. Just as she stood up, she noticed a man walking quickly up the beach towards her. He wore a black nylon jacket and a Cubs baseball cap pulled down across his face. His hands were pushed into his pants pockets.

Why is he coming here? she thought. Just as she turned to leave, a large wave broke against the rocks and enveloped her with a burst of pounding water and foam. Maeve lost her footing on the slippery rocks and fell as another hard wave crashed into the rocks. She landed on her side and started to slip from the rocks into the water. She tried to hold onto the edge of the rocks, but the slippery wet surface did not provide enough traction to give her a good grip.

"Help," she shouted in a panic.

The man ran towards her and held his arm out to her. She grabbed his arm just as she was about to fall into the lake. The man locked hands with her and held her tightly. He grabbed her with both hands and pulled her onto the dry end of the rocks and let go.

"Thank you," Maeve gasped as she tried to catch her breath. But the man had already turned and hurried away. She ran towards him.

"Wait," she cried loudly. She ran as fast as she could, but her gym shoes and slacks were wet and dragged her down so she could not pick up enough speed in order to catch up with him. She stopped and stared as he sprinted up the stairs on the hill leading up to the street. The thought of what might have happened to her and how close she had come to disaster made her shiver violently.

What if she had fallen into the lake? The water was churning explosively now as the mammoth waves smashed into the shore. The sky darkened more and the wind whirled in hard bursts. She heard the clap of thunder and ran to her car. Luckily, she had left it unlocked. She reached for her small mini bag on the passenger side of the car, pulled out her keys and started the car.

Just as she started to shift in reverse, she noticed a piece of paper on the passenger seat peeking out from under her mini bag. She picked the paper up and read the words, You are welcome. Who had written it? Was it he? Was it the stranger who had saved her. Who was he? Where did he come from? Where did he go and why did he not answer her when she tried to thank him? All these questions raced through her mind as she quickly backed up her car and drove it up the winding road to the top of the hill. Another clap of thunder roared above and a torrent of rain fell in strong gusts against her car. Only moments ago, she could have been drowning in the lake during the storm She knew she was a very lucky woman.

Chapter 72
Trouble Is Brewing

Maeve arrived home soaking wet at eleven fifty-five in the morning to find her mother sitting at the kitchen table with her hair in rollers and her hands pointed straight ahead.

"Keep your hands still," Sophia shouted angrily. "The nails must dry." Sophia saw Maeve and motioned to the hairdryer on the kitchen table and said in an annoyed tone of voice, "Your mother's hair can dry with the air or you can dry it. The laundry is still in the clothes dryer. I must go now." She picked up a pen and filled in her time card for the week. For Sunday, she put in eight o'clock in the morning to one o'clock in the afternoon. She had done this many times in the past, rounding her hours up to the next hour and Maeve had said nothing about it.

But today, Maeve became very irritated. "Sophia, did you give Mother and Dad their lunch?" she asked.

"No, I was busy doing her hair and nails," she responded gruffly.

"Well, next time make sure you give Mother and Father their lunch before you leave. That is more important than doing Mother's nails." She looked at her watch and continued, "It is noon. Please enter your correct time on your time sheet and then I will sign it."

Sophia scowled at Maeve and started to say something, but then she reconsidered and changed the time on the time sheet to twelve o'clock and placed the time sheet before Maeve.

Maeve examined it and then signed it. "From now on please enter the exact time you arrive and leave and don't round the hours up," she said intently.

Sophia grabbed her time sheet, her purse and cell phone and left without saying goodbye to Maeve or Therese.

Maeve changed into dry clothes and returned to the kitchen to make lunch for Paul and Therese.

"I was very hungry," said Paul as he sat at the kitchen table with Therese. "It was taking Sophia forever to do Mother's nails and hair."

"It's all right Dad," Maeve responded. "It won't happen again. Lunch is ready. Let's eat."

When they finished, they walked into the family room and watched television. Maeve sat with them and read the newspaper and fell asleep. She woke at five o'clock and started dinner. She made tilapia, broccoli and mashed potatoes. At the end of the five thirty news, Paul rose slowly from his chair in the family room and inched into the kitchen. Therese followed him. They sat down at the kitchen table very slowly and started to eat.

"So, did you have your bath today?" Maeve asked as she sat and ate with them at the table.

"No," Paul answered.

"Why not?"

"Because I was already dressed by the time she came into the bedroom."

Maeve knew exactly what had happened. Each morning, Sophia would arrive at the house and empty the dishwasher. Then she sat in the family room and watched television. This time she must have gotten engrossed in the television show she was watching and went to her parents' room late. Maeve felt herself getting angry. The previous week Sophia did not wash and curl her mother's hair nor do her nails. So she decided to talk to Sophia about her displeasure with the way Sophia was taking care of Paul and Therese.

She also left Sophia a note to be read on Monday summarizing her expectations for Sophia. The note read: Write down your schedule for the each day of the week. I want to know when you bathe Dad and Mom, get them dressed, do Mom's hair and nails, the laundry, feed them and take them out for walks or to lunch and give them their medication. I will talk to you about the schedule on Tuesday.

That night she gave her parents their medicine and put them to bed. She went into her bedroom and called Jeremy. His phone went into voice mail. She left him a voice mail message: "Jeremy, I almost drowned today at the beach. There was a bad storm and I almost fell into the lake. Luckily, a man at the beach pulled me off the rocks just as I almost fell into the lake. I don't know who the man is. He left before I could thank him. Just wanted to let you know. Love you."

Then exhausted from the day, she went to bed, put her phone on silent mode and immediately fell asleep.

Chapter 73
The Neighbor

The next morning, Maeve gave Sophia the note about keeping a schedule with her parents. Sophia's face turned red, but the only thing she said was, "I will keep the schedule and show it to you."

That evening, Jeremy returned from his trip in time to have dinner with Maeve, Paul and Therese. "How are you doing after your accident?" he asked.

"What accident?" Paul exclaimed in a concerned voice.

"It was nothing, Dad," Maeve responded. She gave Jeremy the look that meant keep quiet.

He remained silent through the rest of the meal and after he finished eating, he said, "I am going down to the basement to work. I have a lot to catch up on after my trip."

"As you wish," Maeve commented. "Mom and Dad, would you like to watch television for a while?" she asked.

"Yes," said Paul. They went into the family room and turned on the television.

Maeve decided to take a short walk. She wanted to get out to clear her head and get some fresh air and exercise. She took a turn to the left, down through the wooded areas and back up the street one block away from her home where she saw a woman walking her two dogs. Maeve recognized the woman as a neighbor on her block, but whom she hadn't seen for years, not since Clare and the woman's children had been in high school.

"Hi, Judy," Maeve said in a friendly tone of voice. "Long time no see."

"Hi," Judy answered. She pulled at her dogs and started to walk down the street with Maeve. "I hear you have your parents living with you."

"How do you know?" Maeve asked.

"I asked Dorothy Ryan," Judy laughed. "I saw the Ford parked in front of your home every morning and wondered what was up. Dorothy told me about your parents living with you and that you have a caretaker who parks her car in front of your house. She also told me about the intruder at your home recently."

"Oh, yes, that was certainly a frightening incident, but the police are aware of it and there haven't been any incidents since then. Perhaps my parents moving into the house gives anyone pause if they are thinking of breaking in. I mean, we have our caretaker in the daytime and the four of us are home at night unless Jeremy is traveling."

"Does he travel often?" Judy asked seriously. "I would be terrified to be at home without him."

"Not too often," Maeve replied quickly. She did not want anyone to know about Jeremy's next trip the following week, just in case the news traveled.

"That's good," said Judy.

"How is your family?" Maeve inquired.

"Oh, the kids are gone. They both live on the East Coast. My mother died two years ago and my father still lives on the West Coast. He said he wants to come and live with us when he can't stay in his house alone any more, but I couldn't take it. We would lose all of our privacy. We've decided we will put him into an assisted living complex or a nursing home if his condition deteriorates. I don't know how you can do it with both of your parents in your home."

By now, they were standing in front of Maeve's home. They stopped for a moment while Maeve thought about what Judy had just said.

"Oh, you just do your best, Judy," she commented. "That is all that we all can do." She started to walk up her driveway. She turned around and waved goodbye to Judy. "Take care of your little dogs," she said. "They are precious." Then she paused. "Judy, did you by any chance hear any strange sounds the other night? Loud, screeching sounds about four o'clock in the morning?"

"As a matter of fact, I did," Judy responded.

"Do you know what they were?"

"I reported the sounds to the police and told them that I saw a dead rabbit on the street. They sent someone to pick up the rabbit and he said that a coyote is roaming the neighborhood and killing small animals. It was a terrible sight. All bloody and eviscerated."

"That is terrible," said Maeve. A coyote I can deal with, she thought. Just not an intruder.

Judy waved goodbye and continued up the street to her house. Maeve entered her home and found her parents getting ready for bed in their bedroom. She helped them get their pajamas on and gave them their pudding. After she helped them into bed, she took the stairs down to the basement to see Jeremy.

"A coyote is roaming the neighborhood and killing small animals. Judy down the street heard the noise too and reported it to the police. They told her about the coyote. They said they are looking for the animal. At least it wasn't a human being killed," she said with a sigh of relief.

"Thanks for letting me know," Jeremy replied. "Sorry about asking you about your accident with your parents present. I didn't mean to get them upset. But how are you?" he asked in a concerned voice.

"The experience was horrible. Thank goodness for that kind samaritan. I'd probably be dead if it weren't for him," she said emotionally.

Jeremy hugged her and said, "It sounds like a miracle." Then he went back to his computer.

Chapter 74
The Stuffy Air

The next Saturday, Maeve spent the day shopping for food and giving her parents their medicine and making them breakfast and lunch. Around four-thirty in the evening, she asked her parents, "Want to go out to eat for dinner?"

"Yes," Paul said quickly. He reached for the remote and turned down the volume in the television set in the family room. Therese smiled and shook her head up and down.

The weather forecast called for unseasonably warm weather. Stuffy air permeated the house. Maeve had opened the back door and raised the window in the family room so the screens would let fresh air into the house. She had also opened the windows in the kitchen and bathrooms but the air still hung heavy and thick. Maeve descended the stairs into the basement where it was cool. Jeremy sat at his computer typing in numbers from the company checkbook.

"What are you doing? she asked.

Jeremy did not flinch, but kept working at the computer. "Entering two months worth of payroll numbers," he explained patiently. He leaned forward and pushed his glasses further down on his nose.

"Why do you insist upon wearing those cheap glasses?" she asked in an annoyed tone of voice. "You have two very expensive pair of glasses upstairs that are just sitting on the kitchen counter. "

"Because I can see better with these," he countered cooly. "Besides, I got such a good deal on them, three pair of glasses for twelve dollars from Sal's Bargains. Now that is a savings!"

She walked up behind him. "Want to take me and Mom and Dad out to dinner tonight?" she asked warmly.

"After I finish this work. When do you want to leave?"

"Well, it's four o'clock now. How's about five o'clock?"

"I'll be ready to go by then," he said as he continued to enter the numbers into the computer.

She climbed the stairs and felt the hot air consume her energy. She headed for the thermostat and turned on the air conditioning.

"It's too cold," Paul complained from the family room. "I can feel the cold air blowing out of the vents."

"Well, I am just turning it on for a few moments to get the humidity out of the house," she replied impatiently. She turned the thermostat to seventy-six degrees. The inside temperature was seventy-nine degrees. It would take a half hour or so to cool off the house. They can just sit through the cooling process, she thought. She went into their bedroom and took their sweaters out of their closet and brought the sweaters to the family room.

"Here," she said. "Put these on while the house cools down." She gave one sweater to Therese and helped Paul put on his tan sweater with the zipper in front. Then she went into her bedroom and lay down. At least she didn't have to make dinner tonight, she thought with relief.

Chapter 75
The First Change

Maeve sat in Ruth Stein's waiting room. She arrived early and waited until one o'clock when Ruth opened the door to her office.

"Come in," Ruth said warmly. Maeve entered the room and sat down.

"Tell me, how have things been going?" Ruth asked.

"It's time for a change," Maeve answered nervously. She felt her heart pounding but also felt a surge of confidence in what she was about to say.

Ruth's eyes brightened and she leaned forward. "In what way?" she inquired quickly.

Maeve took a long breath and said, "I am through with talking. It is time for me to make some actual behavioral changes. I no longer will accept being taken for granted by everyone around me."

Ruth smiled, sat back and stared at Maeve. "How did you come to this decision?" she pressed.

"It has been a gradual thing. This past week, I stepped outside myself to see how I act and how others react to me. And it was not a pretty sight. I've decided that I am invisible," Maeve explained. As she spoke, she felt her hands start to sweat.

Ruth leaned forward and asked, "Invisible in what way?" Now we are making some progress, she thought.

"There is no me. I am a composite of trying to please others and make others happy. My life is a nothingness and I am tired of it."

Ruth probed her further. "But there must have been a trigger which brought you to this conclusion."

"Last weekend, I went to the beach and almost drowned. Luckily, I was saved by a passing stranger, but the incident gave me a sense of how fragile life is and how quickly it can end."

"What happened at the beach?" Ruth questioned further.

Maeve recounted the events at the beach.

"You were very lucky," Ruth commented slowly. She shifted in her seat and stared at Maeve's eyes. "What will be your first concrete action in asserting yourself?" she said as though she were speaking to a child.

"I thought about it last night and I've decided that I am terminating my therapy sessions with you." Maeve felt her heart start to race harder.

Ruth stood up and laughed. "Of course, you are not serious," she stated emphatically. Her black penciled eyebrows rose high in her face.

Maeve could not believe that Ruth was laughing at her and that she was dismissing what Maeve had said. "Yes, I am," she retorted decisively.

"You realize that you have a long way to go to feel better about yourself and we have only touched the surface of your feelings," Ruth said in a shrill voice.

Maeve rose from her chair. "I realize that I have wasted all these past sessions with you listening to you talk about yourself and your brother and trying to get me addicted to your mystery pills. And it is over."

Ruth put her hands on her hips and smirked. "Don't you think you'll miss those youth pills I gave you. Look what they have done to improve the lines on your face."

"I haven't taken one pill since my first visit with you. And if the lines on my face are improving, it is because I have decided to make changes in my life." She picked up her purse and opened the door to leave.

"You'll be sorry," Ruth shouted. "Nobody walks out on me."

Maeve closed the door behind her and straightened her shoulders. Whew, that felt good, she thought. She drove home ready to tackle her next problem.

Chapter 76
The Second Change

Sophia stood at the kitchen table setting Therese's hair. "Who cut your hair?" she asked gruffly. She rolled Therese's fine white hair over the plastic curlers and secured them with bobby pins.

Therese smiled sweetly and shook her head. "I don't know," she responded softly.

"Well, these American beauticians don't know what they are doing. Look at how they cut your hair in the back. It looks terrible, all in layers. I do not understand these American women." She finished with the last curler then plugged in the hair dryer. She turned it on and pressed the high hot button and moved it slowly over Therese's curlers.

"Ouch, that hurts," Therese cried. She pulled her head away from the hot air blowing at her.

"This will make your hair curl," Sophia growled over the noise of the hair dryer. "The beauty shop did such a poor job; this will cover it up and besides, your daughter insists that you have your hair curled."

Therese turned her head away from the dryer and pleaded, "Then please make it cooler."

"If it is cooler, the curls will not be as good," Sophia insisted. She pressed the dryer closer to Therese' head and moved it from curler to curler. "Keep still," she shouted. "After this, I still have to do your nails and it is almost time for your daughter to come home."

Just then, Maeve entered the kitchen. She saw her mother's pinched face and the way she squinted her eyes in pain. "What are you doing?" she shouted at Sophia.

"Drying her hair," Sophia answered as she moved the dryer to the next curler.

"It hurts," Therese cried. "Please make her stop."

Maeve jumped around the table, grabbed the hair dryer and turned it off. "Why do you persist in going against Mother's wishes?" she screamed.

"Because you told me to curl her hair," Sophia said defiantly.

"You can curl her hair by using a lower setting on the dryer or letting the curlers air dry," she explained in an angry tone of voice.

Sophia crossed her arms and moved forward. "I think hot air is better. It makes a tighter curl."

"Well, I am telling you to stop using the highest setting. Also, her nails are not done. Why are they not done? It is Friday. You know I want her hair and nails done on Fridays so she looks lovely for the weekend."

"I don't stick to schedules," Sophia shrieked loudly. "I do things when I think they have to be done. If I feel like during her hair and nails on Friday, I will do them, if not, I won't. I am not a schedule person."

Maeve regained her composure. "Well, you won't have to follow my schedule any longer," she said in a steely voice. "You are fired."

Sophia stepped back as if she had been hit with a fist. She started to cry. "I have tried to do the best that I can for your mother and father and this is what happens. You don't appreciate all the days that I have come here and taken care of your parents. They have had good care," she sobbed.

"I think that you have done an adequate job of taking care of them, but you certainly have not exerted yourself. You arrive in the morning and empty the dishwasher and then you turn on the television and watch it. There have been many times when my father has not had his sponge bath because you did not come into his bedroom when he woke up because you were watching television.

I had to tell you to stop watching the television in their bedroom in the afternoon and only knew about it because my father saw that the television was turned on to a different station than when he turned it off the previous night.

You act resentful if I ask you to boil some vegetables or potatoes in the afternoon and told me that you are doing more than you should. Well, I work too, and I don't get paid to watch television in the morning and afternoon or talk to my friends on my cell phone all day as my father says that you do. I cannot keep my job if I act resentful if I am asked to do something. So, I'll say it again. You are fired."

Sophia grabbed her purse and cell phone and stormed out of the house. "You don't know what you are losing," she screamed. She slammed the door behind her.

Therese looked at Maeve in relief. "Thank you for telling her to leave," she said through tears. "She was hurting me."

Maeve heard Paul's footsteps as he slowly walked into the kitchen. "What is going on here?" he asked. He looked about. "Where is Sophia?"

"I just fired her," Maeve replied.

"Good," he said. "Now you can quit your job and stay home and take care of us." He sat down and tapped his fingers on the kitchen table.

"Oh, no," Maeve said in a calm, steady voice. "I am not quitting my job. I'm going to call the agency right now. We'll get another woman to watch you and Mom." With that, Maeve dialed the number of the home healthcare agency.

"What has come over you?" Paul asked in bewilderment.

"I've only just begun," she answered with a large smile.

Chapter 77
The Third And Fourth Changes

Maeve enrolled in an exercise class after work. From five o'clock to six o'clock in the evening three times a week, she went to the class located in the neighborhood recreation gym. There, she walked around the track, rode the stationary bikes, and used the rowers and step machines. She came home exhausted, but happy. Violet, the new caretaker she hired from the home care agency, cooked a full dinner every night and stayed until Maeve arrived home.

Even Paul was happy with Violet. He reported that she was polite, prompt and made sure that he and Therese had their baths, helped them get dressed, gave them their medicines, played cards with them, watched television with them and ate with them.

"She's doing a good job," Paul had said with satisfaction. "None of this staying on her cell phone all day and watching television in our bedroom while we are in the family room."

After the first week at the gym, Maeve began to have more energy and her clothes hung looser on her. Then she made an appointment to get her hair and nails done at Mademoiselle K, a new salon in downtown Chicago that she had read about in the newspaper. When she walked into the salon, a lovely dark haired young woman with impeccable makeup greeted her.

"This way, Mrs. Carey," she said. She brought Maeve back to the shampoo room where she gave her a plush white robe embroidered with the initials MK on it. Maeve sat in the lounge chair and lay her head back over the sink. It felt so good to relax this Saturday morning, she thought. Violet was watching her parents and for once she was alone and pampering herself. The shampoo girl rinsed her hair, then squirted shampoo onto it and rubbed gently, massaging her scalp and her temples and the back of her neck. Maeve felt the tension run out of her body. She relaxed as the girl rinsed her hair and squirted conditioner on it.

Then the girl wrapped a towel around her head. "This way, madam," the girl said. She escorted Maeve to a chair that sat next to floor to ceiling windows that overlooked Michigan Avenue.

The last time she had been in downtown Chicago, Maeve had helped Clare move into her new apartment. She frowned as she thought about this.

"Is there something wrong?" Pierre, the beautician asked as he helped her into the chair at his station.

The sound of his voice broke Maeve's reverie. "Oh, no," she answered. "I was just thinking about someone."

"Well, whoever it is, I hope they bring a smile to your face instead of that frown," he commented cheerily.

Maeve smiled. She happily realized that she hadn't thought about frowning being bad for her face for the past few months because she had been so busy with work and her parents.

"Now tell me, how do you want your hair done?" Pierre inquired as he pulled her hair back to get a good look at her face.

"Well, I would like a totally new look," Maeve replied candidly. "Something to perk me up and make me look younger." She thought he must hear this all the time.

He stepped to the side looking at her from every angle. "Madam, I have it," he exclaimed. "I see you with highlights in the front to cover your gray and we will layer your bob to give it more volume. I will cut bangs and shag it on the sides. What do you think?"

What he suggested was more than Maeve had been prepared for, but this was the new her, so she said, "I am in your hands. Make me a new woman."

He smiled and picked up the scissors. Clip, clip, she heard. She closed her eyes and and felt a lightness as the hair came off. When Pierre was finished, he declared proudly, "Look now, madam. What do you think?" His face beamed with pride.

Maeve opened her eyes and stared at her face in the mirror. Her hair was so different than what she was used to, but she turned her head from left to right and smiled, "I love it," she declared. She ran her hands through her cropped hair.

"Good," Pierre said with pleasure. "Now we are going to highlight your hair." He brought out the foil strips and placed them throughout her hair, and then brushed them with a white paste. "Now, you are to sit and read until I come back," he instructed her. He handed her a stack of magazines.

Maeve glanced through the magazines until he returned. "Now we are going to wash your hair again" he continued. "Then we will blow dry it and you will be ready for your manicure."

She hadn't felt this good in a long time. When he finished with her hair, she stared in astonishment at the woman in the mirror. My goodness, she thought, I look great!

"Thank you, Pierre," she said in a delighted voice. "You truly are an artist."

"No madam, you are lovely and it is easy to make you more beautiful than you are. Now I will take you for your manicure."

Chapter 78
The Fifth Change

Pierre escorted Maeve to the next room where she sat at a table across from a young woman. The woman smiled shyly. "Your hands, please," she said. She held Maeve's hands and looked at them intently. "Why so rough?" she asked as she examined Maeve's split, dry hands with dried blood caked in the cracks.

"I wash my hands a lot," Maeve explained with embarrassment. She pulled her hands back.

"But you need to put cream on your hands. Put cream on them at night and then put gloves on them and go to bed. Your hands will heal," the girl suggested.

Ah, Maeve thought. But you don't know how many times I wash them in a day. She thought of all the times she had washed them just this morning, when she got up from bed, after she went to the bathroom, before and after she put on her makeup, when she brushed her hair, dressed, before and after touching food, medicines, after touching almost anything. She estimated that she had washed her hands at least twenty times since eight o'clock this morning and now it was noon.

Well, at least I have clean hands, rough, cracked and bloodied, but clean, she thought. It always seemed to get worse as the weather cooled. Her hands started to dry in late autumn and by early winter, they were hopeless. She had tried to put cream on them during the day, but her compulsion to wash them never allowed the cream to remain on the long enough to do any good.

"Madam," she heard the manicurist say. "Madam, I am going to start now. Please relax." The girl rubbed cream into her hands and started the manicure. Maeve almost fell asleep during the procedure. She felt so tired from all that she had been doing that she realized that everything had taken a bigger toll on her than she had anticipated. For the next hour, she allowed herself to enjoy the pampering that she received. When the manicurist was finished, Maeve looked at her groomed nails, trimmed and buffed short and painted a light pink. The cream had taken away some of the roughness of her hands and they actually looked smoother and soft.

"Thank you," she said with an appreciative smile. "You don't know how much it means to me to have pretty hands and nails." She handed the girl a ten dollar tip.

"The manicurist took the tip and placed it in her pocket. "Here, I will take you to the reception area if you are finished. Do you have any other appointments after me?" she asked.

"For what?" Maeve asked.

"Well, we have pedicures, massages, facials, makeup. We are a full service spa besides a beauty salon."

Maeve made a mental note to make another appointment in a few weeks. Getting her hair and nails done and a facial next time would be very nice, she thought.

"No," Maeve answered. "I don't have any more services scheduled for today, but thank you for asking." She paid at the reception area. The bill came to one hundred fifty dollars. A bit pricy, she thought, but then on second thought, she was worth it. She left the salon with a happy heart and looked forward to the rest of the day.

Chapter 79
The New Toy

When Maeve arrived home, Jeremy had just pulled into the driveway and was unloading the car. "What do you have in those bags?" she asked.

"Riding gear," he replied cheerfully. He carried two large bags into the house and then went back to the car and opened the trunk of his BMW. He unloaded four more large bags and brought them into their bedroom.

Maeve followed him. What have you bought" she inquired again. She stood by the bed and stared at the six bags sitting on the top of the bedspread.

Jeremy started unpacking the bags. He pulled out a motorcycle helmet, a black leather jacket, leather gloves, motorcycle boots and decals.

Maeve's mouth dropped open in astonishment. "Is this motorcycle gear?" She reached for the helmet and held it in front of her. "This helmet is heavy," she commented.

"Yes," said Jeremy. He turned towards her. "I bought a new motorcycle. This one is a BMW."

"You've got to be kidding," she exclaimed. The blood drained from her face. Another motorcycle? Has Jeremy gone mad? she thought. "But you are fifty-five years old." She lay the helmet on the bed.

"Yes," he interjected quickly. "I am. So what?"

"Well, you will kill yourself on it. By the way, where is it?"

"I am going to get it tomorrow." He picked up the helmet and placed it on his head. "What do you think?"

She stared at him and frowned. She pursed her lips and the brows on her faced pulled together forming furrows on her forehead. "I think that you look ridiculous," she stated firmly.

He ignored her comment and reached for the motorcycle jacket and put it on. "Looks pretty good, don't you think?" Then he whipped out a package of decals from the other bag. "These will go on the front and back of the jacket." He then pulled on the boots.

"You said you are going to pick up the motorcycle tomorrow?" she asked nervously.

"Well, I should have said that I will pick it up if you will drive me."

"Drive you where?"

"To the motorcycle dealership. I am going to ride it home."

"But you will get hurt," she protested.

He put his arm about her. "No, I won't. I'm used to riding large motorcycles. Remember my last Harley? And remember when we were dating and you even rode on the back of my old Triumph with me?"

She closed her eyes in horror. "That was so long ago. We were just in our twenties. It was a lifetime ago. And it was just for one month or so until you sold it."

He looked at himself in the mirror again. "Well, I am bringing it back. I've spent all these years being a good provider, husband and father and now I want something I can call my own."

"But you have your car, this house, the business and Clare and me. What more do you want?

"I want to experience the wind in my face and the freedom of riding on the road. I want to be free." He took his arm off of her.

She felt as though she had been hit in the stomach with a fist. All the air went out of her and she felt the room start to twirl. She sat on the bed. "How much did you pay for it?"

"Twelve thousand dollars," he replied matter of factly.

"But we could have used that money to pay down our home equity loan. I thought you were having financial problems with the business."

He turned towards her and grinned. "The business is starting to turn around and that loan will still be in effect in five years. I don't know that I will be around in five years."

"Are you leaving me?" she asked in astonishment. She hadn't seen this coming. She folded her arms across her chest.

"No, of course not," he laughed. "It is just that I've had medical problems. You do remember the angioplasty that I had last year? The way I feel is you never know when you might go."

"But you exercise and watch your diet."

"Even so, we're not in our thirties any more. Time is passing. I've spent all these years providing for you and Clare. And now your parents are living with us."

"Do you want me to ask them to leave?" she questioned him sadly.

"No, that's not what I am saying. When you asked me if it was okay to let them live with us, I said it would be all right. And, I'm not going to turn them out on the street now. But I need something for myself now too," he continued.

"I'm not enough?" she murmured as she sat on the bed.

"Maeve, you and I have drifted apart these past years. I've been consumed with the business. You spent your time raising Clare and now you are working and taking care of your parents."

"But I have to take care of them. They are helpless."

"I understand. All that I am asking is that you support me with my new toy."

Chapter 80
Great News

Maeve knew the next words that came out of her mouth were very important. Could she give her blessing to this new motorcycle? Should she lie and say that is was okay with her and then resent it for the rest of her life? Then she remembered her last visit to Ruth Stein when she spoke about her need for a new life. Perhaps she and Jeremy were not that far apart in their hopes and dreams. How would she feel if he told her to send her parents away? She took a deep breath and looked directly into his eyes.

"You have my support," she said. "I'll drive you to the dealer tomorrow. Where is it?"

"In Long Grove," he replied. "I already rode the old one there and the dealer drove me home." He took off his helmet and smiled at her. "Now I'm going to sew on the decals."

"Thank you for not asking me to do that," she laughed.

"No, I know you are not handy with a needle and thread. I'll do it myself." He walked to the linen closet and took the sewing box off the top shelf. Then he moved into the kitchen and put the sewing box down on the kitchen table. He reached for his reading glasses from his shirt pocket and placed them on the tip of his nose. Then he carefully pulled a black thread off a spool and threaded a needle. It took him four attempts, but finally he got the thread through the hole of the needle. Then he happily spent the next two hours sewing the decals onto his leather jacket.

"Want pizza for supper?" Maeve asked after he finished his sewing.

"That sounds good," he responded quickly. He peered at her over the top of his reading glasses.

"Where do you want it from?" she continued.

"I don't care," he responded.

"Okay, I'll order from IL Fresno and have it delivered. They usually take less than an hour." She picked up her phone and placed the order. "One extra large pizza with pepperoni and sausage and another extra large pizza with mushrooms and black olives," she said with a smile on her face. She provided their address and clicked off the phone.

Just then she looked at the clock. It was six o'clock. In the family room, her father turned off the television and slowly shuffled into the kitchen and sat down at the table. Therese followed a few steps behind him.

"Mom, would you please set the table?" Maeve asked softly.

Her mother's eyes lit up in delight. "Of course," she said in a happy tone of voice. She walked to one of the kitchen cabinets and pulled out one plate at a time and placed them on the table. Then she moved to the cabinet that contained the glasses and set them on the table next to the plates.

She hesitated a moment while she tried to gather her thoughts. Then she looked at the cabinet where the napkins were placed and opened it and lay them on the table next to each glass. Finally, she moved to the drawer that held the forks and knives and lay them over the napkins. She studied the table intently and when she was sure that the table was totally set, she sat down. She and Paul and Maeve and Jeremy ate blue cheese and crackers while they waited for the pizza to arrive.

Paul cleared his throat. "Jeremy, I want to tell you how grateful Therese and I are for welcoming us into your home. I know it hasn't been easy for you. Sometimes, I find it hard to express myself, but you're a fine man for allowing us to live here. Not every son-in-law would do that."

"Yes, thank you, Jeremy," Therese added. She took a piece of cheese and a cracker and offered it to him. "Please take this. I made it especially for you."

Jeremy looked at Maeve and smiled. "Thank you Therese. I want both of you to know that I enjoy having you live in the house. It has become quite lonely since Clare moved out."

"By the way, Clare is coming over tonight," Maeve interjected. "She said that she has some news for us."

"What time will she be here?" Jeremy asked.

"She said around seven o'clock."

Just then, the doorbell rang. It was the pizza delivery man. Maeve paid him and took the pizza into the kitchen. Then the doorbell rang again. "Hi, Clare," Maeve said excitedly. "You are lucky. We ordered pizza for tonight. Come on in and have it with us."

Clare looked quite happy. She entered the house and sat at the kitchen table. "I have some good news for you all," she declared. "I don't have to move into your home." For a moment, everyone sat silently at the table.

Then Maeve asked, "Oh, honey. Why?"

"I got a job," Clare exclaimed.

Jeremy poured a glass of wine for Clare and Maeve and a diet drink for Paul and Therese. "Congratulations, Clare! Where are you going to work?"

"I will be working for a non-profit doing their marketing. I met the director of the non-profit at a fundraiser last week. We started chatting and before you know it, she hired me. I start next week!"

Paul raised his glass and offered a toast. "To the best granddaughter in the world. You are destined for much success and happiness."

Therese continued, "To you, honey. We love you and are so proud of you!"

Maeve reached over and gave Clare a big hug. "Oh, honey, we are so happy for you!"

Chapter 81
The Police Arrive

Stephen sat at his desk and thought about Rubin's case. When Ruth referred Rubin to him, he thought he had died and gone to heaven. But the case was dead in the water now and he knew it was all over. Stephen picked up his phone and called Rubin's number. He dreaded this phone call.

"Yeah," slurred Rubin at the other end of the line. "I hope you have good news for me, O'Mara."

Stephen swallowed hard. "Hello, Rubin. I'm afraid the news is not good. The court has granted Summary Judgment."

"What the hell does that mean?" Rubin growled.

"It means that the defense has won. There is no merit to your case. You will not get any money."

Rubin threw the phone to the floor. He slammed his fist into a door and knocked a large hole in it. Then he grabbed his phone again. "You'll regret this, you loser. You told me I would get a settlement. Why did you take the case if you didn't think you could win?"

"I did think you had a good case, but you lied to me, Rubin. The video from the gas station across the street from the restaurant proved that you didn't slip and fall on the restaurant's property. Tell me the truth, Rubin. How did you get that slash on your head and sprain your ankle?"

"You haven't heard the last of me," Rubin threatened. He slammed the phone down and raced into his bedroom closet where he kept his guns.

Stephen heard the click of his phone and leaned back into his chair. That guy is nuts, he thought. Just then, the doorbell rang. He unlocked the door to find two police officers standing there.

"Mr. O'Mara, could we step in? We would like to ask you some questions about a Mr. Damien Flynn."

"Damien is dead," said Stephen. "He was my stepson."

"We know, Mr. O'Mara. We would just like to ask you some questions about your whereabouts on the night that Mr. Flynn was killed."

"I have an appearance in court in an hour and was just going to leave. Could you come back tomorrow?" Stephen asked.

"We'll be happy to. Will one o'clock work for you?"

"Yes, that will be fine." Stephen closed the door and locked it. He slunk back to his office and locked that door too. He slouched in his office chair and unlocked the left drawer of his desk and reached inside. A gray gun lay shimmering under the sunlight that streamed in through the vertical blinds.

Should I write a note, he thought. To whom? Sherri was dead and they had no children. It wasn't as if they hadn't tried, but after a few years, they knew they weren't destined to have children of their own. They had considered adoption, but Sherri decided she was not up to raising another person's child.

He never really forgave her for that decision. He would have been happy to raise a son or daughter, but he couldn't do it alone. So here he was, no wife, no children and no relatives. Sherri was an only child and so was he. Their parents were dead. He'd moved to Lake Bluff to get away from living in Chicago and the pressure of the big time well known law firm he had worked for there.

He thought he would succeed in his own law firm, but things did not turn out as planned. His case load had not improved much from the inception of the firm. He made enough to get by, but Sherri wasn't satisfied. It was a shame that she found out about his gambling and the hookers. She wanted a divorce, so he had to get rid of her. There was no way he could have afforded a divorce. It was all her fault and it was such a relief to be rid of her.

When he hired Maeve, he thought he was getting back the happy, young Sherri he had married in another person. Maeve resembled Sherri so much, her brown hair, her green eyes, the way that she laughed at his jokes. But after a while, he realized that Maeve was just like the Sherri that disapproved of him.

When he looked in Maeve's eyes, he knew she had suspicions about his gambling and hookers. She pretended that she didn't know about those things, but he was sure that she was aware of them. And there was that time that she saw the heroin packets in Damien's backpack. After that, he recognized that he had to get rid of Maeve. But telling Damien to do the job was so stupid.

He had warned Damien that if he didn't knock
off Maeve, he would report him as a heroin pusher to
the police. Unfortunately, when Damien botched the
job, Stephen knew that he had no choice but to get rid
of him.   If he didn't kill Damien, he could have
blackmailed Stephen or talked to the police
incriminating Stephen about his part of the heroin
business. And now the police were suspicious about
Damien's death.   That idiot.   He couldn't even try
killing Maeve without screwing it up.

Chapter 82
The Body

Stephen reached inside the locked bottom drawer on the right side of his desk for the scotch that he drank in the mornings, the afternoons and evenings to keep himself going. He grabbed the tall glass next to the scotch, poured the scotch to the top and gulped it down. Then he poured another and gazed at the glistening copper colored liquid swaying in the glass.

"You are my only friend," he spoke sadly to the glass of scotch. "I shall miss you the most when I am gone." He twirled the glass in a circular motion, swallowed the scotch and enjoyed the warmth that spread from his mouth to his stomach. He was beginning to relax. It wouldn't be so bad. He poured another glass and raised it to the picture of Sherri on his desk. He swilled down the third drink, relishing the thought that he would be free of it all. He threw the glass to the floor where it smashed into jagged pieces. Then he reached for the gun.

Just then, he heard a knock at the front door to the law firm. Stephen ignored the knock and placed the gun to his head. The knocking turned to pounding and it sounded so loud that Stephen stood up and hid the gun under some papers on his desk. Who in the hell could it be? he thought. When he opened the door, Rubin was standing there.

"What do you want, Rubin?" Stephen growled.

Rubin pushed the door open and jerked a gun out of his coat pocket. "You bastard. You ruined my case. Now I get nothing and it's all your fault." He pushed Stephen with the gun and said, "Go back to your office and keep your hands up. I'll be right behind you."

Stephen turned around and followed Rubin's instructions. His mind was racing. One moment he wanted to kill himself, but now he had changed his mind and he tried to think of something he could do to save himself.

Once inside Stephen's office, Rubin ordered, "Lock the door and then sit down. I've been dreaming of this since you told me you lost the case."

Stephen moved in front of his desk and said, "I was just going to call you. I have some good news."

"Yah, what good news? Just more of your lies," grumbled Rubin. He pointed to the desk chair. "I said sit down. If you don't, I'll pull the trigger now."

"Rubin, I think you still have a chance to get a settlement. I just want to show you some papers that I just received. The restaurant is afraid that the video is too blurry and won't hold up in court. They want to make an offer to you. Let me show you the papers."

Rubin thought for a moment. "You'd better not be bullshitting me, Stephen, because if you are, you're dead on the spot."

"I'm telling you the truth," Stephen declared. He turned and reached for the gun that was under the papers on his desk.

Before Rubin realized what Stephen was doing, he heard a blast and felt the strength of a bullet piercing his chest. He dropped his gun and looked in surprise at Stephen. He staggered back and fell onto the floor with blood pooling under him.

Stephen kicked Rubin's gun to the side and leaned over him. Rubin's eyes were fixed and dilated and his breathing had stopped. Stephen felt for a pulse but there was none.

At that point, Stephen heard more loud knocking at the front door of the firm. Stephen peered out the front window and spotted a police car with flashing lights parked in front of the firm. Without hesitation, he raced to the back exit door and rushed out.

"Stop right where you are and drop the gun," ordered a police officer. He called to his partner. "Get back here fast. They were the same officers who had asked for an interview the previous hour.

Stephen dropped his gun. "One of my former clients just tried to kill me, so I shot him, officer. It was self defense."

The officer was on his phone. "Send an ambulance and backup. We have a possible homicide. He turned to his partner. "Good thing you wanted to stay outside the back of the office in case of trouble. Wait here with O'Mara while I step inside."

He inched into the back office and spotted the body lying on the floor. "We've got a body in here," he shouted to his partner "Cuff O'Mara and put him in the squad car."

Chapter 83
The Walk

The morning sky faded from a navy blue to powder blue as the sun started to rise. Maeve stepped out of the house and walked down the brick driveway. The birds chirped in the trees and a soft breeze caressed her face. She wore white shorts, a cream colored cotton top, white socks and gym shoes. She stepped onto the street and turned left at the mailbox. The green grass was covered with dew and here and there she observed squirrels jumping onto the trees and climbing to the top branches.

She thought about the previous day when she received a call from the police informing her of Stephen's arrest. The police reported that they had decided to keep an eye on Stephen's law firm after he asked that his interview be postponed. They spotted a man park his car in front of the law firm and knock on the door. When Stephen let the man into the firm, they put the man's license number into their search database and found that he was Rubin Stein. They moved rapidly when they heard the sound of gunfire. One officer covered the front door and the other had remained at the back door.

Stephen was booked on murder charges and put in jail till his arraignment and bail could be posted. The officers found Maeve's name and telephone number on Stephen's desk and called her. She explained that she had worked for Stephen. She told them about Rubin Stein and his case and about

Stephen's increasingly erratic behavior lately. She revealed her suspicions about Damien selling heroin. The officers informed her that she would probably be called as a witness if the case went to trial.

After Damien's autopsy results came in a few weeks later, the charges against Stephen were upgraded to murder in the first degree. The bullets and gun that Stephen used to kill Rubin were identical to the bullets and gun that killed Damien. Maeve could not believe the charges. She couldn't believe that Stephen had killed Damien.

Also, the police told Maeve that Damien's autopsy fingerprints matched the fingerprints they had found in her house after an intruder tried to kill her. So it was Damien who invaded her house and terrified her. In jail, Stephen tried to contact her, but she declined to speak to him. This was certainly a part of her past that she didn't want to open up again.

And now, what about her? She had started to make changes in her life. Where would they lead? She straightened her shoulders and concentrated on taking brisk steps. She had read that thirty minutes of a quick walk gave a person as much benefit as a fast run. Why pay money to go to a gym when she could work out in the house on a cold or rainy day and walk outside every other day.

So far, she had lost two pounds. Also, she felt better and had more energy. At night, she went to bed at nine o'clock. It was all she could do to stay awake that long. But in the morning, she awoke at six o'clock with a sense of exuberance at the start of a new day.

Jeremy was a night person and could barely get up in the morning. He was sound asleep now as were her parents. By the time she returned to the house and took a shower, Jeremy would hear her and get out of bed. He then would move to the other bedroom to work out. When the cold weather came, she too would use the other bedroom to exercise.

But now, as she turned the corner onto the next street, she enjoyed the fresh air and newness to the day. The street was empty. She swung her arms at her side and felt the pull of the muscles in her legs. The homes in her neighborhood were lovely, large brick homes with expansive lots and towering trees. Long, winding drives led to each home. All boasted well manicured lawns, shrubs, perennials and annuals in pastel shades of pink, white, powder blue and yellow.

Tiger Lilly's dotted the sides of homes and Impatiens bordered the trees and driveways. It looked picture perfect. She wondered if life was as perfect on the inside of the homes as it appeared on the outside. She doubted it.

She had heard from Dorothy that a few people on their block were having financial difficulties or were out of work. Who knew what else was happening? Everyone kept a smilie on their face and greeted each other, but conversations rarely occurred. She rounded a corner and picked up her pace.

She passed the half block long two story mansion on the road that wound through this part of Lake Forest. Then, she turned another corner and walked down a hilly road and looked at the pale blue sunlight peeking through the dense trees on each side of the road.   This was her favorite part of the walk.   The trees provided a private refuge from the outer world.   She slowed and listened to the birds chirp as she passed.   What were they saying to each other? she thought.   Were they wishing each other a beautiful day?   She continued the walk and passed the new homes that had been built in the middle of a large parcel of land.

The homes were massive with five car garages.   They resembled English manors with their stone and turrets.   The sun beat hard now and she took a sip from the bottle of water she carried in her hand.   A group of bicycle riders passed on the street and she waved to them with her free hand.   They called back a hello.   Yes, it was a lovely morning and it helped clear her head to take these walks and get the exercise.   She felt better and more able to tackle the daily stresses.

She was still in shock about Stephen's arrest and the charges against him.   He had seemed so easy going, but who knew what demons lurked in a person's head.   She rounded the corner, turned into her driveway and picked up the morning paper.   She lay it on the kitchen table and took a shower.   It was time to get ready to face another day.   After Violet came, she drove to the beach to think about her future.

Chapter 84
The Stranger On The Beach

Gray cotton clouds hung in the sky as she climbed the boulder that braced against the lake. She sat and gazed at the frothy water that crashed gently against the rocks and at the straight, strong horizon that separated the water from the sky. It looked as if an artist had taken a dark blue marker and slashed it against the horizon. She heard the sounds of children playing in the water off the sandy beach. She turned to the right and looked at the Lake Forest flag flapping in the wind off the circular seating area that jutted out over the lake. Turning north, she viewed the far shoreline dotted with smoke stacks and factories; looking east, she marveled at the never ending expanse of clear blue water; and to the south, she peered at the beaches of the North Shore suburbs and in the far distance, Chicago's skyline jutting into the sky.

Seagulls spread their wings and floated effortlessly in the sky circling over the water and resting on the beach until they took off again. A group of people sailed out from the pier. The weather was perfect, about seventy-five degrees and the wind blew in gentle gusts against her hair. What more could I want?, she mused. I am here to relax and think. The wind grew stronger and clouds covered the sun. A chill gust of air blew across the rocks and turned the lake into a murky dark blue that revealed rocks peering from beneath the fluorescent water.

What a wonderful place to be, she thought. She decided that she would come back here more often and give herself time to rest and enjoy the solitude.   Yes, this was the place where she would spend more time.   A seagull flapped its wings and careened in front of her, then met with another seagull and they coasted on the wind and flew away.

A helicopter flew overhead towards Chicago. The clouds started to part and a patch of blue peeked out from behind them.   Perhaps the sun would come out again today.   No matter, all that was important was that she was here and taking time for herself.   Then she glanced at her watch and realized that it was time to return home.   As she scrambled up, the sun broke through the clouds and warmed the air.   It was a good time.

A hand touched her shoulder and she turned around.   She recognized the man.   He was the one who rescued her from the rocks the last time she slipped at the lake.

"Good morning, Maeve," the man said gently.

"You saved me," Maeve replied quickly.   "I'm sorry. Good morning. Who are you?"

"I am your guardian angel," he answered with a smile.

He didn't look like a guardian angel, she thought.   She stared at him and estimated that he was about thirty years old.   His clear, blue eyes crinkled when he smiled and wisps of his dark brown hair fell onto his forehead.   If she had to describe him, she would have said he was a hunk, standing about six feet four inches tall with a trim, muscular body.   He wore faded jeans and a blue windbreaker over a blue top.

"Oh, come on," she said with a grin. "Who are you really? I never had the chance to thank you."

"But you did thank me," he continued.

"And how did I thank you?" she persisted.

"Every time you helped another person you thanked me. Every donation to a charity, every smile to a stranger, every time you were kind to someone, every time you held your temper when you wanted to scream, every time you were good to yourself, you thanked me," he explained

"But I haven't exactly been the most kind person in the world. I have been angry a lot lately," she said quietly.

"Your anger became your teacher. It taught you to explore who you really are. It taught you to be you. It made my job much easier because you took control of your life. I just had to help you out a few times."

"You mean when you rescued me from the lake?" she inquired.

"That and a few other times. Remember your car accident? I called the ambulance for you."

"So that was you. No one had any clue about who made the call."

"Remember the landscapers first visit to your home?"

She felt as if she were losing her breath. "Were you the blue eyed landscaper?"

"Yes. You gave us water when we were so thirsty."

"I knew there was something different about you when I looked at you," Maeve revealed. Then she blushed. "Giving you water wasn't anything special."

He stared at her and said, "It was special to me and the other men. Remember the hobo in the Lake Forest parking lot who followed you to your car and asked for some money?"

"That wasn't you, was it?" she blurted out.

"Yes, it was me. Even though you were frightened, you treated me with respect and gave me some money so that I could survive."

Now she felt ashamed. "Oh that wasn't much that I did. Actually, I was terrified of you."

It seemed as though his blue eyes were piercing through her. "No that was a lot," he stated gently. "Remember those unsigned notes in your mailbox after your car accident?"

"You wrote those?" she said in disbelief.

"Yes, they were reminders that I cared for you."

"All they did was frighten me and make me think that there was a crazy out there watching me."

"I'm sorry about that. But they did get you to think about life in a more broad sense."

"What do you mean by that?" she said quizzically.

"Life as opposed to material goods. What life is all about."

"What is life all about?" Maeve asked softly.

"You now know," he shared as he started to turn. "It's getting late and I must go home."

She felt a sudden sadness. "Where is your home?" she pressed.

He pointed up to the clouds. "Up there, but remember, if you need me, I am always with you. Most times you cannot see me, but in special circumstances, we are given permission to become human. Just know that if you need help, I'll be there for you."

"Please don't go," she pleaded. But he was gone, walking down the sidewalk at the beach. She ran after him and tried to stop him, but he disappeared before her eyes.

She walked over to the food stand and ordered a ham sandwich and sat eating it on a bench overlooking the lake and looking up into the heavens. A seagull flew by and landed in front of her. She tore a piece of bread from her sandwich and placed it in front of the seagull. The seagull looked at her and took the bread into its beak and ate it. The seagull again looked at her and she broke off another piece of bread and gave it to the seagull. It bit the bread, flew around her and then swooped into the sky.

She followed its path in the sky until it disappeared behind a thick, white cloud. I wonder if that was him, she thought. Then she headed for home.

Chapter 85
The Suggestion

The next morning, while getting dressed, Maeve received a call from Jack.

"Annie and I would like to come over to your house to talk about Mom and Dad," he said.

"I'm free today," she answered. "Why don't you stop by at one o'clock?"

"We'll see you then," he replied.

At one-thirty, they still had not arrived. Jeremy was out of town and Violet had taken her parents out for a walk. Maeve sat in the den and wondered what Annie and Jack wanted to talk about with her. Just then, she heard footsteps in the house.

She headed towards the kitchen and saw Jeremy standing there. "What are you doing here?" she asked in surprise. "I thought you were in Las Vegas?"

"I took the red eye home after the last meeting," he said happily. "Maeve, I've got great news. I've just picked up another new account and our money problems are a thing of the past."

"Money problems?" she asked in astonishment. "What do you mean? How can we still have money problems? I assumed they had gone away because you haven't mentioned them to me since Clare told me about them."

"I haven't been very upfront with you. I didn't want to upset you what with you dealing with your parents and Stephen's arrest. You should know that things have not been good with the company for the past year or so." He put down his suitcase and placed his arms around her. "I hope you can forgive me for not confiding in you more."

"I can forgive you anything, Jeremy, if I know about it. I can't forgive what I don't know."

"Let's sit down and talk," he said. "The economy has been in a downturn and this affected sales for the company. I've been trying to keep the business going as long as I could, but I decided it was best to close it down."

The color drained from Maeve's face. "You have got to be kidding," she murmured. "Where have I been this past year?"

"As I said, you've had a full plate and I didn't want to worry you with my problems." He took her hands in his. "But things have changed for the better. Now that I have this new account, we can continue on as we have in the past. It's a big account, so big that we can keep the house and we won't have to sell anything."

"And you kept all this to yourself and dealt with it all alone?" Maeve remarked in astonishment.

Just then, the doorbell rang. "That must be Jack and Annie. They said that they want to talk about Mom and Dad. Can we talk about this later?" Maeve stood up and answered the door.

Jeremy shook his head from side to side and shrugged his shoulders as Maeve left the room. Then he rose and carried his luggage upstairs.

"Come in," Maeve said to Jack and Annie. "Let's talk in the backyard. Can I get you anything to drink?"

"I'd like a gin and tonic," Jack said. Annie shook her head no.

"Have a seat and I'll be right back." Maeve mixed the gin and tonic and brought the glass to the patio. "So what brings you both here?"

"How is their money situation?" asked Annie. She crossed her legs and planted her arms in front of herself. "We know nothing and you certainly haven't been forthcoming about their finances."

Maeve shifted in her chair and stared at both of them. "I'll be happy to share this information with you once I get permission from Dad," she stated firmly. "As a matter of fact, Dad can fill you in on all the details."

Their eyebrows furled and creases appeared between their eyes. "No, that's not necessary," Jack stammered.

"But I am afraid that it is necessary. You see, Dad and I are co-executors of his and Mom's estate, so anything I say or do must be approved by him."

"He'll get mad, like he always does and he'll cut us out of the will," protested Annie. "Do you have any beer in the house? I'm parched."

Maeve stood up and faced Jack. "Would you like another gin and tonic? There's not much left in your glass."

"Yes, and make it a double," he replied. He drained the last of the drink and handed it to Maeve.

"We are in Mom and Dad's will, aren't we?" Annie asked hesitantly. She held her hand in front of her face to shield it from the overhead sun.

"That's another question you will have to ask Dad," said Maeve.   She turned and entered the kitchen.

"Well, that didn't go very well," growled Jack. "You and I better have a talk when we leave here."

"I told you this was a stupid idea.   I should have listened to Peter.   He told me not to come with you," Annie muttered under her breath.

Maeve returned with the drinks and handed them to Jack and Annie.   She poured a bottle of water into an ice filled glass and took a long gulp and then another.   "Any other questions?" she asked cooly.

"Aren't you the comedian," Annie snapped as she took a large swig of her beer.

"You know we appreciate everything you have done for Mom and Dad," said Jack.   "I would have given you more help, but I've been busy with my job and Susan."

"Me too," interjected Annie.   "You know you can call me anytime for help."

Maeve smiled at both of them.   "Well, thank you," she responded with a twinkle in her eye.   "I have a suggestion.   Why don't you both spend a little more time visiting Mom and Dad and having them over to your homes for Sunday dinner.   That would mean a lot to them.   And then you can ask Dad any questions you want."

Jack and Annie looked at each other and stood at the same time.   "We have to get going," said Jack sheepishly.   "Susan is waiting for me."

"I have to get back to Peter, too," Annie uttered.

Maeve stood up to walk them to the front door. "Fine, but think about what I've said.   All it takes is a phone call asking them over." Maeve led them to the front door and let them out. Then she hurried to the master bedroom.

Chapter 86
Things Are Changing

Jeremy was unpacking his suitcase and placing his clothing in the dresser drawers and closet. He felt like a deflated balloon. All that hard work had paid off and just when I confide in Maeve, she blows me off, he thought.

Maeve entered the room. "I'm sorry that I didn't listen to you, but," she stopped mid sentence. "No buts about it. I'm sorry I didn't listen to you." She dropped into the stuffed chair in the corner of the bedroom. "You've had a lot to handle this past year. I just feel sad that you didn't have enough confidence in me to let me know what has been happening."

"What good would it have done? There was nothing you could do." He zipped his suitcase and placed it in his large walk in closet. "At least we don't have to worry now. Things are back to normal and we can continue as we have in the past."

Maeve took Jeremy's face in her hands. "But I don't want things to be as they have been in the past. We've essentially been living like strangers in the house. I want things to change, for us to communicate with each other, to tell each other what goes on in our lives. I want to be there for you when you need to talk to someone."

Jeremy took her hands off his face. "Maeve, I think we are way past being there for each other. I have my life and you have yours. Anyway, we have a full house with your parents. Things are much too busy here.   I'll just keep doing what I have been doing."

Maeve looked at him sheepishly. "You know, I haven't been entirely forthcoming with you, either."

Jeremy look alarmed and his face turned red. "Now what?" he demanded. "I don't know how much more I can take."

"My news is good news," Maeve assured him. "First, I've been looking at smaller homes in the area for a few weeks. Second, I have a feeling that Clare and Sean are going to get engaged."

Jeremy stared at Maeve in disbelief. "What did you just say about Clare and Sean?"

"This is just a gut feeling, but Clare asked if we were free to go out to dinner this Saturday evening with her and Sean.   This is the first time she has asked us out to dinner with them, so I think something is brewing."

"But she is so young.   She's only twenty-two years old."

"I was twenty-two and you were twenty-five when we married. What's good for the goose is good for the gander."

"Well, you're right about that. It's just that she is my baby."

"I know, but our baby has spread her wings and started to fly."

He frowned and moved to the window that looked over the back yard. "Why are you looking for a smaller home?" he asked quietly.

Maeve looked around the bedroom and pointed towards the hall and first floor. "Do we really need all this space? We can live comfortably with half the house and still have room for my parents plus an extra guest room."

Jeremy smiled. "Actually, that's not a bad idea. We could get a good price for this home and plow the profits into stocks or a money market fund."

"Just what I thought too," she answered excitedly. "I found a lovely home on the west side of Lake Forest. It's a single story with three bedrooms and a family room addition in the back. Would you like to go and see it this weekend?"

"Yes," he stated firmly. "And let's call Clare and tell her that we are free to go to dinner on Saturday night."

"Why don't you call her right now? I know it would mean so much for her to hear that from you."

He picked up his cell phone and dialed Clare. She answered on the second ring. "Daddy, how are you?" she asked delightedly.

"Hi, honey. Mom told me that you want to go out to dinner this Saturday with us. We will be happy to go. Want us to make the reservation?"

"No, Daddy. Sean and I will make it. Come down to my apartment around six-thirty in the evening on Saturday and we can drive to the restaurant together."

"Sounds good. Bye honey." Jeremy disconnected the phone and stared at Maeve. "I wonder if you are right about them?"

Just then, his phone rang. Jeremy answered it and said, "Hello. Oh, hi, Jack. Yes, Maeve is right here. I'll put her on the phone." He held out the phone to her.

"Hello, Jack. Why are you calling? I just saw you." She frowned and shook her head at Jeremy as she spoke.

"I just want to invite you and Jeremy and Mom and Dad over to our house this Sunday for dinner. Annie and Peter will be coming too. Will you be able to come?" Jack asked.

"Jack, hold on. I want to talk to Jeremy and ask Mom and Dad. Better yet, I'll call you back."

"Okay, talk to you later," he responded. He disconnected the phone and looked at Annie. "She's going to call back."

"Did she sound angry?" Annie asked nervously. She folded her arms across her chest and leaned back on the sofa.

Just then, Jack's phone rang again. "Hello," said Jack. He smiled broadly and looked at Annie as he spoke into the phone. "You can? That is great Maeve. We'll see you at two o'clock. No, you don't have to bring anything. Just bring yourselves and Mom and Dad. We'll eat around four o'clock. Will that work with Mom and Dad's schedule?"

"Yes. That sounds great, Jack," Maeve replied. "Mom and Dad are very excited to see your new home. We'll see you on Sunday. Bye." Maeve clicked off the phone and laughed. "Looks like things are changing for the better, Jeremy. Now would you like to see the home in West Lake Forest? I'll call and make an appointment if you want."

"I couldn't think of anything I'd like to do better," Jeremy replied happily.

"That is great! By the way, Jeremy, once we have the appointment, I want to drive us to the house.

You know how in the past I always drove in the middle lane free from the incoming traffic on the right and the passing cars on the left. I felt safe and on auto pilot in the middle lane, sort of the way I felt in life. Well from now on, I am leaving the middle lane and will be driving in all the lanes in the street. It reflects how I now feel about the future. It is time for a new start in everything."

Author Bio

Claudia Williams is the author of the new inspirational novel and murder mystery, **Leaving The Middle Lane.** She previously worked as a correspondent writing features for a newspaper and magazines in Illinois. Over the years, she has always been interested in how divine guidance can influence one's actions and reactions in life without one even realizing it.

Claudia now lives in Texas with her husband. Spending time with her husband, children and grandchildren in Texas and Colorado and driving her 2006 BMW rank number one and two as her favorite activities.

www.ingramcontent.com/pod-product-compliance
Lightning Source LLC
Chambersburg PA
CBHW061928170626
46813CB00006B/2338

* 9 7 9 8 9 8 8 7 7 0 3 0 5 *